*f*P

ALSO BY HAVEN KIMMEL

A Girl Named Zippy

The Solace of Leaving Early

Something Rising (Light and Swift)

She Got Up Off the Couch

The Used World

IODINE

✣

A Novel

HAVEN KIMMEL

Free Press

NEW YORK   LONDON   TORONTO   SYDNEY

FREE PRESS
A Division of Simon & Schuster, Inc.
1230 Avenue of the Americas
New York, NY 10020

First Free Press hardcover edition August 2008

FREE PRESS and colophon are trademarks of Simon & Schuster, Inc.

Grateful acknowledgment is made for permission to reprint excerpts
from the following: "Dog," from *Country Music,* by Charles Wright.
Copyright © 1982 by Charles Wright and reprinted by permission of
Wesleyan University Press.
"Sheet Music," from *The Orchard,* by Brigit Pegeen Kelly.
Copyright © 2004 by Brigit Pegeen Kelly and reprinted with
the permission of BOA Editions, Ltd., www.boaeditions.org.

For information about special discounts for bulk purchases,
please contact Simon & Schuster Special Sales at
1-800-456-6798 or business@simonandschuster.com.

Designed by Kyoko Watanabe

Manufactured in the United States of America

1   3   5   7   9   10   8   6   4   2

Library of Congress Cataloging-in-Publication Data

Kimmel, Haven.
Iodine : a novel / by Haven Kimmel.
p.   cm.
I. Title.
PS3611.I46I55   2008
813'.6—dc22   2007049565

ISBN-13: 978-1-4165-7284-8
ISBN-10:   1-4165-7284-8

This one is for Scott Browning

and

for Robert Rodi,

with my love and gratitude

Contents

CHAPTER ONE: Two Dogs • *1*

CHAPTER TWO: Caduceus • *22*

CHAPTER THREE: Pluto • *48*

CHAPTER FOUR: Oneirocritica • *73*

CHAPTER FIVE: Puella Aeterna • *99*

CHAPTER SIX: Revenants • *115*

CHAPTER SEVEN: Nekyia • *137*

CHAPTER EIGHT: Kerberos • *151*

CHAPTER NINE: Eros • *165*

CHAPTER TEN: Familiaris • *186*

CHAPTER ELEVEN: Hekate • *203*

Acknowledgments • *223*

Each dream is a child of Night, affiliated closely with Sleep and Death, and with Forgetting (Lethe) all that the daily world remembers. Dreams have no father, no call upwards.

—JAMES HILLMAN, *The Dream and the Underworld*

"I did this," says my Memory, "I cannot have done this," says my Pride and remains inexorable. In the end—Memory yields.

—FRIEDRICH NIETZSCHE, *Beyond Good and Evil*

It was an easy birth, once it had been accepted, and I was younger.

—Martha, in EDWARD ALBEE's
Who's Afraid of Virginia Woolf?

IODINE

CHAPTER ONE

Two Dogs

Dream Journal

I never

I never had sex with my father but I would have, if he had agreed. Once he realized how I felt he never again let me so much as lean against him while we watched television. I was never allowed to rest my head in his lap, or hold his hand. We gave up our late-night dancing in the kitchen to his favorite records; we stopped camping together. He took away my old hunting rifle, and when I rode behind him on his motorcycle I wasn't allowed to wrap my arms around his waist anymore. I had to let them lie on my own thighs, even when taking sharp corners.

Colt Pennington, Colt a childhood nickname that stuck. He was tall and leggy and too thin. There's just the one photograph of him as a boy, I think—he's standing in a dirt yard in Kentucky with two other boys his age. They are all tanned and barefoot and their hair has been buzzed for the summer, and Colt's head is turned, he's laughing at something one of the other boys has said. Just the *one* picture, and his head is turned. This is a perfect example of, I don't know, I forget, something about . . . Doors that close? Doors that were already closed before anyone knew they were open? The three of them, Colt and his two friends, don't look like boys today, in the same way child soldiers from the Civil War are foreign looking, so long lost. That is another example but I don't know what the word is.

His Gramaw Pennington swept the dirt yard but no one else did. She was the last of her kind in this family, out there swishing a broom around in the fine, dry soil, making patterns. The Last Dirt Yard Sweeper, right up until she killed herself with ant poison. I'm unclear on the details. Colt's mother, Juna? Hold a broom? No. There are a couple of pictures of her around here somewhere; Colt kept them. Juna was a cliché of the worst sort which I know because her type shows up all the time in books and movies, mostly movies, I guess. The too pretty mother who married young and never took to the whole thing, and in the movies there is her rouge and her stockings and the swirl of her skirt as she flies out the door while her little boy begs her to stay—he stands in the door watching as she gets in a stranger's car and drives away. But Juna wouldn't have been cast in that movie; she lacked the necessary . . . refinement. In Colt's photographs she's dressed like a singer at the Grand Ole Opry, the costume party equivalent. All Colt saw going out the door was (I'm guessing) some ratty old shoe and a cloud of cigarette smoke. But he kept those photographs: one where she's holding him, he's about two years old and Juna is so miserable one side of her mouth has collapsed—she has had a stroke of misery. In the other she is modeling her Opry dress (white) (some predecessor to vinyl) and her white boots, along with her big hair which is black like Colt's and does appear to be leading her out of the frame and into whatever her future was, no one knows.

If only he'd been facing the camera you (I) could see his eyes, which were round, irises so black there was no end to his pupil. Hair from Juna, eyes from his father, Clyde Sr., of whom there are a number of photographs but no one is interested in them. Not much to him, as I understand it—he was born to be Juna's victim and live in the same house with his widowed mother and give up on raising his only child after the child's mother left, well what was the man to do but walk slumped over every day to his job at the gas station and . . . am I right—did his teeth eventually melt? I think so, I think his teeth melted. So Colt let his hair grow long and bought a wrecked 1950 BMW R512, which he worked on night and day in place of a formal education, and was it even running yet when he met L

his hair grew long and he rode that bike all the way from Kentucky, over the Ohio River and through Tell City, up up the middle of Indiana until he landed

a day laborer and then a carpenter but no one ever messed with him or said a word about that ponytail because he was fast as a whip crack, afraid of nothing, he carried a switchblade and walked with a slight left-leaning swagger from a childhood accident, he seemed cool in all ways but he was wound tight. His body rang like a piano string: I could hear him coming from miles away, an A note in an upper register, struck and struck and struck again. His hands were ruined with work and before he stopped touching me he would sometimes run his hand over my back and leave a dozen snags in the material of my shirts, he maybe didn't have fingerprints anymore.

In the winter he drove a '73 Ford truck, an F-100 with a 360, brown—that specific shade of brown of 1973. The muddy dogs jumped in the front seat, barn boots weren't even wiped in the grass before driving. The floor was littered with every imaginable kind of trash and tool and cast-off work glove (they assumed the shape of his hands), and the bed was scarred from loads of firewood and scrap metal. He thought only about what was under the hood, he took care where it mattered.

Cold had

Colt had me, his truck, his bike, his ruined hands, he had his black dog, Weeds. And cigarettes, which maybe Juna left him or taught him, I don't know how it happens. The Marlboro red pack, more of the music of my life: my father's barely in-tune A note jittering down the gravel road and up to the side of the house, and the ritual gestures. Peel away the silver strip that seals the rectangular box; pull off the upper cellophane. Throw it on the ground, in the bed of the truck, whatever. Knock the box against your forearm three, four times to pack the tobacco. Flip the lid with just your thumb, choose the cigarette in the front, in the middle, put it in the corner of your mouth and light it with your hands cupped around the match or the lighter even if no wind is blowing, even if you're standing in your daughter's bedroom and she wakes up because of the sound of the flame, and she doesn't know what you're doing there but she sees you, she would give you anything, she would fillet herself to keep you there, to take you in under the cheap coverlet. She is the dying, the cancerous, the starved or dehydrated, and you, he, Colt: morphine. bread. water. But he turns and walks away, as if he has prevented a disaster, and he takes the smoke with him, but the slight and fading sound of him remains.

✦

Trace Pennington pressed her tingling hands against her forehead, read what she had just written. She was supposed to be starting a dream journal for the class that began on Monday: Special Topics in Archetypal Psychology, an invitation-only course for senior Honors students who had either majored or minored in psychology. She was also enrolled in another senior seminar, Archetypal Analysis of Literature, available only to English or classics majors. Trace was both. At the last meeting with her adviser, a woman in a wig that had seemed deliberately stripped of color (it looked less like hair than fishing line) and styled to flip up at her shoulders, Trace had been told that in addition to her two majors and the psych minor, she had enough credits to declare minors in humanities and philosophy, and was one class away from a fourth in women's studies.

"So," Trace said, nodding.

"So do you want me to add them? You want them listed?"

"How did they happen, those minors?"

The adviser, *Mizzz* Birkle, studied Trace over the top of her half-glasses. "You took the classes."

"Yes," Trace said, trying to remember the past four years. When had she earned minors in four different subjects?

"You declaring them?"

"Wouldn't I?" Wouldn't she? Trace wondered if there was a rule somewhere, a code she had broken.

She tore the pages out of what was supposed to have been her dream journal and stuck them in one of the approximately two hundred unlabeled file folders scattered around the room she slept in. There were three bedrooms upstairs, all oddly shaped and dormered; Trace had chosen the smallest, the one at the back of the house, hoping it would be the easiest to heat. She had found a kind of plastic sheeting that attached to the windows with double-stick tape, and that one then turned into shrink-wrap with a blow-dryer. Having neither a blow-dryer nor electricity, she'd gone to the slick and overpriced store on campus that sold camping supplies (Daredevil Outfitting) and asked a young clerk, who was striving mightily to look gentle and outdoorsy and daring at once, if there was such a thing as a blow-dryer that used batteries.

"Sure," he said, walking toward the back of the store. "We've got curling irons, too, but they use propane inserts."

"Can you weld with them?"

"I'm sorry?"

"Nothing—I'll take the blow-dryer."

It had worked; Trace had turned the dryer up as high and hot as it would go and directed it at the loose plastic, which became tighter at each spot she focused on, until finally the window was completely sealed. There was still the hole in the ceiling, but she'd covered that with cardboard, and in the end she was glad to have the blow-dryer because on the very worst nights she could put it under her blankets and turn it on, warming the sheets just enough that she and the dog didn't shake in the way she hated, the kind of shivering that hurt.

She chose a different notebook to serve as her dream journal. There were stacks available to her, as there were file folders and ink pens and sticky notes and index cards. Working at the campus bookstore for four years had fulfilled her every office supply need. She didn't have to steal a thing: if a box of legal pads came in damaged, she was to take them out to the recycling Dumpster and throw them away, then make a note on the Inventory Loss form, which then went to the higher powers for Trace didn't know what—tax deductions or refunds or perhaps just regret. But in four years at the store (daredevilly named the Campus Book Store) no one had ever watched her recycle anything, nor had they seemed to care. As long as she made the note on the Inventory Loss form, and as long as the CBS superiors were satisfied, everything was fine. Their Loss became her Inventory Gain, just like that.

• • •

The scholarship she'd been offered to the University of the Midwest, in Jonah, Indiana, had included room and board, which Trace declined. The money was refunded to her, and for days on end before her freshman year she drove her father's battered Ford truck up and down country roads so rutted and ruined they might have been Coventry in 1945, until she found an abandoned farmhouse set back on a quarter-mile lane she nearly missed. She had been there ever since.

After pulling ivy off the back door (she left the front untouched) and nearly being killed by a swarm of wasps, she and Weeds had shouldered their way into a domestic disaster. Every room was filled with trash: broken toys and abandoned cheap clothes and a series of televisions with shattered screens. It appeared that there had been two separate types here before her: whoever initially abandoned the house (that was the bottom layer—they were fast-food aficionados) and squatters after them, because there was an old upright piano in the living room above which someone had spray-painted the words *La Dolce Vita!* with real feeling, and also she had found a broken-spined and mildewy copy of Paul Auster's *New York Trilogy* lying on the floor, open in the middle and on top of a pile of rotting blankets. The first night she was there she did nothing but read it cover to cover by the light of a hurricane lamp.

There was no heat or electricity, but she had this Inventory Gain: above the well was a hand pump—not the old kind that required literal pumping; this one was orange and all Trace had to do for well water was lift a handle and fill a bucket. That took care of cooking on the Coleman stove, washing the dishes, bathing if she had to (she mostly showered at the truck stop out on the highway), and flushing the toilet in the truly horrifying bathroom just off the kitchen.

Winters in the farmhouse were so cold she often felt as if she were being lightly stung all over her body by a dentist's drill, even with the three kerosene heaters she used: a small one in the bedroom, a large one in the kitchen, where she often worked at the cheap and scarred table someone had left behind, a small one in the bathroom. She and Weeds reeked of kerosene, she knew, but there was nothing she could do about it. At the cheap Laundromat on the south side of town, the one where no one knew her, she was often afraid to wash her clothes for fear of an explosion. Kerosene was in her lungs, her bloodstream, but she didn't have options. Even if the fireplace hadn't been boarded up she wouldn't have dared use it, in the same way she never used light at the front of the house.

Using a clean notebook, Trace described the dream: Colt in a billowing white shirt, walking into the kitchen of a house Trace had never seen, juggling oranges. She tried to hold on to the feeling of the dream but it slipped even as she reached for it. Trace closed her eyes, opened and closed her numb hands. It was early afternoon of a bitterly cold January, in the abandoned farmhouse where she was hiding with the black dog, Weeds, who lay against her leg. She would need to leave soon; today was her standing visit with her oldest and only childhood friend, Candy Warner, formerly Candy Buck. The girl and the dog were as close to the heater as they could get, and yet they both shivered and were loath to leave.

✛

It was a long drive to Candy's house outside Mason—sixteen miles—and all of it on rural roads. And Mason was Trace's hometown, it wasn't safe for her to be there, so she ended up taking strange detours and looking for roads that didn't exist, thinking that eventually she was going to find a route she'd missed, a sudden turn, an iron bridge in disrepair.

Candy lived with her husband, Skeet, and their two little boys in a trailer at the back of Skeet's parents' property. Trace drove slowly down the dirt drive, in which there were holes deep enough to break an axle, past the senior Warners', their garage and workshop (which seemed to be missing part of its roof), to the place Skeet's domain began. It wasn't hard to find, marked as it was by dead cars and stripped trucks, lawn mowers that were unrecognizable in any season. There were tires and hubcaps and busted aluminum chairs. There was an old refrigerator and the hulking remains of a coal-burning stove. Trace had long since ceased cataloging or even see-ing what was in front of the trailer—Candy's front yard looked like a thousand other front yards in Hopwood County.

Trace parked the truck so it couldn't be seen from the road, and stepped out carefully, Weeds following. Some parts of the ground were snow, some were ice. Everything was muddy, mixed with chunks of salt thrown carelessly, so that most of it was on the vehi-cle graveyard and not on the path that led to the steps.

From behind the chicken-wire fence attached to the trailer, one of Skeet's hounds, Blue, jumped and bayed and pulled against his chain. He was behind a fence and yet chained to his doghouse. Weeds stopped and looked at Blue. Trace stopped. Skeet had two dogs; where was the other? He called the missing dog Coon but Candy refused and referred to him as Bon Jovi. There was the sec-ond doghouse, the second chain, no dog. She took the last few steps and grabbed the handrail of the unsteady metal stairs.

Candy wore her hair in a style known as the Mall: permed on the sides, with bangs curled up into a roll and sprayed with Aqua Net. She had been pretty in high school, cheerful and bright-eyed, but had dated no one but Skeet Warner. From eighth grade on: Skeet's sullenness, his cars, his temper, his boots, the chain he wore con-nected to a wallet. The Skoal ring in the back pocket of his jeans.

The issue of him was not up for discussion, not with Trace or Candy's parents or anyone else; for him she revealed a stubbornness that just grew heavier and more inexplicable as the years passed, and now, seven years later, she certainly had him or he had her but in either case the talking about it was over.

They sat at Candy's Early American kitchen table, which was covered with a plastic tablecloth. Candy smoked one cigarette after another and drank six cups of coffee, three of them so hot she burned her tongue and had to go to the kitchen for ice. The tablecloth was sticky from cereal and baby food and runny eggs and spilled beer and soda, so Trace kept her hands in her lap. As she smoked and drank coffee, Candy also managed to wrangle her eight-month-old son, Duane (named after a dead Allman Brother), who sometimes clung to her and sometimes tried to throw himself off her into the smoky air.

"You know how much weight I gained with this one?" Candy asked, squinting past her cigarette.

"You look fine," Trace said, taking note of the bruises on Candy's forearm, the shadow under her jaw, as if someone had taken sandpaper to her face. There was no denying it—Candy was now officially fat. Her legs were wide, her neck had disappeared. She no longer even had any wrists, just creases where her hands bent.

"*Ninety* pounds. I gained seventy-five with Danny Rae and I thought that was as bad as it could get. And I hadn't lost most of that before I was pregnant with this one."

"That's what happens to pregnant women, right? They gain weight?"

"I'm thinking smoking will help." Candy tucked the baby under her arm and patted the tabletop for the lighter she'd lost. "Dusty's got two girls, she didn't gain weight."

Trace studied her, said nothing on the subject of Dusty, Trace's sister.

"Of course, I don't have what she has to keep me skinny, there's one problem right there." Candy laughed nervously. "Seen her? Or the girls?"

Trace shook her head. "It's been a month or so."

"Them little girls is what makes me sad." Candy joggled Duane fiercely, and he bobbed his head up and down on her fat shoulder and fell asleep.

Them little girls, well yes. Erin and Jessie, five and three. Beautiful surprises, blond like Phil's family. After Erin was born Trace snuck into the hospital in the middle of the night and sat for an hour watching Dusty sleep, the baby tucked up next to her, against hospital policy. The last time Trace saw them Erin was wearing pink fingernail polish she'd put on herself. Half was chipped off but the rest still sparkled, and Jessie had gotten mad at her mother for forgetting to put the chocolate in her milk and cried, in a voice so small Trace couldn't imagine how she was able to imbue it with such misery, *You. Breaked. My. Heart.* Pointing to it, pointing at her chest.

"If it comes to it you'll take them, won't you? You won't let them go to the state?"

"I can't, Candy—I can't even talk—"

"You would."

"You don't know that."

"I've been knowing you since we were six years old and you showed up on Granddad's hilltop outta nowhere."

"You *always* bring that up. You must stop bringing it up."

Candy stood, took the three steps from the table into the narrow kitchen. She came back with a box of doughnuts. Duane snored slightly. The cartoons playing in the living room suddenly got very loud and Candy yelled, "Danny Rae! Turn that TV down or I'll put a hammer through it!" Still the baby slept on, and gradually the television quieted. "Today I'm bringing it up for a reason, not to change the subject, and you're just gonna have to sit your college butt still and listen to me. Now I know you don't hold with almost anything, you think most everything was designed for retards, but I have to tell you about something I heard on the radio last night. Take a doughnut, they're good."

"I don't like doughnuts."

"Take a doughnut."

Trace chose a glazed and ate it. It was good.

"Now you know how there are people who have been abducted by aliens," Candy said, as if she were reminding Trace that there are full moons, or a country called Brazil.

"No, I do not know that."

"Well yes you do and apparently it happens all the time, like *constantly.*" Duane raised his head up and made a sound, a roosterish little squawk, then collapsed back into sleep. Candy pounded on the baby's back as if he were choking, and he just snored harder. "And there was a man on a talk radio show last night, I've forgotten his name already after like five minutes, and it turns out that he spent *years* getting abducted by aliens and he described what it was like, how they could come in through his bedroom window and they're little like dwarves and they dress in blue police uniforms."

"Candy? Were you and Skeeter maybe just the tiniest bit high?"

"We have stopped all of that, Tracey Sue, since Danny Rae was born that funny color." She reached over and took the cup of cold, bitter Folgers Trace hadn't touched and drank the whole thing in three big gulps. A stream spilled down her chin and onto her white T-shirt, which said, in gold letters, SLIPPERY WHEN WET, but the coffee blended with a number of other things that had found their way to Candy's chest over the course of the day. There were stains all over her pants, too, which weren't exactly blue jeans but more like the denim used to cover papasan chairs. "And here's the thing about this guy: he was so sane. He was maybe the sanest person I've ever heard talking on the radio. He was so calm and reasonable and you could tell he was not making up *one word* of what he was saying, he was just telling it like it is: he is a one-hundred-percent victim of alien abduction and they want him for something but he doesn't know what. The poor, poor man. He had the sweetest voice, too. And I kept thinking, If Tracey were here she'd tell me if this person is a bald-faced liar or if he's telling the truth, or if, *even worse,* he believes he is telling the truth but he is lying because he doesn't know the difference, in which case he is not sane in any way."

"A conundrum," Trace agreed, unconsciously resting her elbows on the table. A variety of crumbs ground into her sweater, but she didn't react. "If he truly believes it and he's completely sane, it happened. And if he completely believes it and it didn't happen, he's crazy. And if it happened, we are all in a bind here, where the aliens are concerned."

Candy nodded vigorously. "That is it exactly. I wish you'd been here." She rubbed the rim of her coffee cup with her thumb, a gesture Trace had seen her make a thousand times. "Do you want some coffee?"

"No thanks. But get more for yourself if you want."

"And I've got to tell you something else about that UFO guy." Candy swallowed, lit another cigarette. "One thing he kept talking about was how many people have been abducted and don't know it, because their minds protect them by throwing up a *screen memory.* That's what he called it."

"A screen memory."

"Like this: he has a vivid memory of sitting on his grandmother's front porch and seeing a pack of gorillas come up over the hill in front of the house, coming toward him. He's completely sure that the gorillas are a screen memory for the first time the little midget policemen took him up in the spaceship and stole his sperm."

A high-pitched tone pierced Trace's inner ear and she shook her head as if to dislodge it. The sound stopped. "A pack of gorillas, huh?" Trace asked, smiling. One corner of her mouth twitched and she hoped Candy hadn't noticed. "A spaceship? Just to get some sperm?"

"And that made me think"—Candy spun her Bob Seger Commemorative Concert lighter on the table, spun it around until it was pointing at Trace—"about that time when you were six and you showed up on my granddad's hilltop, and when he asked you where you come from, you said you'd just had a picnic with a coyote, and at the end the coyote had put a little rock in your neck."

Trace's elbows ground against the food on the plastic tablecloth even harder. "Why must we always *talk* about this?"

"Is that rock still in your neck?"

"It isn't"—Trace waved the question away—"it isn't a rock— it's a knot. And anyway it's a calcium deposit or some sort of little, I don't know what. It's a little *knot*."

"Can I feel it?"

"No, you cannot feel it! I should get going. I want to visit your parents today."

"The other thing he saw?" Candy moved the limp, sweaty Duane to her other shoulder. "Tracey? Was a man walking through the train station, he was just a little boy with his dad at the time, and they passed another man walking a wolf on a leash. And eventually"—Candy talked faster, as if to make Trace hear it all, everything that could be said—"he gave up on the screen memories and he began to face what was happening to him, even though he was helpless to stop it. I think that's true. Although I seem to recall a moment at a Halloween party when he thinks he's seeing a child in a costume and it's really one of the dwarves, and that was *really* scary."

Trace reached for her bag, which she'd hung on one of the empty kitchen chairs.

"Doodlebug?" Candy reached over and grabbed Trace's hand, gripped it hard enough that Trace stopped moving. "Sit still a minute."

Trace sat back, let her body go limp.

"Your mother—Loretta, I mean—called." Candy's eyes filled with tears, but even so she seemed that same cheerful girl she'd been at fourteen, fifteen; even under all the weight and the bruises and the terrible color her skin had taken, she was a lovely prize, squandered. "It's not good."

"No." Trace could barely speak. Loretta would have asked, as she had asked Candy (and Candy's elderly parents, and everyone else Trace had ever known) where Trace lived, and Candy would have said she didn't know, because she didn't.

Before he knew the truth about her, Colt used to spin her around in the kitchen, her socks gliding over the slick linoleum floor, and he'd sing, *You with the stars in your eyes.* Sometimes Loretta would be there, sometimes she would hum along. She was the singer, after all—the real thing. If she was there she would slip in between them, between Trace and her daddy, and she would dance with him in a way Trace could only puzzle over. Loretta was so short, her hips were wide, and her breasts were enormous—how could she be graceful at all? How could she move so meltingly, and sing at the same time, and look Colt in the eye and keep him there? What was Trace failing to do, how could she possibly do more than master the finicky old Winchester .22 he'd given her, or catch a bigger fish than that largemouth bass last summer? Out on Lake Chapman she knew not to speak; she cast her line like a pro. She had spent hours working on his motorcycle with him, his truck, hand-ing him tools, rolling cigarettes for him on the arched roller with the rubber grip when his store-bought were gone. Patient hours, patient, silent years she had given him, and all Loretta had to do was slip in and sing a few notes, move her body like a snake with an undigested meal, and his youngest child vanished, the other two already gone.

"They found out where Billy is. But he doesn't know they know."

Trace jumped, hitting her knee on the underside of the table. Billy, gone five years? Her brother? Wild angel boy, now *he* had *loved* Loretta, he charmed her and picked her up off the floor to show her his strength. He had inherited the best of them, of his parents. Funny and tall and a great runner, he would hold open his arms to Trace and she could run and jump and he could catch her as if she weighed nothing; he spun her and read to her, and he was the one who took care of her after—

he got shocked a lot. Was that it, electricity? He took some very bad shocks, once while turning on the basement light, standing in an inch of water, and another time he—there was a guy wire, a storm, a bird, Trace tapped her hand against her ear, there was that sound again, but not as bad. "Where. Where is he?"

Candy shook her head; of course she didn't know.

"Loretta said Marty found him through some buddy. She was crying—"

"This is about Marty." Trace nodded. "Candy? This is about Marty, right?"

Candy swallowed but didn't blink. "Yes."

Trace took a deep breath, rested her hands flat on the sticky table. Weeds, who had been sleeping beside her chair, stood up and slipped under the table, to lie down on her feet. "I was the first to see him," she said, which Candy knew better than anyone as Trace was living with Candy and her parents at the time. It had been a

Sunday; Trace had gone home to pick up a few things, hoping her mother would be at church. She had just come through the front door and was about to cross the living room when she saw him walking down the staircase of her father's home, *Colt's* house, Marty Morrison. She already knew who he was—all the girls in Mason knew who he was. He owned an operation that rented out farm equipment; he ran it out of a huge ugly pole barn on 27, the two-lane highway that ran from Mason to Haddington to Jonah. Hell of an idea he'd had, that one, and at just the right time. Because farm equipment did almost nothing *but* break down, and at the worst possible moment, and the time had come when farmers couldn't afford to lose a single minute, and even if everything was perfect— the planting, the rain, the pesticides, the harvest—even then no one could make it anymore. Not one crop turned a profit but everyone was in too deep to sell, and the bank men stopped drinking coffee with the farmers or their hands, and the insurance men stopped coming around at all, and at four in the morning when the combine a man had financed for a staggering six figures threw a belt that had to be ordered, or when a blade broke, and he and his sons and farmhands were bent over in a blinding rainstorm, dropping bolts and wrenches, so afraid of what was right in front of them their chests began to stab, their arms weaken—someone, it didn't matter who, would eventually say, "Call Marty Morrison. Wake him up."

So he wasn't stupid, and he had money—more than anyone else in Mason, which didn't need to be much. He drove a Lincoln Town Car. He was a giant of a man, with a stomach so distended from diner food his back was swayed from supporting it. His hair was always neatly cut; he was clean-shaven and wore white shirts with dark, pressed blue jeans and cowboy boots. He was immaculate, the rarest quality in a man in a farm town, and he smiled and flirted and told jokes that made other men laugh, the men who owed him, and the bankers. At the county fair he always had a big display in the barn, and every time a pretty girl passed he would put his hand over his heart and say, "Come sit on my lap or I'll *die!*" and a few actually did.

Dusty told Trace about him; Dusty, who had never uttered a coarse word in her life. Candy and Trace were walking through the fair barn, and they could hear Marty's loud voice calling out all kinds of things, and then Dusty Ann was beside them. At first all Trace saw was Loretta's red hair, and she froze. But there was her sister's sweet face, and she took Trace by the shoulder and whispered in her ear. She straightened up and glanced in Marty's direction, leaned down, and asked if Trace understood what she'd been told. Trace couldn't answer, and Dusty had to ask again.

I did, Trace thought, her hands trembling on Candy's table. I understood, except I'd never heard of any of it before, what she said. I stood there like some brain-damaged spy: the message had been delivered to me and not one word of it made sense and anyway I didn't know what to do with the information, which government was I working for? Colt was selling elephant ears in the booth set up by the volunteer fire department, Loretta was singing at the talent show in the gym. And where was Billy? If one ride had broken, he was trapped in it. If a single gas line leading to the Italian sausage trailer had snapped, Billy was standing on it. I forget. I wasn't paying attention. Was it before Dusty's missing year, or after?

"Loretta was very upset, Tracey, she said that Marty is going to turn Billy in unless."

She had gone home to pick up a few things and there was Marty Morrison, walking down the staircase of her parents' home. He was wearing a white T-shirt and boxer shorts, and because she had come home at just that moment Trace was the first to learn that Marty carried with him a plastic two-liter Pepsi bottle with the top cut off—carried it up to bed and downstairs in the morning, and sometimes left it on an end table—into which he urinated, because it was time-saving. Also it just appealed to him. It was his own bottle of pee, and later she would learn he defied anyone to say a word about it. However, the longer nothing was said about it, the more prominently it was displayed. Perhaps he was conflicted. Someone was discreet about it too long (Dusty assumed she was the culprit), and the bottle ended up next to the punch bowl when Marty and Loretta were married in the big hall at the Armory. (Trace had asked, "How . . . how much was in there?" Dusty blushed. "A week's worth, maybe? A lot.")

"Why?" Trace asked, leaning toward Candy with a desperate need, like Duane trying to hurl himself to the floor, where nothing waited for him but gravity and whatever Skeet had ground into the carpet with the heel of his boot.

"Why which thing?"

"Why me? I'm not asking in self-pity, I'm not saying, Why me, Lord? I just honestly don't understand."

Candy stood—her shoulders seemed to be aching—and carried the baby into the living room, where Danny Rae had fallen asleep in front of the television. She put Duane in his playpen, stretching her arms and sighing as she walked back to the table. "You"— Candy fell heavily into her chair—"you . . . *denied* him?"

Trace watched Candy carefully, because this woman—a woman who had come to such straits as this—was the sole repository of Tracey Sue Pennington's past. Candy was a Living History project— or, more appropriately, a Civil War reenactor. She lacked verisimili- tude and was far too heavy to serve as a soldier, but she knew her lines and every square inch of the battlefield. Trace would soon have a degree, but it was Candy who would say, "This is where you fire your musket, and here is where you fall, and die."

Candy rubbed her eyes and left her hand there, covering half her face. "You were what he wanted all along, Bug, you are the reason he married her. That's a lot, you know, to marry someone and tangle up your money and your business and your . . . everything private to a person. He'll lose half of everything he owns if he leaves her, and you just—you just slipped out of his grasp." She paused, lowered her hand. "You saw him walking down the stairs that day, but he saw *you* long before—years and *years* before. He saw you in early summer, or spring maybe, riding behind Colt on his bike. You weren't wearing helmets—"

"We never wore helmets."

"—and your hair was so long and so black, a black velvet curtain, he said, and you had your arms wrapped around Colt's waist, you were resting your head on his back. You drove past him, past Marty, as he was walking to his car from the bank." Candy had said all of that while looking down into her ashtray, which was overflowing. She looked up.

Trace reached out and took Candy's hand, looping their fingers together. She whispered, "How do you know this?"

Candy whispered back, "Loretta told me."

In the living room the mayhem in cartoon land went on and on and on; mad, hectic music and ceaseless violence. Each moment seemed punctuated with a blow to the head, a shotgun blast, a fall from a heart-ripping height. The babies slept.

"It wouldn't be the worst thing," Candy said, but with hollow spots of hesitation in her voice, "to save Billy. You could close your eyes and pretend you was someplace else—that's what being married is like. And you did it twice before and survived."

Trace clenched her jaw muscles, nodded slightly. True enough. Once for Erin and once for Jessie, and he had kept his word, as far as Trace knew. She stood, nearly knocking her chair over, grabbing her purse at the same time. Weeds was up with her and almost to the door. Hat, scarf. One sweater bigger than the sweater she was wearing, another sweater bigger than that, her long black Australian bush coat, her gloves. "Where's the dog, Candy? Where's the redbone hound?"

Her friend, her only, remained seated, her thumb resting on the rim of her coffee cup but not moving.

"What did your husband do to him? Do you want me to guess?"

Candy shook her head no.

Outside, the air was so cold her lungs ached after a single breath. She walked carefully down the icy steps and onto the path to her truck, Weeds running ahead.

She was nearly there when Candy came flying out the door, jumping down the steps as if she were weightless. She ran to Trace and grabbed the sleeve of her coat, Candy's blue eyes wide and thrilled, as they had been long ago. "That man on the radio?" she asked, gasping in the frigid air. "Tracey? Remember the bobcat? I'm just saying. Do you remember the bobcat you found asleep on your bed?"

CHAPTER TWO

Caduceus

Dream Journal

My great-uncle, or maybe he was my great-great-uncle, Eugene, kept bobcats in his barn. They were his pets and they never hurt him. I used to sit on the porch swing with him in Kentucky and hear them screaming, but he said to pay them no mind, they were just talking.

One day he took his favorite out on a leash—her name was Sammy Cat—and led her to the porch to sit with him. She became interested in his right hand, so he put it down for her to smell and she licked the back—one swipe—and took his skin off in a sheet. He told me their tongues are barbed, just like a house cat's, except the barbs are so sharp and the bobcat's tongue is such a powerful muscle it can strip meat away from the bone like a knife.

The back of Uncle Eugene's hand was ruined as if he'd been burned. A surgeon grafted skin from his thigh, and the skin had grown tight and shiny. I asked him why *that* day, why that hand, because sometimes I have problems with my hands, and also with my ears, a bell ringing, and he laughed and said, "I'd just finished lunch—a tuna sandwich." He was right-handed.

"Were you mad at Sammy Cat?" I asked him, keeping the swing going with my foot.

"Naaah," he said, looking at his scar. "She was just being a bobcat."

After

Before I. There is no one I can ask now. I walked into my bedroom at the top of the stairs. Mine was the smallest room in the house, so small I kept my clothes in a chest of drawers in the hallway. My bed was covered with a scratchy quilt in a pattern of tropical flowers—I hated it every day. I hate it now, in retrospect. There was a bobcat curled up in the middle of the bed, sound asleep. They are bigger than you think; their ears alone are enough to make a person nervous. This one had paws as big as a Saint Bernard's. His fur was gold, with black stripes on his front legs, and spots and patches of brown and gray everywhere, a complex pattern. Tufts of black fur, baby fine, curled out of the tips of his ears. In his sleep he purred, a soft throaty hum. I stood as still as I could, I stood a great long time, I memorized every detail, until he

I don't have an uncle Eugene, great or otherwise, or so Loretta told me. I described his house, every room, right down to the sprung nail in the wood floor of the laundry room, a nail I cut my foot on. Uncle Eugene pounded the nail flat, put iodine on the cut. He was a widower; my aunt Nell had been dead for five years. There was a knothole in one of the barn doors right at eye level for me, and I had looked through the hole and watched three bobcat kittens play in the straw.

I was about to tell the part about the tuna sandwich and the barbed tongue when Loretta, who was sitting on the couch in the living room folding towels, said, "It was Colt who wanted another baby, not me. Your brother and sister were already too much, and pregnancy was very, very hard on me, Tracey Sue, because of my size, and it was the worst with you, I don't know why. I had heart-burn every day and I was dizzy—I've never suffered so, we'll just leave it at that. I don't know what Colt thought he was going to prove, or if he thought you'd be like a bit in my mouth." She shook out a dish towel with a snap. "But I don't have a bit in my mouth, do I? And he didn't get the boy he wanted, did he? It's like he has one mission in life, and that is to tame me, break me like a saddle-bred. Now tell me, do I look tame to you?"

I looked into her Appalachian blue eyes—ghostly pale—but not for long. Her red hair was curled and teased and sprayed into an elaborate dome; there were waves and . . . like the outline of pais-leys, it was busy, stiff, bright hair. Not the red she was born with—this was the color of a ripe cantaloupe mixed with blood. I glanced at her small nose, the slight upturn on the end, and her doll's mouth, spread with waxy Avon lipstick in a color that matched her hair. She didn't move or blink; she sat as if for a portrait.

"No ma'am," I finally said, looking down at the floor.

"No ma'am what?" she asked in her fine, playful voice.

"No ma'am you do not look tame to me."

"Good. Come sit by Mama and help me fold these towels, it's almost time for my story. You can watch with me and then we'll go pick gooseberries. If you lie again to me—about uncles or moun-tain lions or anything else—I will beat the life out of you and throw your remains in a ditch, you hear?"

I nodded.

"Well don't just stand there!" She smiled, and there were her teeth, small and round—not square like Colt's—as if she'd been gnawing on something for years. Grinding them down. "Come! Sit down and we'll turn on my story. Maybe today will be the day Nancy gets to leave the kitchen." She tipped her head back and laughed. "Laws, I doubt it, though. And you just watch: one of her sons was born the exact same time as Billy, and by the time Billy was three, that other boy was a *doctor*! I guess that would be called 'television time.' Different than ours."

Gooseberries. So it must have been summer. I loved them; they were like little planets, the faintest stripes running from top to bottom. I sat down next to my mother. I folded the rest of the towels and tried not to touch her, but she pushed her leg against mine every time she talked back to a character, or made some point to me about their lives. She was wearing white shorts, very tight, and the heat coming off her was unbearable; it felt exactly like looking into the open door of the huge furnace in the basement of my elementary school, which I had done once and never again. The one time had made my eyeballs feel melted and I'd singed my bangs.

When *As the World Turns* finally ended, I stood up to fetch the colander to gather gooseberries. The outside of my left leg, the one closest to her, had gone beyond scarlet into white. Within a few days I would have a water blister there so big I was afraid for anyone to see it. Dear Nancy, the soul of kindness and patience and maternal love, had not left the kitchen. Loretta, though: she could *cook*.

I was followed by a hawk as I walked down our country road. Bees circled my head but didn't sting me. One night I woke up and there was a pig standing in my bedroom doorway. It had a kind face, so I tied the belt from my bathrobe around its neck and led it downstairs and out the back door. Its hooves, those hard, devil-shaped shoes, made no sound on the wooden stairs and I hated that part but I'd already figured out a person has to get a pig out of the house any way she can.

I was swimming in the Taylors' pond and a black snake wrapped itself around my neck until I nearly lost consciousness. It loosened its hold, turned its head toward mine, and flicked its tongue into my mouth.

One evening I walked into the kitchen and there were seven rats standing on the kitchen counter. They watched me, moving nothing but their twitchy noses, until I gave up and left the room.

A fawn lay down with me under a tree. I was trying to make arrows from a kit Colt had gotten me. I don't remember what happened to the

I sat on our porch one afternoon, watching a turkey buzzard circle a narrower and narrower spot. I crossed the field until I could see the bird's aim: there was a newborn calf, split stem to stern, its intestines unwinding like carnival balloons.

The weasel.

The raccoon hung by its neck from a tree in the woods. Hung with a rope.

Three dogs in the cemetery, running toward me from beneath a spreading tree. A wolfhound, a shepherd, a square-headed terrier. The cemetery dogs, looking for my remains in a ditch.

Those were all a rehearsal for what came later. Uncle Eugene had been training me, he was my mentor. The bobcat was a lesson; so too the pig, the snake, the bees. I was learning something the old-fashioned way, by rote, as they say, and didn't realize it at the time. I caught a glimmer of it when Colt gave me back my old Winchester and asked me to go out in the woods with him. (He was carrying his 12-gauge, which I shot once and dislocated my shoulder.) It was raining so hard I could barely see the back steps, and we weren't wearing hats or jackets. I'm not sure I'd had time to put on any shoes. Weeds ran ahead of us, ran as if the weather suited him. Our guns were soaked, which Colt would ordinarily never allow. I followed him. I don't think I was wearing shoes. We came to the canopy in the center of the woods, and Colt reached back and broke the rubber band holding his ponytail. He shook his head and a shower, diamonds, flew from the ends of his hair, the blackest hair I've ever seen, it reached his waist by then. He pulled me toward him and broke the band in my hair too, and I spun around and around in the canopy's wet, green light. We danced and danced, Weeds ran around us, barking, but the rain never let up, not for a moment, *You with the stars in your eyes.*

That was our last semester, and then came the final exam. I stood at the front of the room, beside his open casket. Watkins Mortuary, Serving Your Needs Since 1957. I never made a sound, nor could I hear what was being said around me; it was as if my village had been hit with a concussion bomb, one that landed at my feet. I was deaf, and then suddenly was not, because I heard the front doors of the funeral home open with their soft *shisk* sound; I looked up, and in walked a black horse. It came right up the aisle toward me, and it wasn't a special horse—it smelled like a stall with a dirt floor, and there were knots in its tail and mane; its only exceptional trait was one brown eye, one blue. I had known a horse very like this one, once. Rain. The horse I knew was called Rain. My aunt Elbetta stood up and started screaming, and Loretta began to act faint, so I grabbed the horse's mane and climbed up on his back and left.

We rode and rode; it felt like hours. We rode to the end. Nothing. At one edge of my memory we are cantering down a gravel road; at the other edge it is morning, and I am in my small bedroom. Loretta hits me again and again, she makes threats, she has something in the pocket of her bathrobe. She makes vows, strikes harder. I stop her, finally, and rise from the bed. There is no way to measure how much taller I am than she, how much I have grown, how I am of an entirely different order than my pretty, ripe little bloody melon mother who can sing, who can sway against a man and steal his fight, this spitting, tiny thing who has a special name for me and will not stop screaming until she has branded me with it forever: the demarcation cutting through my lifeline. Before. After. I take one long step, cup the back of her head with my left hand as if drawing her toward a kiss; I slam my right palm over her mouth and nose. I shut her mouth. I look at her, much longer and harder than on gooseberry day. I ask her if she has ever seen an arcane map—say a map of the sea. Her pale eyes widen with fear, because I could break her neck, and she knows it. She doesn't need to answer; of course she hasn't seen such a map, not unless Nancy happens to be holding one in the kitchen in Oakdale.

I allow my left hand to slip down to the lip of her skull, to her brain stem. I slowly pinch the upper vertebrae—not hard, but enough. I tell her that maps used to end, the world had edges and no one knew what was past them. I tell her she and I are standing on such an edge; all the rest of the map is blank parchment, and one sentence. Beyond This Point: *Monsters*.

I let her go. She says no more, although there is something in her pocket. I begin to pack; I even turn my back on her, because at some point during our conversation Weeds has come into the room and he is sitting at my feet, watching her. I take very little. I take what I am honor bound to keep with me, and I go straight to Candy, to Paul and Esther Buck, who still call their daughter Candace, and they do not hesitate. They take me in. I am sixteen. In one year I will graduate from high school at the top of my class, the recipient of the Lilly Endowment, along with countless small scholarships that add up to

until he walks down the staircase on that Sunday morning with his shorn plastic bottle. Twice: once for Erin, once for Jessie and her broken heart, and I don't even have to do as married women do and pretend I am somewhere else, because both times there is a red fox sitting on the floor, positioned so that I can look directly into his eyes. They are obsidian, and hold no light. Twice. A fox.

This is from one of my favorite poems, by Charles Wright, called "Dog":

> *If I were wind, which I am, if I*
> *Were smoke, which I am, if I*
> *Were the colorless leaves, the invisible grief*
> *Which I am, which I am,*
> *He'd whistle me down, and down, but not yet.*

On the streets of my university, in the hallways, I pass frat boys and nearly invisible girls studying to be kindergarten teachers, and serious young men who eschew vanity. There are athletes and the high school academic stars who don't understand what has gone wrong here, why they must plunge so frantically just to touch mediocrity. Everyone moves away from me; my path is never obstructed. I am a girl who rode away from a funeral on a black night mare, and they know it, they feel it like the swipe of a barbed, insistent tongue. I am that girl.

✛

By the time she wrote the last sentence, Trace's hand and forearm ached, her shoulder was frozen, hours had passed. *What on earth,* she thought, flipping back through page after page of her angular handwriting, which was difficult, on occasion, even for her to read. She had adapted to life without electricity by writing faster and faster. She had a thick callus on her middle finger where her thumb pressed against the pen; her entire right hand seemed misshapen, now that she thought about it. To have a typewriter, to not have to go to campus to use one, what heaven that would be. Instead of tearing out what she had written, she stuck the whole notebook in a file folder and tossed it aside.

Dream journal, dream journal, dream journal, she repeated, digging in the pandemonium around her bed. Where was the one she began yesterday? She had acquired *mountains* of books, and although she periodically endeavored to stack them, they slid around like every-thing else and became part of the general population. *Hundreds* of books, maybe a thousand. "Good god," she said, catching a sock on the hook end of one of the spiral-bound notebooks. Even after squandering an entire day writing . . . what? Some sprawling, sham-bolic thing, not a word of which she could recall; her dream of the night before was still right there, she could see it all. Plus she had had the foresight to wake up and write the key words on her arm with a Sharpie, in order to keep the events in order. So she would use a new notebook; sometime between now and Monday she would find the first one and combine them, and who cared any-way? Her coffee was ice cold, the bedroom heater was nearly out of kerosene. Trace blew against her fingertips, reached over and pushed play on the paint-splattered boom box she'd found in the salvage shed at the dump. It was a little yellow Sony that looked like a small school bus and ate C batteries like a shark. She listened for a moment to the new Dead Can Dance cassette, then wrote: a game show, a woman who became a chair, a chair that became a machine, a room that lifted off the earth and flew away.

Every weekend she drove into Jonah and bought the same things: kerosene, Sterno, batteries, coffee, dog food. She stayed away from campus and distant from all central shopping locations, but the city was still too small and everything about her was conspicuous; there was no place she could *blend*. It helped that at her freshman orientation a kind assistant provost had simply told all the white children the parts of town they should avoid. Trace had written down the names of cross streets, restaurants, a Mexican grocery, whole neighborhoods, then taken out a map and discovered an Inventory Gain: all Dr. Berry—kind woman that she was—had needed to say was Do Not Cross the Planck River. Every address she named was over that line.

Trace found a Standard station for the kerosene in what was, essentially, a ghetto; Jonah natives called the area of town the Low End. Trace loved it there, and sometimes found herself sitting on the lawn of the Hallelujah Israelite Tabernacle and Its Army, listening to Reverend Willie (who sat on a metal kitchen chair with a shredded yellow vinyl seat) declaim from the Scriptures in what struck Trace as a nonsensical way—the Reverend was perhaps not entirely sane. Even when his rhetorical juggernaut gathered steam and he ordered the death of all blue-eyed devils, Trace lay on her back in the grass, content. Her eyes were violet, after all. She was a Mud Person; she carried a curse. She was forced to sing the songs of Zion, yet be content to stay in Babylon. That's how she chose to think about it anyway, all the while aware that she stood out among the Israelites like a leper in the Roman Senate.

No one in the Low End spoke to her; they barely glanced in her direction. But she didn't think they'd hand her over, either, if given the opportunity. They didn't care enough one way or the other.

She found a Big Lots not far from the gas station—a ghetto Big Lots where not one person from the university would ever be seen; an Aldi's; and most miraculously of all, an anonymous brick building in the center of an abandoned lot. There was nothing on the building to indicate what went on there—not a word. There was no sign anywhere on or near the lot. The only clue was a flag flying near the door. Trace wasn't quite sure, but she thought it was from Afghanistan . . . Iraq? She drove past it four or five times; one day she simply turned the wheel and parked in plain sight. She got out of her truck and walked toward the door feeling nothing but the gut sensation of slowness, the rubbery stretch anticipation adds to time. If anything she was slightly giddy; no one knew better than she how much there is to fear, and that the threat is never where you expect it to be.

Inside she was faced with a sight so strange she nearly laughed aloud. Her shock must have shown on her face, because a number of the men standing (frozen and postured—each looked like a combination of a sentry and a mannequin) at the various stations in the building said hello and welcomed her.

She was in the supply outpost for members of the Nation of Islam who were preparing for a violent revolution. They explained themselves directly, with a mesmerizing tone of respect and chivalry. No weapons were sold there but nearly everything else was: large gas- or diesel-powered generators; cases of batteries; flashlights and lanterns from Russia with hand cranks, should the batteries run out. There were floor-to-ceiling cases of prepackaged military rations: MREs, waterproof matches and jackets and hats, mink wax for waterproofing everything else. There were safety flares, emergency medical kits with surgical field training manuals. Blankets, tents, night-vision goggles; Trace couldn't take it all in. Her chest began to ache and she had a hard time swallowing. She rested her hand on her throat, took the measure of her rabbiting pulse. It was the men themselves causing her heart to race: the bespoke suits that were both subtle and proud, and the way the men stood, the depth their faces conveyed while remaining expressionless. One man gathered his things to go home, and when he emerged from the back room he was wearing a cashmere overcoat, a brown derby hat, a silk scarf, leather gloves.

Trace turned away from him, rested her forehead on a cold metal shelf. She was in the presence of purity and conviction and beauty and rage—they were all woven together in these human men. Purity alone was rare, maybe impossible; conviction unlikely; beauty an indictment. Their rage was not corruption but clarity. Here was alchemy, Jung's intoxicating metaphor. She felt she should confess something to them but couldn't grasp the nature or name of her sins. How facile and childlike, anything she might say; even the sword above her head was shopworn and dull. They were prepared to kill, and to die, while Trace cowered in the dark, in the cold, in garbage, listening for the sound of antlers crashing through the trees around the house. Or hooves on the rotting roof beams. Wings at the window. A Town Car slouching down her hidden lane.

She turned back to the men—soldiers of discipline and the perfect silk/wool blend—and they were watching her. "I—" Her voice failed, broke.

They had a case of Sterno that would have lasted her for months, those gorgeous, misogynistic, vain men, and she often thought of going back to buy it but didn't. Never. She never would.

+

"IANTHE?!?"

The voice cut through the air of the restaurant like a sniper's bullet. She gave herself a single beat, composed her face, looked up.

Myka Holloway and Anastasia . . . Fortinbras or LaFramboise, it changed from week to week, there they were, in *her* barbecue restaurant, which she called either the Murder Shack or the Surly Hut, depending on whether there was actual gunfire or merely extreme rudeness. Trace herself had just sat down—she hadn't taken off her coat or gone to the counter to order. How did they get *here*?

Anastasia was a tiny, multiracial, half-transgendered (the taking-of-estrogen half) drag queen who was famed for ending every relationship with screaming and violence and suicide threats. The Jonah Police Department knew him quite well, and had stopped bringing their rottweilers to his domestic disturbance calls because dogs terrified him and made him cry. But when he didn't have a boyfriend, Anastasia was also known as a generous person and tireless caregiver.

"Hey, you two," Trace said, smiling at them. "What brings you—"

"Look at"—Anastasia pursed his lips, waved his tiny hands up and down the length of Trace's body, peeking under her table—oh, and also he interrupted people with his exuberance—"all of it. I *love* this, the fingertips cut out of your gloves, OH MY GOD THAT IS SO PUNK-ASS but also urchiny, you know, Myka? Like that *Oliver* movie? Little urchins on the street? And what do you call this?"

"It's a hat."

"Yes, I see that it's a hat, but of what variety? What is its relationship to the gloves?"

"They have no relationship. I think this style is called . . . I think this is a hunter's cap."

"Thus the earflaps, mmm hmmm. Could we also call it a—who is that, Myka? A Davy Boone sort of thing?"

"Why not." Myka kept her eye on the door.

"Now, Ianthe, let me ask this. What is wrapped around your neck?"

"It's a . . ." Trace looked down to remind herself. "It's a black-and-white prayer shawl, goat's wool. You're welcome to join me," she said, gesturing toward the chairs opposite her.

"We just stopped in for Diet Coke. Myka would *never* eat here, oh Jesus hold the phone," he laughed. "And *where* did you get the coat? I want the man who originally owned it."

Trace ran her hand over the right pocket, absently. "I forget. Where this came from."

"I see layers and layers here." Anastasia studied Trace's black sweaters, the black wool leggings over which she wore two skirts. "I'm trying to move Myka toward layers like this."

"Hello, Myka."

Myka smiled coolly. "He'll let me know when I'm allowed to talk."

"Tell me about these boots. Because I'm thinking of giving Anastasia a whole brand-new style, the eighties have been a HOR-ROR for me, you have no idea. I thought if I embraced glam in eighty-one, eighty-two, I mean really *embraced* it"—he grabbed Trace's forearms and squeezed for emphasis—"I would be set for a while, I'd develop the look that IS Anastasia, not just what she wore, *n'est-il pas?*"

What was the right answer? Trace wondered. "It is. Not. I understand."

"And now everyone is Goth. I mean no one in Indiana, but other places, like Seattle, and whatchacallit, Nova Scotia. EVERY-ONE is Goth, but what does it mean?" He leaned toward Trace with a pleading look in his eye. "Maybe if I understood it better I could decide if it's right for the New Me."

Trace shrugged. "I'm sorry, I don't think of myself in that category."

Myka raised an eyebrow. Anastasia said, "Oh REALLY? What is this style called on your planet, then?"

"I—"

"What was the last movie you saw?"

The last movie? She had seen . . . two films last year? "*Betty Blue.*"

"Uh-huh. And tell me your five favorite bands or records right now, quick."

She pictured the floor of her bedroom, the cassettes without cases and vice versa. Which were the ones she protected? "Okay. Leonard Cohen, everything. Joy Division, *Closer*. The Cure, Bauhaus, the Sisters of Mercy, Roxy Music, *Avalon*. The Smiths. Tom Waits, *Frank's Wild Years*. Kate Bush, *Hounds of Love,* oh, and I adored someone I heard in a club a few months ago, a man, a composer named—I forget—with women singers. The project is called Black Tape for a Blue Girl."

"I thought so."

"Wait—that's just off the top of my head. I also love Penderecki and Miles Davis and—"

"Too late." Anastasia held up his hand.

"Come on," Trace said, "it's not like I mentioned Killing Joke or Theatre of Hate or Fields of the Nephilim, for heaven's sake."

"Hmmm." Anastasia thought about it. "I've never heard of those people, but *you* have, Ianthe. And what about this hair color, what do you think it is, Myka?"

Myka didn't even glance at Trace. "Jet Grape."

Trace said, "I don't dye my hair, I never have."

"Then what about your lipstick? You weren't born with lips that color."

Myka said, "Jet Grape."

She was right about that one, so Trace said nothing.

Anastasia and Myka wore the same smug smile. Myka said, "Come to our party tonight—it's just the regular scene. Do you know Vintage Crest apartments? Yes? Apartment 42."

"Thank you, really, but I don't—"

"But I want you to. And you know," Myka said, leaning close to Trace, "I understand you have a hideaway somewhere; maybe I'll try to find it. That's how much I wish you would come."

The two women studied each other. If Trace were standing

she and Myka would tower over Anastasia so completely he might have been their toddler. "When you put it like that," Trace said, taking a notebook out of her bag and unwrapping her scarf. She dismissed the two as if she'd been roped into a social engagement she was too busy for; she affected that, at least. In fact she had felt threatened, and she would go, and if little Anastasia *really* wanted to know the meaning of Gothic, Trace would tell him.

✝

The truck stop Trace preferred for showering covered what had been an entire farm, and was situated just before the ramp onto the six-lane highway leading to Ohio. There were always twenty-five to thirty trucks parked there, engines running as the drivers slept a few hours, or refueled, showered, ate lunch. It had gone through various owners, but each chose to call the business by a single, inappropriate word: Star, Love, Rainbow. The Love Truck Stop: a noble wish for an establishment. These days it was Sunshine, even though the most frantic activity there occurred at night.

The Star Love Rainbow Sunshine One Stop Truck Stop had eaten up a couple hundred acres, but the back of the parking lot was still bordered by an ungoverned field. The sleepers parked there, farthest from the bright lights over the pumps and surrounding the building. Trace parked close to the building but hidden from the highway, as far from the sleepers as she could get while still being near them.

Night or day (but especially after dark), the moment she stepped out of her truck Trace could see them, women moving like shades, weaving through the bank of tractor-trailers. They were there at the height of summer, in torrential rains, and now. The temperature on the digital readout on the towering Sunshine sign read nineteen degrees. Sound carried farther in air this cold and clear; as she had before, Trace could hear the stream of conversation, negotiation, conducted in the shadows and just above a whisper.

She carried her bag through the glass doors and into the blinding light of the gift shop. The women's shower was rarely occupied, and when it was Trace sat in the cafeteria with her homework. Tonight there was no waiting list, and Trace took the key from the clerk and recorded her name in the log as she had for four years: Angela Linton. She paid in cash. The clerk (tonight it was Wanda) had obviously originated at the factory where the supply of truck stop clerks for Star or Sunshine came from. They all had wiry gray hair, glasses. They smoked, were spherical, and devoid of personality. The Unattractive Stepford Clerks of Love. The exception was Louise, who worked the day shift. She met all the requirements except for size; she was gaunt; moved like and resembled a chicken.

Trace moved past the video games, the Harley-Davidson display, and the portion of the store devoted to Christian merchandise, down the hallway toward the restrooms and showers. The door she went through was blue, a metal as heavy as steel. The paint was scarred, gouged away in some places. It was ugly, but secure. Inside Trace hung her bag on one of the hooks, then locked the sliding bolt at the top of the door, the dead bolt, the doorknob, and stepped on the flat surface that pushed a bolt lock into a hole in the floor. The tiled walls and floor of the shower were decrepit but rarely dirty; the Wandas seemed to have a certain respect for the room. Trace began the arduous process of removing her (as it turned out) stylish layers, stacking them on the metal shelf. After she pulled off the last sock from each foot, she stepped into her shower sandals; she never let her feet touch the floor here. She carried her towel and her toiletry bag into the shower stall and turned on the hot water.

For a long minute, maybe two, she couldn't move or think. She was warm. She was standing in water and she was warm. Her skin, her actual cells, opened up in the steam; her shoulders relaxed. During winter break she hadn't worked at the bookstore and of course there were no classes, so she had rarely gotten any relief from the cold, from the way she kept her body coiled, preserving what heat she could. It was only here, in a room that could have been in a prison, that she unwound.

She washed her hair and thought of Myka Holloway. They were both English majors and had come to U of MW at the same time. It was amazing to think that only four years ago Trace used to see Myka hanging out in the convenience store parking lot, the Village Pantry at the edge of campus, dressed like a boy and in the company of many boys, skateboarding and wearing a Black Flag knit cap or a Circle Jerks T-shirt. Her hair was long and blond and she always wore it down and loose. With the cap if it was cold. One day her Doc Martens were brand new and the next day they had been scuffed (all ten eyelets) so thoroughly Myka might have kicked Nancy Spungen to death with them.

Myka had been quiet in the classes they took together, worshipped by all the boys in the skate punk fringe (Jonah's anything "fringe" was so far removed from the cultures on the coasts that mimicking a style was akin to playing the game Telephone: the original message lost a word, assumed an uncomfortable adjective, and eventually bore no relation to what was first said). In years to come the Black Flag hat would be replaced with the Red Hot Chili Peppers, and Circle Jerks would give way to Jane's Addiction. Myka's clothes got tighter, her hair color changed with frequency. Her parents bought her a black Honda CRX. Different groups of boys loved her, and she often had a boyfriend in a local band. She became more talkative in class, and there was *something* there, Trace thought, but she didn't know what it was. It was as if Myka wanted to be a performer but had been given no particular talent. She was an actor who couldn't act, a musician with no instrument. Most important, she was a famous, worshipped, wealthy, gorgeous legend, with only a small audience of boys.

In a single day (it seemed) she had made the change to her current incarnation: a gliding walk, Edwardian dresses and gowns, her hair a delicate strawberry blond curled into tendrils. She often wore it up, bound in elaborate, antiquated styles, leaving a single curl at the side of her face, and another over her collarbone. The Honda was gone—Myka no longer drove, but was driven. It was the campus poets who adored her now, and the male faculty members.

Trace combed conditioner through her hair, stood with her face in the jets of the water as the conditioner did its work. Myka had grown up not only in a town like Mason, but in a subdivision outside it, in a ranch house with a mother who collected Disney paraphernalia. Such straight white teeth Myka had, though, courtesy of her orthodontist father, whose office was between a Dairy Queen and a little shop where women paid money to decorate teddy bears in pearls and wide-brimmed hats, using a hot glue gun.

Trace turned and tipped her head back, rinsing out the conditioner that smelled not like kerosene but sandalwood. The water reflected off her hair as if off black ice, and it was so long now it nearly covered her one tattoo: a snake, rising up from its coils, its jaw yawning to swallow the base of her spine.

The Vintage Crest apartments were off campus but attracted only college students. The two-story buildings dated back to the seventies, and if the residents of the Low End had their projects, the students of U of MW had this.

Trace opened the door that led to apartments forty to forty-three; Myka lived on the second floor. Dreadful, the notion of attending a party, and Trace's feet were leaden as she climbed the stairs, which were carpeted and ruined in an unparalleled fashion. She entered the party without knocking, as no one would have heard her over the sound of the music anyway: Orff's *Carmina Burana,* playing not at a particularly loud volume but with the bass so high the floor of the apartment had a vague shiver, like a struck drumhead.

The room was lit only by candles and a lamp with a dark purple bulb, and there were maybe twenty people standing in little clusters, talking, Trace presumed, about death.

"IANTHE!" Anastasia floated over the room, an inappropriate accessory in Myka's decor. "Come here, come here, I was just getting ready to tell this story." He dragged Trace over to a small, round dining room table with a smoky glass top. "Move, you," he said to an overweight girl in various leather garments that appeared to have been applied with double-stick tape and a blow-dryer. She rose as if accustomed to such orders. "Now, take her wrap and her goat scarf and . . . hat and put them in *my* room, not in Myka's room, thank you."

Trace watched the girl go. "Is she your slave?"

Anastasia wrinkled his little nose. "Well, God did create fags so fat women would have someone to dance with, but I draw the line there. She is a thing. Now," he said, turning to other people at the table, "I was just saying that we had gone to visit my Granny over in the projects because I had this form I had to fill out for health insurance and on the form was a box for race. I was in the student health office and I saw it and I said, *nicely, I thought,* to the desk girl, 'I don't know what to put here.' She glanced up at me and said, 'Just check *Black.*' I *looked* at her and *looked* at her and then I said, 'My mama is half black, half Mexican, and my dad is half white, half Korean. You think I'm *black,* BITCH?' " He paused for laughter, which he got, and continued, "So I went to Granny's and showed it to her. I asked her what I should do and she didn't even look at the form, she handed it back to me and said, 'Honey, you just check *Human Being*.'"

"Sweet," someone said, without feeling.

"Then we went to the most ghetto barbecue hole I've entered since I left Granny's and who do we see there but *this one*!" He patted Trace's shoulder. She looked around the table at the faces staring back at her, all of them pallid and slashed with lipstick and eyeliner. Virtually everyone was smoking French cigarettes. There was a great deal of architecture going on with hair, too.

A young man leaning against the wall next to Trace said, "I know you." He too was dressed all in black leather and studs, but his clothes fit him. He was tall but not gaunt, as was generally prescribed. The longer she looked at him the more Trace saw; there was a lot of him, and between his size and his piercings and his intense stare, she imagined he frightened old women and little children everywhere he went.

"You do?"

"I've seen you." He held out his hand; the back was tattooed in a black Celtic pattern and his palm was bleeding. "Todd."

Trace shook his hand. "You're bleeding."

"I know."

Myka appeared, as if on cue. Trace wondered if she'd been waiting in her bedroom for a timed appearance or if she'd simply run out on hearing the twentieth retelling of Just Check *Human Being*. Her costume for the evening was stunning: she was dressed like a girl in a photograph by Lewis Carroll, a barely pubescent waif who had spent most of her life in bed, ill with something wasting and unnameable. She was too tall to pull off part of it (the pedophilia), too old for all of it, for the entire business of the gown, the vintage robe, the dead flowers in her hair. But she was striking, and everyone was looking at her.

"COCKTAILS!" Anastasia shouted as he ran into the small kitchen, began talking about something.

Barely an hour later the glass tabletop was sticky with Chambord liqueur and vodka, and everyone was drunk except Trace.

"Did you know him—Dante?" Myka asked Trace, with a pained expression. Myka's eyes were green, her lips were scarlet, and she was quite drunk.

"I don't think so."

"So you didn't know he died?"

"No."

"He"—Myka reached across the table and rested one hand on Trace's sleeve while finishing her fifth drink with the other—"I used to go to his apartment and we would read Rimbaud to one another in the dark. Or Verlaine. He used to have dreams so frightening he couldn't repeat them." Her eyes filled with tears. "His apartment, that's where he died, it caught fire, he died in the fire and there were people outside who told me that as he died he was calling my name. His pit bull died too." Myka covered her face with her pale hands and began to sob.

"I'm sorry," Trace said, unsure what to do next. It *was* very sad, and Trace loved pit bulls. She and Colt had had six at one time, and as often happens one of them killed another and the remaining four were confiscated and humanely euthanized, because, as Animal Control explained to Colt, it's better for people to kill the dogs than for the dogs to kill one another. Colt had said, "But they *love* to kill each other, it's their reason for living at all," which didn't sit well with the officer.

"Ah," Myka said, taking a handkerchief from the pocket of her robe and touching her face with it. "Forgive me. Have you read much Rimbaud?"

The hair, the lips, the gown, every gesture. Where inside this

woman was Black Flag? Where were the Misfits for that matter, or
the skateboard and the black Honda CRX? "Yes," Trace said, pushing her untouched drink toward Myka. "Yes, I've read Rimbaud."

She rinsed out a glass in the dark kitchen, filled it with water. There
were three or four people clustered in front of the refrigerator.

"Did you hear about that kid at the truck stop?" one of the girls
asked.

"Which truck stop?"

"The one way out, close to the bypass. Peace or something like
that. No—Roses? I think it's called Roses Truck Stop."

"What kid?"

"Apparently there are prostitutes there—truck stop prostitutes,
and one of them brings her kid with her. He's a boy but she dresses
him like a girl and sells him to the truckers. He's only like eleven or
something."

The group paused. Someone lit a cigarette. "That's entirely im-
plausible," a young man said.

For the next hour Trace was confined to the couch, where numerous people explained their positions on sex and death, the general
consensus being they were coequal. There were ten minutes of All
Penetration Is Rape (would that never go away?), followed by
Death as Rape, the Rape of Love, I Was Raped in a Dream and
Woke Up Bleeding. *Blue Velvet* was on Myka's very expensive-
looking television, muted, via her expensive VHS player. Dennis
Hopper pulled the mask to his face again and again (someone kept
rewinding it) but Trace couldn't remember whether he was asking
for his mommy or his daddy. On Myka's sound system, which took
up an entire wall, Siouxsie was singing "The Quarterdrawing of the
Dog," and from somewhere in the apartment Anastasia yelled,
"Can't we dance NOW? Myka, don't you have ANY Wham!?"

• • •

A number of candles had already guttered; there had been sickness and weeping, and the room kept getting darker and darker. Trace would have left but for the scene playing out in front of her. A young man named Jeff was demanding that his girlfriend cut open her chest with a razor, for him, to prove her love. What seemed to have started out as a joke had grown completely serious, and the girl was crying, holding the razor blade.

"Just do it," Jeff said, not with any menace, but the way one might tell a child to finish her homework.

"Why? Why is this necessary?" The girl—Melanie—had already asked that question a dozen times and each time she got the same answer.

"Because I'll break up with you if you don't."

"But I let you do that one thing!" she wailed. This point, too, had been made sufficiently. The first few times she brought up "that one thing," she had whispered it, but by now it was common knowledge and the whispering part was over.

"This is not. connected. to. that."

Trace begged to differ, as she could see a number of ways they were connected, "that" being a demand that Melanie allow Jeff to pull a bloody tampon out of her body with his teeth at an illegal bat-cave club somewhere in Ohio. On the dance floor, obviously, not anywhere private.

"We've been together two years!"

"I have a *calendar*, Melanie. Now are you or aren't you?"

Trace was about to stand up—this could go on all night—when Melanie tore her thin black shirt, tore it straight down from the neckline, and dragged the razor horizontally across her chest, over her breastbone. The cut was at least four inches long, probably not deep, but her hands were covered with blood from the moment she lifted the razor.

Todd said, "Ouch." He was leaning against a different wall.

"Dear God!" Anastasia said, running from the kitchen. "You people are just *asinine,* get out of the way! Stupid girl, press this towel against your chest—let's get some of the blood off and see how deep it is. If you need stitches you WILL go to the emergency room because I WILL drive you there myself. You are NOT going home—"

"Damn." Jeff was standing back, watching Anastasia tend to Melanie. He seemed genuinely stunned, although Trace couldn't imagine this being more shocking than the tampon in Ohio. "Damn." He began to pace, then disappeared around a corner in the hallway. When he came back he was wearing his leather jacket. "Melanie, I'm breaking up with you anyway. You're *crazy.*"

"I'm out of here," Trace said. She decided to stop in the bathroom before going home; a person of indeterminate gender was passed out in the hallway, so Trace stepped over it. In the dark bathroom she reached for a light switch and felt two. She flipped them both on. This was the first time a light had been turned on since she arrived and she was stunned. She had no idea what was going on in the bedrooms, but this was not what she had expected *at all.*

There were vomit stains all over the beige carpet, and no toilet paper, and the shower curtain was gray with mold, and even the most basic amenities like hand soap or a towel were missing, apparently because the work of worshipping both Thanatos and Fashion is very time-consuming and one can't simply be dropping in at the drugstore for trifles. Although there was, Trace noticed, quite a large wooden box filled with makeup and hair supplies and spray-on temporary color and shiners and blow-dryers and expensive makeup brushes to apply the white mineral powder that allowed Myka to float down the hallways of the English department embodying Poe's maxim that there is nothing more tragic than the death of a beautiful girl.

• • •

When she stepped out of the bathroom the girl in the shrink-wrap leather was waiting with Trace's coat and scarf and hat. Maybe she's *my* slave, Trace thought, thanking her.

She was out the door as fast as she could move, saying good-bye to no one. She had no interest in how deep the cut was, or how humiliated Melanie was, or how Anastasia would fix it. And she certainly didn't want to know how Myka would retell it.

Just as she reached her truck Todd slammed the trunk of a vintage Ford Fairlane, parked next to her.

"I know you," he said, smiling at her.

Trace smiled back, opened the door of her father's truck. "No you don't."

She stopped at the nearest Village Pantry (they were everywhere) to use the pay phone. The temperature had dropped into the single digits, and Trace was so cold, the phone was so cold, she could barely dial the number.

Skeet answered, furious to be awakened. *"What?"*

"Let me speak to Candy, please, Skeet."

"What the fuck, Tracey? Do you know what time it is?"

In the background Candy said, "Who is it, what's wrong?" Then, "Tracey?"

"I'm sorry to wake you, but could you do me a favor?"

"Of course. Yes."

"Will you call Loretta and tell her yes but that it has to be tomorrow? Seriously, it has to be tomorrow or not at all."

"Okay."

"You won't forget?"

"I'll call her now," Candy said, sounding fully awake.

"Good." Trace nodded and shivered at the same time. "Now's a good time."

CHAPTER THREE

Pluto

Dream Journal

I went where I was told to go although I don't know where that is and could never find it again. Once I was inside, the room felt familiar—it was the same room. It was a room from before. The iron bed frame, almost free now of the flaking white paint I remembered. The ragged patchwork quilt and single flattened pillow. The walls had yellowed with age and neglect, and the veneer on the dresser top had curled in strips like dark candy. Weeds had been in a panic when I left, barking and turning in circles and finally throwing himself against the back door after I had closed it; there is no way to explain it to him—the binding narrative of not just the Dog, but the Black Dog, his place in myth and thus in *psyche,* the Soul, my soul. I could try to explain his work as the guide into death but that seems like a lot to place on the shoulders of such a sweet boy, his floppy ears and feathered tail. He would break under the weight. He is no Anubis, the blue-black jackal. Hekate doesn't want him, not with even one of her three heads. She isn't waiting at the cross-roads for gifts of garbage and black puppies. I know he is no figure, no shadow, because I was there when Colt found him. I remember the fly-bitten ears, the worms, the swell of his ribs. The vet said he was no more than seven weeks old. Today I walked away as if I couldn't hear his panic, because there was nothing else I could do. This door required a key that I somehow had in my possession, and the key required turning, but that escapes me now as well. I was on the outside of the room and then I was inside it. I don't *crave* liminality but neither do I despise an actual threshold. I can't stop thinking about how, a few months ago, a guy I work with named Jim was talking about the decline of Christianity—the ways it's disappearing so slowly no one seems to notice. He said, "I mean, take Hell. Do we still have Hell? What happened to Hell?" I had laughed at the time but a few nights later I was reading a conversation between Michael Ventura and Hillman, and Ventura asked, in essence, the same question. Hillman said, "The realm of Hades has become childhood." I put the book down and thought about what he meant; the way our culture, at a loss to grasp the Underworld (even when it is right in front of us), has taken the whole inexplicable mess, the Bottomless—it was Heraclitus, I think, who said we could never find the ends of the soul though we traveled every way, it is so deep—and placed it in the province of childhood. Now the whole of the past, even what belongs to someone else, is not what happened but what happened *to me;* dreams are not autonomous, they are messages *to me* about *me.* Hell is material and the material is mine—it is bound to my ego with a thick cord, and in order to amplify the pathos until it deafens, I pick up the dead thing, that dense lump of materialism and ego, and throw it backward at the perfectly innocent and helpless child I imagine is standing behind me. And when it hits her I say, *The child is* ME.

From the moment this door closed I knew there was something in the corner, behind the dresser. I knew I shouldn't look at it directly so I didn't, but I could feel its life, its patience. Hades is Invisible, Hidden, Unseen, and He fathered Nothing. No one. But Zeus was rumored to be the brother of Hades, and the *daemon* of Zeus was an eagle. Not an eagle here. Around the corner of the dresser there appeared a face like a small bear and I blinked; one paw and then another, it stopped. Those two front paws pointed inward slightly, the claws long and curved. He stepped all the way out and I. For a moment I thought it was a badger or a weasel, they are such *thieves,* but this was far bigger, fur the color of mahogany with a blond ring around its neck, a brilliant face—a wolverine. My brother, Billy, loved comic books, country music, and going to church. He always had a job—from the time he was fourteen until. He worked at a car wash, he delivered pizzas, he took tickets at a movie theater. Eventually he got on with Colt's crew and took up carpentry, and from that point on he stomped around in work boots, carpenter's jeans, and T-shirts, with sawdust in his red hair. He stomped into the kitchen and ate vast amounts of food; he stomped through the living room and yelled out, *Where is everybody?* When he danced with Loretta she kept her feet far from his and he made her laugh like no one else could. The River Styx is freezing and its etymology is Hatred. Sacred water. Its dead and deathly cold runs through the frame of everything; it is an *original* principle, just as is Eros, or Chaos. Styx has children: Z—not Zealous but something like that (Zeal); and Nike (Victory—that's an easy one); Cra— Cratos, Craton, I forget (Strength); and Bia (Force). Styx is the icy mother and her children are the children of Hatred, which requires a great deal of thought as Styx is the site upon which the Olympian gods pledged their oaths. No one pledges oaths to Medea or Susan Smith, and that is how we know that Hatred is part of the *logos* of the soul, and that it probably doesn't stand in direct opposition to Love. That Love and Hate are opposing, or are two sides of a single coin, is an arbitrary convention. They may not be connected at all, any more than trees are the opposite of pie. Maybe they run parallel, never to touch; or like a ball rolling downhill, one is ceaselessly becoming the other. I can't imagine how many mornings I looked out the window and saw Billy and our dad standing in front of the open hood of the truck, scratching their heads, or trying to turn a bolt just out of reach. Billy kept the bike running, too, and he learned the art of trimming trees wearing just a harness. He had no complaints—that was his genius—and he never begrudged anyone anything; not favors or loans or calls in the middle of the night. I can't picture him saying no to anything. He was spontaneous and tireless and he was guided by a moral code all the more trustworthy and natural because he never expressed it (probably couldn't have) and didn't inflict it on anyone else. The room was barely big enough for the wolverine to move; the musk, his stealth, made my heart tumble in my chest, my stomach turned, too. I swallowed, took a deep breath, faced him. He leapt up to the dresser top and then down to the iron footboard, wrapping his claws around the frame with a terrible slowness and a series of slight clicks as the nails touched the metal. I was shaking so hard I had to grab the edge of the mattress to steady myself; I felt as if I were being split in two. Beauty and Terror: are they oppositional, are they wed? Do the two principles twirl like a double helix? Imagine how many people have seen the open jaws of the shark bearing down on them, or been shaken like a rag doll by a bear, just before his teeth crushed the skull. The animal could kill me, there was no doubt in my mind. Everyone (doesn't everyone?) has a list ready: under these conditions I would fight with as much violence and ferocity as human

beings are capable of, but under these I would surrender immediately. I would offer my throat and pray for a swift end. It's all well
and good to say, *I would have rushed at the SS and taken one of them out
with me.* Please. After you have been stripped naked, your head
shaved, your teeth extracted; after you have been made, along with
your family, your neighbors, your entire village, to dig your own
grave and then stand at the edge watching as, one at a time, everyone you loved fell backward into it, what difference does it make
whether you fight back? There is nothing to fight, because the Underworld isn't *under* anything. It is upward and downward and in
every direction, just at the tips of your fingers. If you want to give
Hades to your childhood, if you want to rest it on the frozen banks
of your mother, fine; if you want to say that the architects of the
Final Solution were attempting to literalize ancient descriptions of
Hell with the ovens, the smoke, the ashes, the bodies stacked like
firewood? That seems inarguable. They were combining art and religion, a tendency as old as our species. The Nazis were grandiose,
the Ego Encrusted Children of Styx. We needn't set our sights so
high, though, not when there are women wrapped in old carpets
and tossed in Dumpsters, and children left to starve to death in
locked closets or cages. There are rats in the nursery, in the pantry;
there are truckloads of blood-soaked bandages and sponges leaving
the local hospital right now, gangrenous limbs being amputated,
weapons being brokered. There were two hounds at Candy's and
now there is only one. If this animal has come for me I won't move
or make a sound.

Except I know better, and before Marty can imagine what is
happening, I have pulled a length of rope from under the mattress
and bound his wrists as if he were a rodeo calf. I leap over the head-
board, taking his wrists with me, and tie the rope to the iron railing.
He is so shocked he forgets to struggle, or else he thinks I am im-
provising, bartering for something extra, which he would gladly

give me for playing rough. He would love a boot to the head, the brute heart of the brute he is. One thing I've never understood is why Hades, the Unseen One, is also called Pluto. What is wealth in the Underworld? What currency, what is traded? Does Pluto merely hoard, does he steal? Maybe the answer is simple: money is power, and allows Pluto to have anything he wants, which is every-thing. And he gets it, in the end.

As I dress and gather my things, reestablish the first principles of my life, the wolverine leaps from the bed rail and lands next to Marty's hip. Ole Hoss, the Entrepreneur and Friend of Foreclosure, looks like his heart might just give out, especially when the first claw is lifted and lowered onto his vulnerable white gut. I see the nails sink into Marty's soft flesh, and then in a single fluid movement the wolverine is on top of him, they are face-to-face and the little bear has been replaced with a hiss and a display of teeth so sharp they might have been filed. I'm tempted to remind Marty—who isn't after all himself a Natural Man, merely their lending officer—that a wolverine has enough jaw strength to crush bone, but I don't. In-stead I lean over and say, quietly (if there are other guests I don't want to disturb them), "He will eat your intestines while you lie there awake." This doesn't appeal—I can tell by the man's ghastly com-plexion, the cold sweat. "Now you tell me where my brother is, and not just the country or the city or some vague neighborhood in Mexico—I want the street address and his alias. Don't lie."

He tells me everything and I write it all down carefully on a church bulletin Marty had in his pocket; I go over the information with him a few times, as blood streams down the sides of his torso, soaking the bed. I *could* tell him they are just holes being gouged out of his appetite by the nails of a predator—Marty isn't *dying,* he's just bleeding—but I don't offer reassurances of any sort. I gather my coat, my scarf and hat, the urchin gloves. The window in the room is impossible to open; there appear to be at least twelve coats of paint binding it shut. I take Marty's flat pillow from under his head and bend it around my fist. The window shatters the first time I strike it. I pull all the shards out, sweep the inner frame with the pillowcase, and move to the opposite corner. The animal turns his head ninety degrees, regards me with one savage eye. Then he is in the air, landing on the ruined dresser. Blood drips from his paws as he leaps out the window; he is gone without another glance at me, which I don't mind. He isn't mine.

I turn the cab of the truck upside down gathering change. I dump my bag on the seat, raid the Laundromat fund in the glove compartment, then I drive to the nearest Village Pantry and get change for all the bills I have as well. My coat pocket is filled with quarters when I run back outside to the pay phone. I dial 0, tell the operator I need to reach a number in Ontario, the number Marty had written on the back of a church bulletin and tucked in his coat pocket. She tells me to deposit four dollars for the first three minutes and I'm not sure I can do it. My fingers can barely grasp the coins; I'm shaking so violently I can't insert them. I pray, I breathe, I think of the last time I saw my brother, how all of it is my fault and my doing. I push the quarters into the phone, one after another, until a mechanized voice tells me Thank You. My Call Is Being Connected. I listen to the foreign telephone ring once, twice, three times, and then a man is saying hello and I use his alias, I haven't heard his voice in five years but I know it as well as my own. As fast as I can form the words I say this is your sister Tracey; Marty and Loretta know where you are, you have to move, go now. He is silent so long I think he has already hung up, then he says, "Tracey Sue? The little black-haired girl I love?"

+

I think, I will tell Dusty Ann. Then I think I will go there, I'll see what has happened, and make the decision, depending. I catalog possibilities by genus and species, which is time- and thought-consuming. The truck's engine is racing, I'm pushing it so hard, and I realize I'm on the highway and only a few miles from Dusty's house. I know where I am, but I have no idea where I've been. The bell ringing in my ear is fading, my hands ache. I take my foot off the gas and try to picture the moment I dove into the cab of the truck: Where was it parked? What was around it? I can't see anything. How did I get to the convenience store, by what streets, which store was it? A hundred different gas stations and parking lots scroll across my memory, and not one of them is it. I take the left turn that will lead me to my sister, and pull over. I rest my head against the steering wheel a moment. It is freezing, and hard. I raise my head and check to see if I have a fever but I don't. I relax, attempt to stretch out the ache in my shoulders. The back of my neck is so stiff I feel it might shatter—I push against the muscles with my fingertips, and there it is. A knot, just below my hairline. But it isn't a knot, or a calcium deposit, or a spider bite, or an undeveloped twin: it is a stone, and it's been there for fifteen years. At the picnic we had eaten a chicken, a pail of mulberries, and crackers I found in my pocket. He stood, he walked on his hind legs the whole afternoon. We drank water from a creek nearby and then the coyote turned me around until I was facing west. He told me to close my eyes and hold my breath: he was going to give me a great gift. I felt the stone enter my skin but it didn't really hurt; it seemed to fit. He licked the place where the stone was buried, as a dog would, and bumped me with the top of his head. He said, "Run up to the top and over that hill. Your best friend is waiting for you on her grandfather's porch. Go on, now." I did as I was told, turning back only once to wave at the coyote, who held the handle of the mulberry pail by a single black claw. He waved in return. I ran up the steep hill as if the earth had no hold on me; I couldn't wait to meet my best friend. I would never be that happy, or that weightless, again—which was no fault of the coyote. I recognized Candy the second I saw her, and she knew me in return. We played together for hours, until it started to get dark and her granddad offered to take me home. So I'll never know what the gift was, whether it was the stone or the girl. We got in her granddad's truck and he asked me where I lived and I told him the truth: I didn't have the slightest idea.

✛

Trace pulled into the gravel drive in front of her sister's house. She didn't get far, as there were vehicles everywhere, seven at least. The truck door slammed in the quiet rural air, and within seconds Dusty Ann was out the front door and headed toward the drive, wearing a summer dress and white heels, a blanket wrapped around her shoulders. The small, tilting cube of a house she shared with her husband, Phil, and the girls looked so much worse than the last time Trace had been there, she wondered if there had been a weather system or natural disaster she'd failed to notice. The dark green paint was *leaping* off the wood siding; it couldn't get to the ground fast enough. Two shutters were missing; the screen door was hanging by a single hinge; the porch swing had fallen and remained where it landed, splintered on the cement porch.

"Tracey, hello darlin' girl, hello," Dusty said, a fermented kindness in her voice. She rubbed her forearms through the blanket, and marched in place.

Trace couldn't speak. She stared at her sister openly, unwilling to disguise her shock. Dusty, who was not as tall as Trace but at least an average height, appeared to weigh as much as a nine-year-old girl. Her hair was the color Loretta's had been when Colt first heard her singing with the jug-and-bucket band at the county fair, deep in the swept-dirt yards of the past. It had been Dusty's vanity and glory. Now she was bald in patches—Trace could see her scalp clearly—and the hair she had left was thin. It looked dead. The rings around Dusty's eyes were so dark Trace thought at first someone had hit her, twice, but they weren't bruises. Dusty seemed not to notice, or to care, that she was being scrutinized so thoroughly. She scratched at a bald spot, pulled against a section of remaining hair. She clawed at her neck, thrust her chin up in the air, stood on her toes in the odd shoes.

"Dusty, are you having a seizure?"

Her sister's eyes flickered toward Trace; she pretended to laugh. "Whaaaat?"

Had she seen— "Are you *missing two teeth*?" The mountain-beautiful Dusty Ann Pennington? President of the Home Ec Club, treasurer of Future Homemakers, the girl who could have been a cheerleader but said no, their behavior was immodest, she would choose the Pep Club, thank you. Middle child, Loretta's child, her devotion to her mother was absolute and genuine; Dusty made them matching dresses, matching aprons, they sang together at church. Loretta's shadow, a perfect girl who had shocked them all (Loretta nearly to death) by running away at sixteen with a group of bikers just passing through Mason. She was back in a year— something wearing her skin was back, at any rate, and she'd married Local Phil Wilson in an appropriate church service, and it had seemed she would Home Economize after all. Two little girls, Phil at the Chrysler plant, Dusty so pretty, the disposition of an angel. But three—had it been three, four?—years ago, Phil was laid off and he and Dusty Ann took their babies and stepped on the escalator going Down, an escalator that moved swiftly, as it turned out.

"Yeah," Dusty said, looking back at her house, "I had to get 'em pulled they were botherin' me. It's great to see you though, what brings you out this—?"

Trace started for the door. "Where are the girls?"

"Hey, hey hon," Dusty grabbed Trace's arm so hard her fingers bit through the coat, the layers. "Where are you going, the girls aren't here."

"Really? Where are they?"

Dusty shook her head, clawed at her jawline, ground her remaining teeth. "A friend's."

"What friend, can you give me a name?"

"Tracey Sue, sweetheart? Phil's got company right now, forgive me for being, I don't mean to be unwelcoming or nothing like that but I need to get back inside and also I'd love it if you came back another time okay?"

What a difference three inches and a normal body mass make, Trace thought, looking down at Dusty's scalp, her brittle, wasted body. This was her big sister, eight years in the lead—the one who, in swearing fealty to her mother and vowing never to leave home—had been the only one to escape, at least for a while. A brilliant maneuver, in Trace's opinion. Candy had asked recently, "How do you think it started, for her?" Trace knew what she meant: Phil brought it in the house, said, *We can make more money this way than all my years at the factory put together.* And he sold it but didn't use it, and then one day he was tired and tried it. He probably pushed her for months before she acquiesced, but that first time must have felt like a miracle. And every time after, year in, year out, had been an attempt to re-create the first. The beginning is innocent: everything that follows is just nostalgia.

"Dusty Ann, stand still a minute and look at me." Trace reached out for her sister's shoulder but didn't touch her. "I want to tell you one thing and ask you one question, and then I'll go and let you get back to your company."

"All right, honey, go right ahead I'm standing here waiting as you can see."

"The question first. Tell me one thing you remember about Billy."

"Billy?" Dusty blinked, eight or ten times in rapid succession. "Now is he dead right? Is Billy dead or where is he? He could have been a basketball star or or a minister even he was a, Billy? Billy was a good boy."

"Yes, he was good. But tell me something specific about him, something you remember."

Either the question or the cold or . . . everything, everything in the house and in the air, acted on Dusty like a toxin. She bit her lip, her hand, she jumped around shaking her head no. If Trace hadn't known better she would have suspected Saint Vitus, or the Tarantella.

"Hmmmmm." Dusty pressed her jaws together, shook her head. "Awww, Tracey, no. I had this dream once but but this isn't a good time for me to think about it I'm sure you understand, this was when you and me shared a room right remember? But I don't want to talk about it. I got so scared I sat up in bed and you were gone, dead of night six years old or thereabouts. I don't know why, I ran to the window, I don't know why I did that when what I meant to do was go tell Mama and Daddy she's gone we have to go find Tracey. Like I said I looked out the window and Billy was carrying you back toward the house, you had been hmmmmm"—Dusty ground her teeth—"sleepwalking? or whatever and he carried you back to the house. Then him and Daddy were talking in the hall-way, I don't know what they said and Billy came in our room and put you back in bed and you didn't wake up at all, and Daddy nod-ded at him and Billy laid down on the floor next to your side of the bed, between you and the window and he slept there for the next year, right, yes, a year?"

She was telling the truth; Trace had forgotten that year (how *could* she?) but there it was, almost too vivid to consider. She would never re-forget, either, she was stuck with everything *in* the memory and everything behind it and below. "What was the dream, Dusty?"

"No no no honey." Dusty became even more agitated, pulling at the edges of the blanket, rocking from foot to foot. "This is *not* a good time for me to be remembering that dream although I think the world of you and I need to go back inside is the problem."

"Okay, I understand. You just tell me the dream and I'll let you go," Trace said, calm and unmoving, as if she could affect her sister by example.

"Aaaaaaaaa ALL RIGHT! Forgive me I didn't mean to shout, that wasn't nice but, there were bugs—they were like tree roaches or something like that each one was as big as a, hmmmmm"—Dusty's face was so twisted with effort, so ruined, Trace almost stopped her—"A BANANA, each one was as big as a banana but fatter shiny black they moved fast, the window was open and the bugs weren't coming in or flying in or crawling whatever they were being *poured* in out of this big metal ummm, like a pitcher, there were thousands of them being poured in, a *wave,* and I screamed and scared myself sat up it took me a minute but then I knew you were gone. Tell Mama and Daddy they had to get up, go find you, you were just six or so the dead of night."

"But instead you looked out the window."

Dusty squinched her entire face up into a single pucker, like an apple doll. Seconds later her face relaxed so completely she might have been in a stupor. "Yeah."

"It was a full moon."

"It was a full moon, I don't know! Forgive me for shouting, that wasn't polite, ummm I guess there was a moon because I could see Billy walking across the yard clear as day holding you against his chest, from sleepwalking is Billy dead?"

"Did you stop being afraid when you saw Billy?"

"Whaaaa? Did I stop being afraid when I saw, NO, you are kidding right, hon? NO I was scareder than ever right? I got a fright on and kept it on for what, two years? it got worse and worse until, ummm, those gentlemen came around and I went to California which in case you didn't know is nothing like"—she waved her hands around, presumably at rural Indiana. Everything at which she directed her spastic gesture, however, belonged to her: *her* body, her house, the cars in her driveway.

"The sunlit world," Trace said.

"Right, sweetheart? Most beautiful place on."

"The sunlit, upper world."

"Mmmm hmmm."

"That's where you wanted to go, the place you fled to? On purpose?"

"Those gentlemen came into the gas station as I was paying for a candy bar I could tell you what kind even, said they were on their way to *Lost Angelees* was how they pronounced it and I *knew* it was the place for me I'd of ran after them in my bare feet to get away from—but I didn't have to run because they said sure introduced me to a gentleman called Cooter who made me his girlfriend, sorta. It was different. But yeah."

"And when you got there was it what you'd hoped for? Was it what you had imagined?"

Dusty looked up, quick, met her sister's gaze. Her eyes shone with a clear light; Trace felt as if a radio station she'd been trying to find suddenly reached her, static-free. "Remember in eighth-grade biology that thing with the peas, the pea chart well I didn't do so well in that class but no matter how I looked at the peas I couldn't figure out how you came to have eyes colored violet or sometimes lavender you're standing here in front of me and I recall how confused I was, Billy had blue eyes and I have blue eyes like Mama where did yours come from?"

Trace opened her arms and Dusty stepped in, allowed herself to be swallowed in Trace's embrace. Where were the aprons, the Butterick patterns on onionskin, the countless attempts at Boston cream pie, in this woman? Where, for that matter, was the bed they shared, or "Blessed Assurance"; where were her daughters? Trace closed her eyes, rested her chin on Dusty's head—but gently—and they stood that way, exile and relic, until Dusty pulled herself free.

"I love you sweetpea, Mendel's pea, I surely do don't you ever think different." Dusty turned in a jerky half circle and walked unsteadily toward her door. Trace watched until her sister reached the porch, then she headed for her truck. Dusty called, "Hey, though! Tracey, hmmmm, ask a question and say something to me was how it was supposed to go right? What do you want to say?"

What was the point? The grave was dug, the village lined up, one bullet per person. All Dusty had to do was fall backward, as if into a hijacked swimming pool under the California sun. You. Breaked. My. Heart. "Nothing. Not a thing except I love you, too, Dusty Ann. I remember everything."

Trace got in her truck, slammed the door a second time. Dusty was still standing on the porch. She twitched once, an eloquent lift of the shoulders that was, for Trace, the sum of every individual loss.

Her final stop at a pay phone (for the day, at least) was far less eventful than the first. She had nothing more complicated to do than dial Information and write a number on her hand: the after-hours emergency line at the Department of Children and Social Services.

The woman she spoke to, Mrs. Yardley, listened with interest. Yes, she was well acquainted with amphetamines in their various states.

Mrs. Yardley typed as they spoke. "Describe your sister's behavior to me?" Trace did so, and she could hear in the social worker's voice, in the speed with which she took notes, something frightful: Trace had begun the turning of a bureaucratic wheel, *she* had done this, and her sister and two children she loved were about to be caught up in it. The *government* was going to enter the lives of Dusty and Phil. She considered hitting her head repeatedly on the pay phone but she was already freezing, she was tired of standing outside, she was

"Miss? Are you still there?"

"I'm sorry, were you saying something?"

"I was just wondering how *you* are. This must have been a hard day for you."

She couldn't breathe, it was too cold to be out like this.

"Miss? Are you somewhere I could meet you? There's nothing I haven't seen or heard and——"

Trace hung up, backed away from the phone. She laughed—oh really? Nothing you haven't seen or heard? There was no one in the parking lot, fortunately, so she could stand there a little longer, her eye on the receiver, gasping for breath, until finally she was doubled over as if she was going to be sick. It seemed she was being pushed from behind; the ground was rising to meet her. She was on her knees as if before a master, and still there was no easing of the pressure on her chest. If she had to she would lie facedown on the asphalt, she would eat the gravel and the glass, which sparkled in the streetlight, she would eat it and go on, to paraphrase the epitaph on the tombstone of a fine poet.

She sat back on her heels, her coat spread out around her, and the feeling passed. She stood up as soon as she was able and went back to the phone. Candy said hello. Trace asked her if Skeet was home and he was not. "Maybe I'll stop by then," Trace said, casually, as if she cared very little either way.

"Please do," Candy said, as if she cared very much.

✛

Trace paused in front of the pen where the remaining hound was chained. He was lying on the freezing ground and didn't raise his head when she said, "Hey, Blue—are you feeling all right? Come here, come to the fence." He looked at her, his eyes followed her as she knelt, and as she stood back up. But he wouldn't move.

The trailer was hot, or it seemed so inside Trace's camisole, her many sweaters. She peeled off a number of layers and sat down at the kitchen table, as Candy put the boys back to bed. Candy joined her briefly, then returned to the shouting children for—who knew? The tenth time? The twentieth? She never seemed flustered by the repetition of her life, or the labor; the laborious repetition of every minute of Candy's life would have driven Trace mad in the first hour.

Candy sat down across the table from Trace for the third time and Trace slipped the book she was reading, volume eight of Hillman's *Eranos Lectures,* into her bag. During the rush of getting the boys to sleep Trace hadn't paid much attention to Candy; now she was shocked to see that Candy was still wearing the same clothes she'd had on . . . three days ago? Yes, Trace was sure of it because there were the stains on the shirt. She had been sleeping in them, too, Trace guessed, by the way the neckline of the T-shirt had collapsed. There were folds pressed into the fabric, a long line down one side.

Trace looked away, afraid of what else she might see. There was no place to rest her eyes; if she looked at the table she would be horrified, and if Candy saw the horror on her face she'd run to the kitchen and come back with a moldy sponge. She'd make a half-hearted attempt to clear away the debris and the gluey foods the children ate, but in the end she would give up and the only thing accomplished would have been the introduction of the moldy sponge, which would lie unceremoniously on the table between them, making Trace slightly ill.

"Tracey?" Candy said, so Trace had to look at her. She raised her eyebrows in acknowledgment; ordinarily that was all Candy required to be off and running on some topic she knew only her oldest friend would be patient enough to pay attention to. Often it was the cost of things on *The Price Is Right*. Over the years Trace had heard so much about *The Price Is Right* she could have declared a minor in it. She was about to tell her, to say to Candy that she nearly had enough credits for a minor in her game show (an idea Candy would find very amusing), but was stopped cold.

The light hanging over the kitchen table, a miniature imitation wagon wheel with a bumpy white globe, was swaying, causing the light on Candy's face to shift. Why was the lamp swaying? Neither of them had touched it. The night wasn't windy, no door was ajar. Trace looked up at the light, back at Candy. Candy's face was a painting: a landscape of bruises, with a periodic cut for composition, like a stream used to draw the eye toward the subject, or toward the source of light. Trace looked back up at the wagon wheel, which continued to sway but more slowly now, in a smaller arc. Her friend had obviously tried to cover the evidence on her face with all the makeup she could find; her forehead, for instance, was a different color than her chin.

Trace studied Candy steadily, without blinking or glancing at the rest of her (if he would do that to her face, what was happening in the hidden places?).

"I have—well, I have something to tell you," Candy began, picking nervously at a hole in the plastic tablecloth, one she'd made with a cigarette two weeks ago. Wait, Trace thought, wait—why isn't she smoking, and where is the coffee, bitter as hemlock?

"So tell me," Trace said as patiently as she could, given that in her mind she was already getting her old Winchester out from behind her truck seat. It was clean, it was loaded, but she would check it carefully anyway. Then they would wait for him to come home, as they used to wait for Loretta or Marty to show up at the Bucks' house.

"I think—I think something has happened to me and I don't know how to say it to anyone."

"It's fairly clear, Candy."

"How could it be? Are you saying you knew, you guessed, what?"

Trace shook her head; one of them was very confused. "You are covered with bruises; your face looks like raw hamburger under all that makeup. How many ways could that have happened?"

Candy sat up straight, gave Trace a look that was close to a glare. "Not the way you're implying. But I get it," she said, nodding. "You walked in here, you saw what you wanted to see. You wanted—you have *always* wanted for me and Skeet to end—so you'll make it up if you have to, you'll draw the assumptions that fit what you're after."

Trace was stung but not surprised; they had had this conversation many times over the years. Never over a matter as urgent as Candy's face, but the difference between this argument and those in the past was one merely of degree. "I'm sorry," Trace said, trying to be. "Tell me how you got beaten up so thoroughly. I know it wasn't a car accident; I saw your car as I came in."

But Candy didn't answer her; she sat perfectly still, staring at a spot just to the left of Trace's head. They sat in silence—Trace apprehensive, Candy seemingly stunned—for so long that Trace said, "Have you seen a doctor? Do you think you could have a concussion?"

Candy's eyes jerked from the spot at which she had been staring, unfocused, to meet Trace's gaze. Seeing that one moment—the way Candy had gone from being in a bovine trance, as stunned as if she had been hit with a hammer but not hard enough, to a sudden presence—frightened Trace more than the bruises, or the clothes, or the absence of cigarettes or coffee. She said, "Candy, just tell me. Please."

Candy leaned toward Trace and began speaking, fast but quietly, as if someone in another room were listening. "I'm one of them, I'm one of those people like I heard on the radio, I've been abducted, taken—it's happened every night since I saw you last—like I *made* it happen, I called them here. They've been . . . doing things to me, experiments, and that's how I got these bruises. I've become an interest to them because ordinarily they don't leave bruises or marks of any kind, they don't leave any evidence of themselves on the people they take, but I'm different, the *process*—that's what they call it—the process of initiation and transport are harder on me, but other parts are easier, like I can hear them better than anyone else in the room, I understood what they were saying from the first moment they came in our bedroom, and that's very unusual, because they don't speak and they don't have a language the way we think of it, they communicate telepathically, and I can hear them and understand everything they say—they even tried tricking me by using . . . nonsense, well, thoughts, nonsense thoughts and I just began thinking back to them, Don't be ridiculous, I know the difference between one and the other, I gave them a hard time really—which is another thing the others don't do—I said, If you want to kidnap people out of their beds and take them someplace and do harm to them, and your only way of talking to each other is a way I can hear and understand, then that's your problem not mine, and they didn't punish me but there isn't a lot of punishment/reward anyway, it's more like just—complete helplessness, utter and total helplessness, and we have to accept their will because there's no choice. We can't fight, we can't hide, we can't report them or use our law enforcement, nothing like that, we have no recourse and so night after night I lie awake and wait and think I'll be able to stop them or fight them but I never can. One time I was awake when they came in through the bedroom window and I looked at them and I must have thought I'm gonna scream, because in a flash I was down, they had me paralyzed and they hadn't moved at all they were just looking at me still, but I might as well have been under the influence of that vet drug, the one that paralyzes large animals but they're still conscious—"

"Succinylcholine," Trace said.

"—that's how I felt, I could see everything going on around me, I knew what was coming next, but I couldn't raise a finger." Candy paused, shook her head. "You're probably wondering about Skeet, well, they deal with that every night of the week, spouses, they paralyze him first—they hypnotize him is more like what happens, and he has no memory of it at all or of anything that follows it. I haven't asked him but I know that if he knew what was going on in this trailer, his house, and to him while he was sleeping? Oh my god he'd be so mad, he would try to kill them, he'd set traps and rig bombs and we'd all end up getting killed, so I've not said anything to him and I won't until I have to, he hasn't noticed the bruises, or maybe he's been *programmed* not to notice them—that wouldn't surprise me at all, if that's what they did."

Trace let her mind go blank. Without fully knowing why she asked, "What about your babies, Candy?"

The air felt electric around them, both women on pause, and then Candy collapsed onto the table, sobbing and wailing and pounding her fists on the sticky plastic; she eventually fell to the floor, where she rolled around as if she had been slain in the spirit on a televangelist's stage, except this was real and it was awful to watch. Trace got down on the floor with her and tried to keep her from hurting herself on the furniture—she acted as a human bumper pad. At one point she was greatly tempted to say, "So Candy, would you like to hear what my day was like?" but didn't and was glad as soon as Candy began to wail, "They've already taken the children once, I saw them through a glass wall lying on these little bedlike pods. They—the visitors—said they thought I'd *feel better* if I could see the boys weren't being hurt, but it wasn't like that at all, it was the worst thing I've ever seen, Tracey." She clawed at Trace's sweater. "You can't imagine how I feel, I want to die to make this stop, to protect the babies from . . ."

Trace held her friend, so sick inside she was afraid she was falling again, and much farther this time; through the floor of the trailer, into the dirt below, farther still. "From what, Candy? Protect the babies from what?"

Candy sobbed harder, couldn't catch her breath. She raised herself up and looked at Trace, and most of the makeup was gone now, rubbed off on the grimy carpet and onto Trace's clothes, and whatever had happened to her had been a hard place to run into, that's what Trace was thinking, how hard she must have taken it to look the way she did, when Candy said, "From whatever happened to you, Tracey. I want to protect them from whatever happened to you."

Trace parked behind the house, in the place that had formerly been overgrown with tall grass and burrs and even a couple stray and sickly sunflowers. After four years it was just a parking spot. The truck ran on a few seconds after she'd turned the key and removed it; she couldn't remember what caused that. She'd known once. The engine shuddered, stopped, and the truck's cab was flooded with a silence so dense it felt anticipatory. And dark; the lights from Jonah could be seen on the horizon only occasionally. She had gone out and also back, and the darkness here was true; sitting as she was—her breathing shallow, her body still—was a deprivation of her senses, and she might have stayed that way all night, but she was worried about Weeds, left alone all day.

She gathered her belongings, backpack, Winchester, and made her way to the door, pointing the beam of her Maglite at the ground before her and then scanning the area around the rear of the house. Same as she'd left it: rusted oil tank and dead circular saw to the right of her path, and to the left a small mountain of debris, including (but not limited to) a hibachi-esque thing and two Weber grills; an old lawn mower—quite similar to the one in Candy's lawn collection—and a bathroom medicine cabinet missing its bathroom. The cabinet was big, metal, and the mirror was intact. Trace tried to avoid the mirror with the flashlight beam.

The back door opened into the kitchen, and she set about lighting the hurricane lamps, the candles, the kerosene heater. She put the kettle on the Coleman stove, then moved aside the heavy wool blanket hanging in the kitchen doorway and called for Weeds. He barked in reply and came tearing down the steps. He'd known she was home long before she got there, but this was his favorite ritual. She could imagine him lying on her bed, his head on his paws but his ears twitching, his eyes bright, waiting for her call so he could bark and run to her. He tore through the living room and ran circles around her legs, his feathery tail high and waving.

"Hello to *you*," Trace said, laughing. She knelt and took his head in her hands, rubbing behind his ears and kissing the space between them. "I'm sorry, I'm sorry I was gone so long and you were here all alone." His tail swept the kitchen floor. "Outside? Then dinner?"

Weeds ran to the back door and Trace let him out. She filled his bowl from the plastic bin she kept his food in; the bin sealed tightly.

She opened the spigot on the seven-gallon water container she'd found at the army-navy surplus and filled his water bowl.

At the back door she called for him, unable to see anything in the yard. The sky was overcast, low clouds; no shadows, outlines. Ordinarily he was waiting when she opened the door; she called again. Nothing. Trace stepped outside, still in her coat and hat, and called a third time, an upward-gliding edge on her voice she hated, because there was no reason to be this afraid, he'd been outside a few minutes at most, and Weeds didn't wander; okay, he was sometimes shy about where he used the bathroom, and he had to look for the correct spot, but he never went farther than the collapsing outbuildings unless Trace was with him. In one minute (she began counting) she would go back in for the flashlight or one of the lanterns, and as she counted she prayed—if a prayer can be directed at no one—Please please please. Before she reached sixty she heard him freeing himself from the undergrowth around the raspberry bushes, and then he was flying at her again, just as joyful as he'd been when she called him down from their bedroom. Same joy. He hadn't meant to scare her, of course—he often crawled into that labyrinth, crouched low, and out again, as if he were some endangered jungle animal. They went inside and Trace poured the water for her tea and sat at the table as it steeped, watching him eat. Even as he chewed he wagged his tail.

So I'll never know what the gift was, whether it was the stone or the girl. We got in her granddad's truck and he asked me where I lived and I told him the truth: I didn't have the slightest idea. Trace put down her notebook and pen, stretched. It was already one in the morning, according to the travel alarm clock next to her pillow. She wouldn't write anything about Candy's announcement—not yet. What was there to say? Trace pressed her fingertips against her temples, drew her knees up, and rested her head on her crossed arms. This was—it was *so* far beyond her reach. Candy might as well have asked Trace to perform brain surgery, or write a symphony. Maybe Esther and Paul—she kept meaning to go see them anyway, but couldn't seem to get there—maybe they should be told? Those dear people, Paul in his old recliner, asleep with the news on, and Esther always moving. She was forever picking things up and putting them down, cooking or cleaning up from cooking, straightening the picture frames on the wall—no sleeping in front of the television for her. Trace sighed. What Candy had said would scare them to death. Weeds kicked in his sleep, his back pressed against Trace's hip. Didn't . . . didn't Jung write a book about flying saucers? Was that *possible*?

She retrieved her daily planner from her backpack; it was stuffed with memos and reminders and letters from graduate schools, and somewhere in the miscellany was her . . . there. Her course schedule, classes beginning tomorrow. Today, technically. She looked at the truncated course names, the times and locations of the last classes she needed to graduate. The prospect was fearful and thrilling and disorienting, all at once. Special Topics: Archetypal Psychology. Special Topics: Archetypal Analysis of Literature.

Trace had asked to be taken off the schedule at the Campus Book Store, in order to focus more fully on the classes that were bound to be difficult, but she'd told Jim to leave a note in her campus mailbox if they needed her. It would be the first time in her college career she hadn't worked as many hours as possible—juggling her schedule and reading behind the counter, staying up all night with regularity. What *luxury* she faced.

She had only one other class, the final requirement for her Women's Studies minor, taught by the head of the department. WS 510: Wounded Women in Literature.

Tonight she was able to find her dream journal (one of them, anyway) without any trouble. She wrote.

CHAPTER FOUR

Oneirocritica

Journal

Colt didn't leave much to go on—his head turned in the photograph of the three boys, Juna already leaving the frame she was in, Clyde Sr. and his stomach acid—but it's still more than anyone knows about Loretta. When Colt saw her at the fair he stood with the small crowd and waited until the show was over, then made his way to her and asked her if she would join him on the Ferris wheel. I imagine he walked with purpose, and that people stepped aside to let him pass. Loretta agreed, and that part, too, is easy to picture: her eyes, her hair, her primitive figure flooded with youth and adrenaline from performing.

On the ride she teased him, asked him question after question, made him blush. Colt had dignity—this isn't anything that could ever be explained to Loretta—and she violated it from the moment they met, and that must be why he married her. So he asked her a few questions but learned nothing. She was an orphan girl, she said, alone in all the world, trying to make her way to Nashville. Seventeen—that was the age she gave—although she might have been twelve or twenty-one, as she has no birth certificate and would never be called upon to prove anything. For all the fact that the world is the world and human nature the same, it was a different time. If I were to meet Loretta as she was then I would look all around me for the band of Irish Travelers who were using her as the prop in an elaborate con. Such a thing never crossed Colt's mind.

I got to the library as soon as it opened this morning and I've been reading ever since. Jung did indeed write a book about flying saucers; some of it is valuable and intriguing, some is unreadable—typical of the leaps Jung took in his own active imagination. He might start on a rock in the river of his argument, a rock called "saucer," and from there jump to "sphere," to "circle," to "mandala," to the shining metal "alchemical" brilliance of the saucer's surface, a symbol of our yearning for wholeness, which reminds him of zero and also that all things are subject to gravity except the psyche, and then he *somehow* ends up here: "Ten is the perfect unfolding of unity, and the numbers one to ten have the significance of a completed cycle. $10 + 1 = 11$ therefore denotes the beginning of a new cycle. Since dream interpretation follows the principle post hoc ergo propter hoc, eleven leads to eight, the ogdoad, a totality symbol, and hence to a realization of wholeness, as already suggested by the appearance of the Ufos" (page 78). I found this less than helpful. However, he also believed that flying saucers were an external projection for an internal psychic state, which falls under the general category of Anxiety: anxiety about the Cold War (the first UFO sightings were reported in 1947), the nuclear age, and the swift replication of destructive technologies; and also about our inability to distinguish fact from fiction when our political leaders make such discernment impossible. Everyone is lying to us all the time and all that misinformation feeds into a single conspiracy, which can take many names. And the collective unconscious *changes,* of course, it moves with us; Jung says things change in the constellation of the psychic dominants (the gods, the archetypes) at the end of one Platonic period and the beginning of another. As the constellation shifts, long-lasting transformations occur in the collective unconscious and thus in the psyche.

Colt asked her where she was staying and her answer was vague—a Christian boardinghouse for young women—something he'd never heard of, and he'd lived on that mountain his whole life. He still wasn't alarmed. She was a righteous young girl, orphaned (Orphaned where? By whom? Show me the graves, Loretta, that's what I would ask), looking for a break. And he was pulled toward her, tugged as if by a rope through the ring in his nose; he couldn't get close enough and he would have liked to take her in, all the way inside his body, to protect her.

Their courtship was marred by events neither would recount but they must have been doozies to drive Colt away, to push him so far he ended up on his bike and crossing the Ohio, through Tell City and up up

I'd like to stop the story there, Colt alone and out of money in Mason, looking for work. That would be a fine place, but I can't stop there because she followed him, she found him, he married her. And at the courthouse special provisions had to be made for the luscious little orphan tart who had no birth certificate or any knowledge of where she was born or who her parents had been. Her last name, Vaughan, was an alias she had assumed but she could no longer remember what came before it. The clerk pushed her: What are your earliest memories? Who is tending to you? And Loretta would get a faraway look in her eye, longing, and say, "My earliest memories are of singing in a church with no electricity or heat." No faces or names. If I'd been at the courthouse I would have said to the intrepid clerk, "Friend, forget it. You won't get the truth out of her with pliers or a Sodium Pentothal drip, because *the truth is not in her*." To paraphrase the Bible.

I think he knew then. I think at some point Colt felt it—the shiver down the spine that denotes you've passed a critical point—and he went forward anyway, not understanding it was a decision he was making not just for himself, but for his children and all of his future and his dying. The decision affected even the staircase of the house he worked so hard to pay for, because someday Marty Morrison would be walking down it in his underwear, cradling his bottle of pee and taking each step like he owned the place because as it turned out, he does.

That person Candy heard on the radio is Whitley Strieber, of all people, and the book he was discussing is coming out in a couple of weeks in the U.K. Why did she hear him now? On what frequency, on what sort of radio, is a discussion of a book coming out in England broadcast in a trailer in Mason, Indiana? If I asked her she would say maybe its origin was no place we would recognize, maybe the broadcast was for her and her alone. I say Whitley Strieber of all people because of course he wrote *The Hunger,* the book that launched the film that launched a thousand capes and bloody kisses, awkward attempts at Sapphic coupling, and stabs at the cello. The book, as I recall, had nothing of the film's Byronic lushness, or its tender soul sickness. Nothing even remotely like the moment Susan Sarandon, the sleep expert, has made eye contact with Catherine Deneuve at a press conference and later dreams of her; in sleep, Sarandon's face unmoving, a single tear rolls down her temple, exactly as it would for anyone in love so suddenly, with a force beyond mortality. And all of that juxtaposed with scenes of ferocious violence.

The only thing I remember from the book is a single description:

that the vampires are like mosquitoes. They are always hungry and they smell blood the way mosquitoes smell the exhalations of our breath (that's what they really smell, although I think Strieber said they smell meat). And there's an image that made it from the book to the film, the way the hip, gorgeous vampires drain a body so dry what remains is leaflike. When they toss the bodies into the incinerator there is nothing in the garbage bags; some hair, I guess? Bones sucked free of marrow, a wrinkled parchment envelope of skin?

In a shoe box in the bedroom where Weeds and I sleep I have Colt's pictures in a cigar box, and a few from when Loretta's official story began: a snapshot of the civil wedding, Billy and Dusty as children, Loretta and Colt as parents. Who knew what the truth was, but the pictures speak of a certain normalcy. And then the few artifacts that interest me the most: my own birth certificate, listing Loretta and Clyde Pennington Jr. as my parents, their signatures. It's real: I've taken it to the County Records Office and they attest it is their seal. I have a photograph of the three of us arriving home from the hospital, Billy and Dusty waiting anxiously. They were ten and eight. And then a documentary, if the pictures were moving and if the director knew the outcome ahead of time. Loretta, Billy, and Dusty on one side, with their uncanny resemblances, and Colt with his black-haired, violet-eyed girl. Sometimes he held me, sometimes Loretta. It appears I was loved, the way late babies often are. We went to church; there were holidays. I sit on Loretta's lap and Dusty stands behind us, or I'm riding on Billy's back as if he were a pony. Years passed, five, six. But something is happening during the last three, if you know where to look. After the age of six I will not again appear with Loretta. She doesn't take photographs of me, either—I can tell because Colt had a tendency to either cut off the top of our heads or capture the tip of his own thumb. A few of those—Dusty Ann looking nervous and overly conscientious, Billy laboring to appear carefree—and the record stops altogether.

There is a lot in the library about flying saucers and things seen in the sky; more than I could take in, even photocopying articles and taking page after page of notes. The key to understanding so much data is to look for the metaphorical conceit, or the dominant archetype, and then read backward. I tried to sort through them, beginning with the neurological hypotheses: epilepsy, temporary schizophrenia, various parasomnias, hypnagogic states, sleep paralysis. Many abductees seem to have had memories implanted during hypnosis—memories then "recovered" by the very person who put them there.

The modern abduction scenario began in 1961 with Betty and Barney Hill, who were plucked from their automobiles. There is a lot of plucking from automobiles; I have a whole category for that. And the details they provide seem to be connected to films that came out years prior, as though they needed cinematic images on which to hang their abduction hats.

There are Gray, Reptilian, and Nordic aliens. They are humanoid, telekinetic. At some point in the victims' narratives—I didn't have a timeline in front of me but I could see it coming clear—certain claims were persistently made: sexual experiments, the implantation of devices, the harvesting of eggs and sperm. Eggs and sperm. I went back and read some of the accounts recorded under hypnosis, and then I saw it: A woman said that all her life she'd known her mother wasn't her *real* mother, and now she realizes it's because she (the speaker) is a human/alien hybrid. A man, describing the moment he opened his eyes and saw a Gray for the first time, said he expected to find his grandfather abusing him, but found an extraterrestrial instead. Phantom pregnancies; nurseries filled with sickly, failing hybrid infants.

Loretta prayed

Did Loretta pray, is that right? Maybe at the little church in the wildwoods where I had been welcome all my life. And God gave unto Loretta the knowledge I was a *changeling.* I was rebellious and proud, defiant. Sometimes I frightened her, she told the congregation; sometimes she thought she saw a demon in me. Sometimes the *human* in me seemed to *vanish.* A makeshift exorcism was undertaken, but the brackish fundamentalists of Mason were uncertain of what to do. They had no pomp, no script, no Holy Offices. The movie would have been quite helpful, in terms of conventions, but it hadn't come out yet. At least I would have known to vomit and say blasphemous things in Latin.

I don't remember much of it except I was confused and cooperative and willing, I did as I was told, and I lay down on the red table the way they told me, the basement of—the church didn't have a basement. Someplace else then. Loretta was there but no one else, Billy Dusty Ann Colt, Loretta had taken me out of the house saying she wanted time alone with me and they believed her, which I find difficult

Jesus drove the demons out of a man and into a herd of pigs, then sent them tumbling over a cliff, which looks like a simple story but isn't, because pigs are sacred in the chthonic. He put the "demons" into the sacred animal and sent them back to Dis. To Pluto. Mr. Money. "The boar is the beast of death," Graves wrote in *The White Goddess,* but I don't know the chapter and verse, and also pig's blood was used for purification rituals. The Indo-European root for pig is *su*—no kidding—and here we are still calling *soo-ee!* There are things buried in our language and we never get free of them, they hold us *captive,* just as Wittgenstein believed. Pigs are filthy or pigs are sacred; either way they are the rare barnyard animal that will eat you alive as happily as they eat their young, and that's nothing to sneeze at. A bull will kill you but he will not devour you. Some cannibals referred to human flesh as *Man Corn;* the . . . who, people somewhere in the Pacific called it *Long Pig.* I don't dwell on the name. What really interests me here, and I don't have any of my books with me—if I go try to find what I need off the library shelves I'll lose track of what I'm trying to say—is that other old story. Demeter and Persephone. Hillman says that Hekate watched the rape of Persephone—she actively watched but did not intervene—by Hades because it was "a priori." I believe it. When Hillman uses that phrase he knows his readers will read "time and space," as well as "prior to," and we are right to do so, he is right to suggest it. Hekate knew all along. Persephone fell into a hole in the earth and her footprints were trampled by a herd of pigs, who fell in with her, down down. Animals who are able to interfere with or injure gods were once gods themselves—their godhood *is buried in the language*—and both Demeter and Persephone were once pigs or Swine Goddesses, but that was *long* ago, long before the Eleusinian Mysteries cult, itself established at least fifteen hundred years *before* Jesus drove the demons from the villager and put them in a herd of swine, and by the way the Mysteries began with a ritual purification in the sea and the sacrifice of a piglet.

I most assuredly would not have clung to or otherwise protected any demon in my body; I showed no resistance at all, and still I couldn't satisfy them. I kept asking what I was supposed to do, was there something I was supposed to say, a song to sing, clapping? No clapping, obviously, as I was bound to the red table and everyone around me was sweating and worried, because exorcism turns out not to be so easy and I think there was also the concern of what would happen should the little scrap of Satan in me come barreling out, like out of my mouth, where would it go? Would they try to trap it in a cage, a net? Would it float free until it found another little girl to eat? What I realized, sitting here in my carrel at the library, was that there is a thread one can hold on to in the abduction stories. It isn't perfect, it isn't uniform, but it seems to have something to do with a whole lot of otherwise normal people (people riddled with anxiety but nonetheless) saying, *My family isn't my family. There is a way to explain everything I felt growing up, including this pain under my rib cage where a transmitter is resting. My children are not my children; they were taken from me and these surrogates were left, and the fact of it has caused me to lose my mind.* It's more complicated than that, I know. I don't remember anything else until I was in the woods behind our house, wandering home. I wasn't afraid of the dark—I wasn't afraid of anything—even though I felt as if I had been split clean with a new ax head, or maybe that feeling left no room for fear. I don't know what I was thinking, but I must have assumed it had worked, given the level of my effort and my sincerity. I saw Billy at the edge of our yard, I walked out of the woods. He opened his arms and I went to him and as soon as he had me I fell sound asleep. I had been sleepwalking, Dusty Ann told me the next day, and I nodded. She said this as she gently rinsed the blood off my body—she stood in the tub with me—she repeated it like a prayer. *Silly little girl.* She never let the washcloth touch my skin; she squeezed the warm water out and it ran over me. Ointment on the cuts, gauze. We stripped the bloody sheets off our bed and I said to her, "They didn't mean me no harm," and Dusty said, *Shhhhh,* and I knew then, knew in my heart it hadn't worked, whatever Loretta had attempted had failed, and she would try again. For a year Billy slept between me and the window because he didn't know any better; he thought that whatever had taken me had come in that way and it would be disastrous long before he understood his mistake. Colt's mistake. But I don't blame them, I never did.

The twelve students enrolled in the Archetypal Psychology seminar were silent at their desks. Everyone had removed from their book bags what could be removed, and straightened their notebooks and pens. The clock ticked. Trace sighed, but not loudly, and tapped on her desk with her fingertips.

At last the door opened and Dr. Richard Scherring swept in, a battered valise tucked under his arm. "Hello hello," he said, not looking up at the class. He put down his coffee cup, ran his hands over the sides of his hair, removed his class list and notes from his bag. He glanced behind him, checking the tray of the blackboard for chalk, sat on the edge of the desk, made eye contact with his students. "I don't know any of you—or maybe I've met a couple of you—I teach exclusively in the graduate school, as you probably know, and this is my first class of undergraduates in quite a long time. You all seem . . . young. So." He slapped his thighs.

Trace scanned him, head to toe. Balding but vain, an intelligent face, expensive eyeglass frames. The blue suit was wrong, though; old but not old enough, and the buttoned vest was straining against his gut. Fifty, or approaching it. Scuffed oxblood loafers and black socks. He was divorced. Shoes (or socks) always gave it away. There was something in his carriage, the way he had arrived, that carried a scent of Cheever; of cocktail parties, the primacy of gin in the early 1970s, a conviction—formed when Scherring himself was a grad student—that academia was the Good Life. He would be clinging to that now, at his age, with that stomach. Trace realized she was squinting at him, her eyes narrowed, and she quickly looked down.

"I'm interested in knowing how you all came to be here, so I'll tell you a bit about myself and my background, and then you can introduce yourselves and say a bit about your interest in Archetypal Psychology. Okay. I'm Dr. Scherring; I grew up in . . . Michigan"—he spoke the last word as if struggling to remember. "I earned a B.S. in psychology at Colgate—not an Ivy but the Patriot League, a first-rate institution—where I played on the football team, if you can believe it. I have pictures to prove it. Uh, let's see.

Then I earned my M.A. and Ph.D. at a little place called Yale; maybe you've heard of it." He smiled at his audience.

Trace put her pen down. She smiled, too. He didn't *really* just say that, she thought, biting her bottom lip to keep from laughing out loud. How perfect, how delicious, she would never forget it. She wished there were one person she could tell, someone who would understand the riches of the statement—so revelatory it was bottomless. He was trying to intimidate *them*? These twelve who had done nothing but hold on for four years, at a school where half the students in every freshman class were the first in their family to attend college? A university where, in an honors class, a young woman had burst into tears over the professor's reference to the Bible, telling him if he didn't say out loud that the Bible was true every word she would have to tell her mother and her mother would make her come home? (She'd gone home.)

Now he was pulling out the big guns: listing his association with the Something Institute, his numerous publications, his service on the board of . . . his delivery of a critical paper at the conference of . . . how many doctoral theses he had directed. Trace took a deep breath, closed her eyes. Her money was on him forgetting to ask their names, or how they came to be interested in the subject, and that was just fine with her.

"Good." Dr. Scherring stood, walked toward the chalkboard. "I know you're all seniors so I'll make this recap brief."

Trace prayed, *No recap No recap,* picked up her pen while waiting to see how far back he intended to go. Dr. Scherring picked up a piece of chalk and wrote on the blackboard: ONEIROCRITICA. As if taking notes, Trace wrote, *Oh dear god.*

"*Oneirocritica.* A work of dream interpretation by Artemidorus that dates to the second century. A lot of people believe Freud was the first to take up the analysis of dreams, but in fact we've been studying the mind's manifest throughout recorded history.

The ancient Greeks read dreams for portents; the Egyptians had special . . ."

Trace had hoped he would start with Freud—she loved Freud—and the Vienna School, but the second century? As his lecture continued, Trace made notes to herself: Find a book by Budd Hopkins, abduction researcher and artist. She wrote, *Paul and Esther?* Maybe she would wait, see if Candy had . . . what? Been prompted by what she heard? Was it possible she'd forget, let it blow over? She needed to look for a book by . . . von Franz, maybe, a study of starving women. What was it called? *Starving Women.* Not von Franz; Spignesi. Or von Franz's *The Feminine in Fairy Tales.* Dusty and Candy: both under a spell, some sort of enchantment?

She checked back in to the lecture, and Dr. Scherring (she wondered if he'd ever made his way home via his neighbors' swimming pools) had proceeded to the nineteenth century, hallelujah. If he had decided to spend the hour on the Asclepieions she wouldn't have been surprised; undoubtedly she had missed biblical prophecy revealed through dreams. He was flying now; she saw he'd scribbled—was it possible?—*The Unconscious; Three Essays on the Theory of Sexuality; The Aetiology of Hysteria; Aversion to Religion; Totem and Taboo; Beyond the Pleasure Principle; Civilization and Its Discontents* (which he was *not* recommending at their age); and finally *The Interpretation of Dreams.* Under *Dreams* he had written *Guardians of Sleep,* as well as *Censors and Wish Fulfillment; Infantile Sexuality.* His voice, his tone, was constant, making her drowsy, so she casually wrote what he was saying to stay awake. But he had those things in the wrong order; *The Interpretation of Dreams* was as much a veiled autobiography as a work of speculative science. Freud had begun with Wish Fulfillment, and then he had separated out the latent from the manifest contents. For instance, Freud would be very interested in uncovering what was latent in Candy's dreamlike tale of abduction, and he would do so with . . . *Condensation.* Not, Trace wrote, what runs down the side of your glass in the summer or forms on the inside of the windows of hot kitchens, although there was a connection. Two latent images combined to make a single dream drama or object. *Displacement.* Not my weight in the water, Trace wrote, and this was what Candy had meant by a screen memory. Freud *invented* the phrase, didn't he? Trace rubbed the back of her neck—yes, he applied the phrase to *infantile amnesia,* he said we create visual memories, like snapshots, that are screens, distortions, that keep us from remembering what really occurred. We distort in memory, and in dreams we pick up the too-strong feeling or the desire and transfer it to something less potent. Take it from the Reptilians or the stocky little uniformed blue men and put it on . . . a pack of gorillas, like Whitley Strieber? Well, to each his own. Dr. Scherring wrote: *Symbols.* How to accept the sexual wish fulfillment, how to bury it, as it were, or move it aside? A diversion, often from the sexual content of a dream, wherein the . . . he might as well say it, Trace thought . . . phallus is disguised as something similar but more acceptable. She wrote, JUST GET TO IT ALREADY. Phallus phallus phallus, Dr. Scherring made it sound as if you read enough Freud, you'll lose the ability to pick up a Magic Marker without considering it first. Forget basting your turkey, or sitting through a history class watching a film of missiles being fired from gunships, not to mention every other object in the world, basically. But Freud began with the Emperor and the Empress, the King and Queen, our parents. And then he moved on to where Dr. Scherring, because it was a new age, had rocketed toward directly: symbols of female genitalia. On the board he wrote eyes, swamps, ovens, all variations on boxes and suitcases. And houses. Almost anything, Scherring said, could symbolize the sexual act itself, something as simple as opening a cabinet door, walking into a small room, or climbing a ladder or a staircase. If Candy and Dusty were under a spell or curse, who would save them? What were the words, the act

IODINE

of heroism, the cutting through of briars on a steed? HA! Trace
wrote, imagining what Scherring would say about the Prince's
slashing of the briars in order to *penetrate* the *door* of the *castle* where
Beauty was sleeping, dreaming; Dr. Cheever here would never get
so far as Freud's essay "The Theme of the Three Caskets," his most
perfect jewel, in which he attempts to discern why, in *The Merchant
of Venice,* and more importantly in *Lear,* there are three daughters
and the youngest is chosen, once for marriage and once for death,
and well, yes, it would take a man like Dr. Scherring quite a long
time to get to the point that the youngest daughter is both Beauty
and Death, and that when Lear holds Cordelia in his arms *she is really holding him;* she is the Goddess of Death, her father's death.
There are three sisters because there are three women: the woman
who gives birth to him, the woman he marries, and the woman
who destroys him. Trace had read that essay many times. And the
Secondary Revision, the reordering of the dream in order to slip it
into the quotidian and bury its contradictions and threats. (But
whence censorship, where the Guardian of Sleep?) Trace wrote,
Onward PLEASE. How long could they remain on elementary Freud
when they still had to understand Freud as a pioneer, as the father
not just of psychoanalysis but of literary criticism? What about his
relationship with Jean-Martin Charcot; Freud's extremely unpopu-
lar claim that men too suffer from hysteria? What about his embrace
of homosexuality and bisexuality? What about Ernst Brücke and
Otto Rank, and *how* how would they ever get to Jung? And they
had to have Jung and Freud meet, Freud had to faint when he realized Jung had appointed him a Father Figure and that the Father
would have to be slain . . .

"That's all the time we have," Dr. Scherring said, brushing the
chalk dust off his hands. "Now if I'm going too fast for any of you
please don't hesitate to say so. As I said before, I haven't been out of
the graduate school for years—they keep me locked up there." Dr.

Scherring smiled. "Pick up a syllabus on your way out. Oh, and Wednesday we'll go over Jung."

☩

"Iaaanthe?"

Trace was spending the two hours between classes in the coffee shop; there was a single booth in the corner where she could sit with her back to the door and rarely be seen or bothered, but apparently the top of her head was now well known to Myka, who was sitting in the seat opposite her.

"Hey," Trace said, closing the book on flying saucers. Today Myka was resplendent in a long, gray silk blouse (quite possibly it was another nightgown) under a black velvet smoking jacket. Her hair was gathered into a complicated structure at the crown, but barely. The hair itself seemed so full of life it defied being contained. Around her throat she wore a strand of yellowing pearls, and earrings (platinum, it seemed) from which teardrop pearls hung at the end of a column of diamonds. Orthodontia must be lucrative, Trace decided.

"Are you excited?" Myka asked, widening her green eyes and taking the lid off her coffee cup.

"Excited?"

"About this afternoon?"

"Is something happening?"

"Dr. Matthias? Hello, our three o'clock theory class?"

Trace puzzled over the question a moment. "Am I excited about the class, you mean? Yes, I guess so."

Myka looked down, stirred her coffee with a plastic stick. "You're being coy."

Trace pointed to herself. "Me? I'm never coy."

"Have you met him before?"

"Oh, I see." Dr. Matthias was to be Myka's conquest, thus Trace was supposed to be excited. "No, I haven't. I've seen him in the halls a few times but I understand he's rarely here."

Myka took a deep breath, sighed. "He's never here. He has a course reduction, so he only teaches two grad seminars; one *entire year,* our sophomore year, I think, he was away on a Fulbright; he does that Oxford thing every fall semester. He's *never* in his office. When we were freshmen his wife left him and no one saw him outside of class for weeks at a time. Wait. I think we were freshmen. He goes to retreats or something, I don't know, some kind of religious thing. It's like, is he even employed by this university? Why can I never sit down and talk to him, why?"

"What do you want to talk to him about?"

Myka stared at Trace. She didn't blink. "What do you mean?"

"Is there something you want to talk to him about?"

"Are we . . . are we talking about the same man?"

Probably not. Trace shook her head. "Maybe not."

They both sipped their coffee. Myka feigned remembering something she'd been meaning to ask. "Oh, you know, can I ask you something?"

"I don't know."

"We were wondering—this came up at the end of the party the other night—is it possible, I mean, are you Jewish? Because that would be so cool to have a Jewish Goth in our circle, very rare in Indiana."

"I'm sure Anastasia is partly Jewish. He covers every other category." Trace opened her notebook to an empty page.

"No." Myka scanned the crowd in the coffee shop, over Trace's head. "He checked."

"What happened with Melanie?"

"Who is Melanie."

"The cutter?"

"Oh god. She needed stitches, if you can believe it, she's gonna have a scar there, what an idiot. Anastasia said it looked like a mastectomy gone wrong."

"What about Jeff?"

"Jeff."

"The boyfriend? Who made her do it?"

"Oh, him. He left town, I think. First he went to her house and ran over her cat, then left town. But you never know with those two; they broke up after the Ohio thing, too, and he came back."

"So it's a pattern?"

"What, which part."

"Myka, I'm not Jewish *or* Goth."

"Whatever you say. Love? For me, though? When it arrives it won't look anything like what those two do, the Ohio thing and the stitches."

"It will be beautiful, I bet."

Myka looked into the distance, in the general direction of where a group of frat boys were stomping on condiment packages. "You have no idea."

Trace walked from the coffee shop to the opposite end of campus, listening to Kate Bush on her Walkman. She was thinking how interesting it was to consider what Dr. Scherring hadn't included in his whirlwind tour of Freud, but then she hadn't really been listening, had she, she had what she considered to be enormous problems on her mind. She was crossing a busy street when, in the song she was listening to, an older woman's voice, clear and mixed above all the other tracks, said, "Wake up, child!" and Trace jumped, nearly tripped. As she walked on she tried to steady her pulse, but just as the song ended a man whispered, loudly (if a whisper can be loud) into the silence, "Wake up!" Trace dropped her coffee cup and watched it hit the sidewalk and splash into an inkblot pattern in the snow plowed up against the edges of the walk. She picked up the empty cup, the lid, walked on to class.

✣

The ten students in the Archetypal Interpretation of Literature class had gone through the same motions as in Trace's earlier class: the removal of notebooks and pens, the shuffling and reshuffling of belongings, the sitting still, only this time the door didn't open and continued not to open. When it finally did, it was the department secretary, Cheryl, informing them that Dr. Matthias's plane had gotten in late from a layover in Chicago but that he was on the way and would be here any minute.

Ten minutes later the man himself flew through the door with such haste the door hit the wall and bounced back, nearly knocking him into the hallway. "Whoa!" he said, his arms full of folders and what appeared to be a carry-on bag. "Sorry I'm late, sorry, there was weather in . . . could someone grab this door? You? What's your name? Good to meet you, Chris. My checked luggage is lost, well, it's missing anyway, so if someone from the airport shows up here with it don't be alarmed. Oh, thanks—did I drop that? Thanks." Dr. Matthias put all of his belongings on the table (where there used to be a desk), and pulled something yellow from his pocket. "This," he said, "is a speeding ticket. Just so you know I was trying."

Trace couldn't help but glance at Myka, who had affected a dancer's posture and was sticking to it, statuesque; she was trembling, Trace could see, her eyes glistening as if she might cry. And over what? Trace turned her attention to Dr. Matthias, who was still fumbling with his folders and his books and traffic tickets, explaining that his flight from Paris had been due to arrive hours and hours before it did. He was tall, his salt-and-pepper hair was cut so short it stood up at odd angles, but maybe he'd been wearing a hat. He had fine bone structure, Trace would give him that; he wore small, round John Lennon glasses on his straight, prominent nose. He had the ever-present, unfortunate earring, just one; a white dress shirt under a loose black fisherman's sweater. Trace was very taken with the sweater, which was going ragged at the sleeves—her favorite thing. He wore blue jeans and—she bent down as if to pick up something from the floor—black tennis shoes. She couldn't see his socks. Even so, she knew he was divorced, because he'd disappeared one of her four years in the English department, according to Myka, who would know.

Perhaps she was looking at him with a bit too much concentration, trying to imagine if she could feel what Myka felt or, more to the point, if she could ever allow this man among all men to approach what belonged, permanently and without question, to Colt. She might have been addressing the issue, in her mind or with her eyes, with a bit too much force, because he suddenly looked up and was staring at her. She held her breath and didn't move, but she felt *robbed*—how to explain it? She felt, as Greta Garbo had after seeing Cocteau's *La Belle et la Bête,* when the spell is broken and the Prince is transformed back into himself, *Give me back my Beast!*

Trace looked down at her desk and he, too, looked away. There were plenty of desirable professors on a campus this size, and everyone was aware that having a Ph.D. and a tenured professorship was akin to being in a candy shop filled with young women; an enormous candy shop, your credit card has no limit, and your metabolism is high. And such men gained a reputation—everyone knew which ones were making which offers—but Dr. Matthias wasn't one of them.

"I've been at this school a long time," he said, giving up on ordering the papers on his desk, "twenty-two years. Longer than many of you have been alive. You wouldn't believe the people I've watched come and go from my classrooms, the university, and I won't bore you by telling you, but I will say that the human drama that plays out in our lives, often right in front of me, is enough to convince me that all these thinkers I love, Jung and Hillman and Campbell and Frazer and Frye, are dead right. They're right about literature and art and the collective unconscious and the archetypes, and even how the spring is comedic and autumn is tragic. We'll spend a lot of time talking about what the archetypes are, or if they are, although I subscribe to the idea that they are autonomous—inborn forms of intuition—a way of describing experiences that come upon us with the power of fate.

"Everybody knows that all literature can be mined by Freudians. But Freud was a physician; he believed in analysis, a code, a key. The archetypes are something else, the way they come visiting and won't be denied, how they show up in dreams and in the way— once you've learned to read a text in this fashion—you'll see the color silver in a story and you'll know Mercury has been there, and so you'll also know there's a trick somewhere even if you can't figure it out. Colors and numbers, and you will ask yourself, 'Why seven?' You'll see how each archetype is associated with so many specific attributes that each work of literature just gets deeper and deeper as you recognize them. Oh, there is Hephaestus, you'll say, and you'll wonder if you dare see a soul at the white heat."

Trace sat very still, not doodling or thinking about Candy or anything else. She looked at the ragged sleeves of Dr. Matthias, his dark eyes behind the small glasses, and a thought entered her mind unbidden, *Oh no oh no oh no.*

"Here's your syllabus"—he gave a stack to the first person in each row—"and you'll see the standard things there, Frye's *Anatomy of Criticism* and *The Stubborn Structure,* Campbell's *Hero with a Thousand Faces.* Also Annis Pratt's *Archetypal Patterns in Women's Fiction,* and a lot of handouts from Hillman. If I could I'd have you read everything, but my department chair has warned me against it. I'll give you handouts from Jung, too, because if I assigned whole books you wouldn't read them and that would be a waste. But we'll also be reading a lot of fiction, starting with Chopin's *The Awakening*, which has the most beautiful ending . . ." He paused, as if remembering, as Trace was remembering, the way the air *pinked* before the woman drowned herself; the cavalry officer's footsteps on the pier. The old dog chained to the sycamore tree barked and the air *pinked.* "We'll read a lot of Hawthorne, and oh, anyway it's all there on the syllabus, you don't need me to recite it to you. But we'll start with one of the most perfect stories to analyze for archetypes: Sarah Orne Jewett's 'The White Heron.' " He paused. "Have you read it?" No one moved or offered yes or no.

And then he did the most amazing thing: he began to recite it. He knew the entire story by heart and he just spoke it. It was about a nine-year-old girl, Sylvia (no accident there), and a hunter she meets. The hunter realizes she knows where the elusive, desirable white heron is and he wants her to lead him to it so he can make a trophy of it, and Sylvia and her grandmother are poor and the hunter will make them rich, and besides the little girl is in love with him, there's no way around it. Dr. Matthias recited the story and no one moved or made a sound, even as the class hour ended and he continued speaking. He said, *The murmur of the pine's green branches is in her ears, she remembers how the white heron came flying through the golden air and how they watched the sea and the morning together, and Sylvia cannot speak; she cannot tell the heron's secret and give its life away.* Green, white, golden, the sea. Alchemy.

Trace could barely hear the last paragraph, the one that began with "Dear loyalty," but she heard the last two sentences: "Whatever treasures were lost to her, woodlands and summertime, remember! Bring your gifts and graces and tell your secrets to this lonely country child!"

The pause in the room was heavy, then Dr. Matthias said, "Go, go—I kept you too long," and everyone was rushing to get out the door, late to another class, and Trace stood up so fast she slammed her knees against the bottom of her desk. She was so terrified of what she felt she grabbed her coat, her notebook and bag, and nearly ran over a short boy traversing the doorway at a normal pace. "Sorry," she said, looking back at him. The first restroom she came to was for faculty but the door was unlocked and Trace threw her bag and her coat in, locked the door behind her, and leaned against it, as a giant, a leviathan, rose up in her throat. She grabbed her scarf and shoved it into her mouth to keep from sobbing; she bit down on the wool and pressed her head against the wood of the door and even then she couldn't stop herself from making a sound like a hare, pierced and claw-tucked against the breast of a hawk.

As soon as she was sufficiently recovered Trace walked calmly to the English department's main office and asked Cheryl for the faculty directory.

"How's your semester going so far?" Cheryl asked, in a secretarial way.

"Great, fine—I just need the office number of my professor in Women's Studies."

"You can leave the directory on my desk when you're done," Cheryl said, walking toward the copy machine.

Was it here, would he dare to publish his address, his phone number? Trace flipped through the alphabet and there it was: Dr. J. Matthias, Department of English. There was his office number, his mailbox, and his home address. He lived in Jonah, in the same neighborhood as lots of other professors—the Westside Historical District. Trace wrote everything down, put the directory neatly on Cheryl's desk, ran to her truck.

· · ·

Please please don't let there be a line, she thought, signing in at the truck stop. There wasn't, and this time Trace didn't stand languid and open-celled under the hot water; she washed the kerosene off her skin and hair; she hung her clothes in the shower with her, to steam them. Using the hand dryer she tried to get some of the water out of her hair so she didn't freeze to death, then she put everything back on and ran out to her truck.

It was dark by the time Trace found his house, a Queen Anne at the end of a block. Half the houses were pristine, half were derelict; Dr. Matthias lived in one of the good ones. He didn't appear to be home, but she rang the doorbell anyway and knocked on various side doors. At the back of the house was a screened porch, obviously recently added. Trace looked in and saw a glider covered in a thick floral pad, and a wicker basket swing, attached by a thick rope to one of the house's original beams. In front of the glider was a trunk, three wine bottles covered with melted candle wax and dust, a metal tray on which rested two dusty wineglasses. She tried to open the door but it was locked with a hook and eye, the sort of thing easily undone with her student ID. Trace let herself in, put her bag down. She turned on the switch for what had originally been an outdoor light, and sat down on the glider. Because it might be a while before he got home, she got out her notebooks, the textbooks she'd purchased that morning, and a copy of "The White Heron," which she read again and again.

He opened the back door and walked in. "Hello," he said.

"Weren't you afraid?" Trace asked. "Seeing someone had broken into your house and was sitting on your . . . couch thing?"

Dr. Matthias sat down beside her with a sigh, dropping his bags on the porch. He still didn't have his suitcase. "No. A little. I probably took a moment to prepare a face to meet the faces I would meet."

"To both murder and create?"

"Something like that. You're in my theory class? This afternoon?"

Trace nodded, couldn't look at him.

"It's cold out here; do you want to come in the house?"

"No." She shook her head. "I'm used to it. I just wanted . . ."

"Yes?"

She couldn't say it. She had been prepared to say it all the way up to the last second. "*The Feminine in Fairy Tales.* You must not be part of the Western Canon Protection Committee. Or else you teach in the Women's Studies department and I didn't know it."

He laughed. "I'm an enemy of the canon, according to my colleagues, yes. And no, I don't teach any Women's Studies courses but I date a woman who does."

All the blood in Trace's body fled . . . somewhere, leaving her toes tingling. Her hands would shake if she weren't sitting on them. "Oh? Who is that?"

"Dr. Cohen," he said casually, without any expression of passion, no secret pleasure in her name.

Trace swallowed. The Wounded Woman, her professor tomorrow.

"Are you . . . in love with her?"

Dr. Matthias tipped his head back, let it rest on the floral cushion. He closed his eyes. "Not really, no. Are you here for a reason, or did you just want to make certain I didn't miss my suitcase, should it arrive in my absence?"

The moment she opened her mouth to tell him, her throat closed. She tried to say a single word, and then he was reaching toward her, pulling her against him.

"Hey," he said, his mouth on her hair. "Don't cry."

"I never cry." She spoke into his chest, breathed in the smell of him. She realized she had a handful of his sweater, just the way Candy had clutched at her on the floor of the trailer. She let go and sat up, smoothing his clothes under his coat. "I'm sorry. I just came here to tell you that—yes, the archetypes are inborn forms of intuition—but *everything* comes to us, every experience, with the force of fate. Because it all is that force."

"I know." Dr. Matthias nodded, watching her carefully.

"I'm *your* fate." Trace looked at him directly and when he didn't respond she said, "I'm your fate, and you are mine. That's what I came to say."

The professor, a man whose first name she didn't even know, sat as still as Myka had earlier, frozen. He didn't speak.

"I've—I've got to go, I need to—" She didn't say she needed to get home to her dog, because in the moment she couldn't remember anything, she barely remembered why she was there.

"Wait." Dr. Matthias stood and they bumped into each other, Trace trying to stuff her books and papers into her bag, digging for her keys.

"I've got to go." Trace slipped around the table with the tray, glasses set for two, burnt ends of candles in wine bottles. She'd made a mistake.

"Wait," he said again as the door slammed behind her and she ran.

✝

She took Weeds out to the deserted country road in front of the house and let him run. He tore up the road, turned, ran back to her. It was a pattern that never seemed to grow old. Eventually they went back to the dark house. Trace had warmed the kitchen in their absence, and she made them both something to eat and sat down at the table. The situation didn't bear thinking about. Either he would tell Dr. Cohen and everyone else he worked with or he wouldn't. Either he would ask her to leave his class or he would not. There was no way to read him. She blew on her tea, took out her books and folders. Where was it? She took everything out of her bag, tipped it upside down, but it wasn't there—her favorite pen was gone. She'd been using it at his house, making notes on the short story; she must have left it there.

Weeds lay down in front of the heater with a sigh. Considering all she had to lose, the pen was of little consequence; it was her favorite only because it was. She took another from the cup on the table—the bookstore had provided her with plenty. There was a great deal to do tonight. The dream journal she'd been keeping would never reach the hands of Dr. Scherring, so she was going to have to go back and re-create one that bore not the slightest scent of her. She made a list: flying dream; teeth falling out; had a baby and misplaced it; found my true love but was forced to wake up.

CHAPTER FIVE

Puella Aeterna

Journal

For the year Billy slept between me and the window, Loretta had a variety of tricks for getting me out of the room. She would come in late, after we were all sound asleep, and take my hand. Dusty always woke up before I did; she slept with her arm around me, to keep me from leaving the bed. Loretta would whisper, "It's okay; I'm taking her into bed with me and Colt—we'll both keep an eye on her." I held Loretta's hand and followed her dutifully, but when I looked back at Dusty Ann she was wide awake and watching us with an expression that wasn't fear, really, it was blank, absent. From his pallet on the floor Billy slept on, unaware. Nothing was going to get through the window—nor would I go out it—on his watch, and nothing ever did.

After a certain point I think the attempt to remove whatever foreign thing in me Loretta feared, and called a demon, took on its own life; she and her little gang of miracle workers wouldn't be defeated: not by the spirit indwelling nor by my stubborn refusal to let it go. By and large I didn't know the people in the basement, around the red table; if they were members of the church I hadn't paid attention to them. There was a man with curly blond hair who suggested I be untied, in case I needed to levitate. I had no idea what that word meant, but when they untied me I just lay there; I didn't try to escape or fight. I waited for the levitate to come and finish the mess.

They prayed frantically. Hands were placed upon me, hands filled with healing power. A man read furiously from the Gospels, mostly Mark, and a section of the Acts of the Apostles, the same things over and over. A—a section of 1 Samuel, I think. Cold water was poured over me, to shock the demon out; hot water, too, but not boiling. I was beaten with reeds through the wet nightgown, my mouth was propped open with matchsticks, so I couldn't hold the spirit in deliberately. They left the match heads on, and then claimed they could smell sulfur drifting up from my soul and out of my mouth.

That was the first year.

Dusty turned fifteen, Billy seventeen, and Loretta prepared a room for me at the top of the stairs by cleaning out a large closet, ostensibly so Dusty could have privacy. She swore she didn't need privacy, but Loretta said all girls do. The room was just big enough for a twin bed, and when it was all set up Colt asked me, with an innocence I can't believe he still possessed, if I was excited. I nodded.

I could no longer go to church on Sundays with the family, so Colt stayed home with me. I never asked him what he'd been told, or why he agreed, but that was the beginning. We made the best of it and went fishing; he gave me a gun. We went hiking by the river, even when it was frozen and I feared what was under the ice. I slept with a stuffed dog Colt had won at the fair—these days such things are called "transitional objects"—and at night the dog, Fipper, served that purpose and all the rest of the time it was Colt. I wanted to hold him or be held by him just as I slept with Fipper under my arm or against my chest. Outdoors I was cool with him, I was his faithful companion, but in the house or in his truck, or riding behind him on his bike, I was like a little chimp. He carried me on his back, he danced with me in the kitchen, I memorized his shoulders, his spine, the way his hair grew from the crown of his head, its shifting color in various lights, the veins on the backs of his hands, the black hair on his arms. When he pulled off his clothes in the mudroom after we'd been fishing my eyes opened and closed, an aperture, on his chest, the ladder of his stomach, the way his jeans hung precarious on the hooks of his hip bones, and there was a dip on either side, just above where the bones jutted out. His body was a map a friendly guard had slipped me in prison; you will have one chance, the guard said, memorize every detail, never ever forget a single turn or tunnel. Eat the map when you're sure.

From the Women's Studies/English Department Newsletter, three years ago: We are delighted to welcome to our faculty Dr. Elizabeth Cohen, who comes to us after finishing her doctoral work at the prestigious Hofstra University. Dr. Cohen's dissertation, which will be published by the University of Pittsburgh Press this fall, is entitled *The Blubber of Moby Dick: Canonicity and the War Against Patriarchy.* Professorship is Dr. Cohen's second career. She worked as an epidemiologist for the World Health Organization for a number of years before deciding her true calling was academia. Welcome, Dr. Cohen!

Budd Hopkins is of the opinion that abductees are no more likely to be neurotic, delusional, or open to suggestion than anyone else in the general populace. Their stories are remarkably consistent: They wake up and can't move (thus the argument for sleep paralysis), sensing a presence in the room, or they are hurtling through the air, out an open window. Occasionally they believe they're being electrocuted. The extraterrestrials (not a word I want to write over and over) surround them, wordlessly. Virtually all agree that the e.t.s communicate telepathically.

1953: *Invaders from Mars* (robotic aliens)

1955: *This Island Earth* (large-headed robotlike humanoids—the introduction of reversible amnesia?)

Early 1960s: *The Outer Limits* (Reptilian). Season 1, episode 21, *The Children of Spider Country* (An alien father, Aable, from the planet Eros, comes to reclaim his four hybrid sons fathered by human mothers. Aable has a big head, big eyes, primordial nose and mouth—beginning of sexual experimentation?)

1963: Betty and Barney Hill undergo hypnosis—abducted from car—their descriptions provide the template for most abduction claims that follow.

Six, seven, eight. Every couple of months, maybe not that often. Sometimes I would wake up and Dusty would be in bed with me, Billy asleep in the doorway, and I don't know what Loretta did then; gave up, probably. On the nights I was alone Loretta would take me by the hand, a new white nightgown each year, and later she would arrive home before me, slip into bed beside Colt, who slept like a rock, that was the reason Billy had been given the assignment in the first place, and I would sleepwalk out of the woods and sometimes on into the house and Dusty would be waiting with the washcloth or the sponge. Then Dusty went to the gas station for a candy bar—she even remembers which kind—and left with the gentleman for the sunlit world. I assumed I was, as they say, screwed. Except

well. I was nine, I had no friends but Candy, we were entirely dependent on one another, and Candy never asked. No matter how often she saw evidence she never asked, which I respected at the

time and still to this day. If only someone had given me . . . *anything*
. . . a script of *any* kind, I could have ended it and saved us all so
much trouble, but no matter how often they tried, those earnest
men and women (just two women, including Loretta), nothing was
accomplished. *Until* one night we had gone through the early hoo-
ha and the middle, I was tall already and harder to manipulate physically, we might even have been in the late-stage hoo-ha and I saw,
near the door, a black rabbit. It was just sitting there looking at me.
It lifted a large back paw and scratched behind an ear. I shouted, "It's
out! The demon is out—it's right there by the door!" Although
even as I said it I couldn't believe any demon would take the form
of a sweet little rabbit, that didn't make any sense at all. Everyone
around me, all the Brothers and Sisters in Christ, turned and looked
where I was pointing and they saw nothing. Doom. If not for Sister
Whatever Her Name Was, Loretta would have beaten me to death.
Instead she decided to call in the Big Gun. But no matter; from that
night on the black rabbit was always there, and he led me home
when I became confused. He never let me get lost, not once.

Jung describes extraterrestrials as *technological angels.* There is an
enormous amount to unpack, in just those two words.

✝

Dr. Elizabeth Cohen's class was full. Trace sat at the back, in the corner, in the least conspicuous place in the room. And Dr. Cohen herself was not late: no blowing in from Paris, scattering speeding
tickets for her—no breathless trek from the rarefied air of the graduate school. She came in on the hour, carrying precisely what she
needed. Trace watched her every move.

Dr. Cohen's hair was short, sensible, black going gray. She wore
glasses, no makeup. Under a complicated, long batik jacket she
wore a T-shirt that read, *If You Can Talk You Can Sing; If You Can*

Walk You Can Dance, in some bright, faux-African font, black children dancing around the words themselves. Her brown linen pants flared at the ankle; her shoes were brown lace-ups with rubber soles that squeaked as she crossed the classroom floor.

She placed her books and notes on the table and turned to the classroom. "Hello hello! I know . . . most of you. I'll know all of you very shortly. This class"—Dr. Cohen's voice dropped into an intimate register—"is called Wounded Women, and here, in an atmosphere of safety, we will work on that subject: Healing the Father-Daughter/Male-Female Relationship."

All the women in the class sat breathless, enthralled. They couldn't *wait* to begin; they had been waiting for years for this day, this hour. Trace had read some of the source materials in question last night, after finishing her fictional dream journal, and had been shocked by their simplicity—or rather, the lack of depth or complexity. There was a lot about self-esteem, and healing oneself by acknowledging one's inner strength, one's inner father, or forgiving a father who was too rigid or too much a *puer aeternus.*

"Hi, my name's Kaitlyn?" The class had started without Trace. She knew at the next session the chairs would be in a circle. "And I want to heal the wound in me that's about my dad? He never really paid me much attention, he works at a bank and is really busy all the time and his job is important to him and also he plays golf on the weekends and when I look at pictures of my growing-up time it's like he's standing in the corner? And I don't know." Kaitlyn's eyes filled with tears and the person sitting next to her reached over and covered Kaitlyn's hand. Dr. Cohen wore a pained expression, one of genuine empathy. "I don't know if I'll understand how to ever choose a mate, like who will make a good husband or father when all I know is this . . . hole where mine was?"

Dr. Cohen nodded. "Kaitlyn, I think that's something we'll be dealing with a lot in this class, the absent father. One of the problems is he didn't give you the tools to access your own animus, the father figure *inside you*. A number of the books we'll be reading will discuss that problem." She nodded at the next speaker.

"Hi, I'm Jessica, you mostly all know me already from being one of Dr. Cohen's groupies." Many people in the class laughed. "Yeah, ummm, I'm taking this class because I've taken all of Dr. Cohen's classes and also because I want to heal my relationship with my dad, who isn't like Kaitlyn's dad, he's, I don't really know how to say this, it's like he's—I'm embarrassed and I'm glad he can't hear me—he's *weak,* you know, my mom was really mean to him and he never fought back, and he never *ever* defied her, she told him what to wear and what to eat and what job he had to take, and then she left him and now he's married to my stepmother, who does exactly the same thing. So like if my mom was mean to me or wouldn't let me do something my dad *never* stood up for me, and now my stepmom isn't nice to me or my sister, she doesn't really want us to see him, and he doesn't stand up to her, either. So."

The professor had adopted a complicated pose: her left arm over her chest, her right elbow upright on that arm, her chin resting on her fist. For a moment she stood that way, then turned (dramatically, Trace thought) and walked to the blackboard. She wrote, CINDERELLA.

"Where was Cinderella's father?" she asked, her head tilted to one side. She wrote, SLEEPING BEAUTY. "Who forgot to invite the right person to the christening of the Princess?" She wrote, NAME A FAIRY TALE. "Dead mothers; weak or absent fathers, fathers who would sacrifice their daughters. That's always the launching-off point of the story, isn't it? There would be no tale if our heroine was held in perfect safety, being reared by two parents who were strong and wise and independent." Dr. Cohen put the chalk down. "Except for one story, which I've been finding very interesting lately: the story of Bluebeard and His Wives. How many of you are familiar with it?"

There were a few tentative hands raised.

"Bluebeard might be a retelling of the story of Gilles de Rais, who was decapitated in the fifteenth century for murdering hundreds of children. But probably Bluebeard is a, let's say, archetypal figure, a husband. The short version of the story is that he marries a very beautiful young woman—in some illustrations she is barely more than a child—and he offers her wealth and pleasure beyond imagining." Dr. Cohen spread her arms wide, to indicate such bounty. "In early versions the bride has no name, although her sister does—Anne—and later the bride is called Fatima. Bluebeard gives his young bride everything she could possibly want, but he tells her there is one thing she absolutely must not do, she cannot have. She cannot open a locked closet door." On the board Dr. Cohen wrote the words CLOSETS, GATES, KEYS, LOCKS, FORBIDDEN ENTRANCES. "He decides to go on a trip and he hands to his wife the keys to the entire estate, including the closet. Now let's think about that a moment." She paced. "All the early versions of the myth suggested that what happens to Bluebeard's bride is the result of her disobedience, and her curiosity, both of which were very unattractive in women, if not cause for violence. And what do you suppose the girl does?"

The room was silent. Trace knew the story very well, but hadn't thought of it in years. She stretched out her hands, which had begun to tingle.

"She called her sister Anne over, and the first thing they did was unlock that door." Dr. Cohen underlined the words CLOSETS, LOCKS, FORBIDDEN. "And what she found in there were the first six of Bluebeard's wives, dead, and hanging on hooks. In some illustrations she finds merely their heads. The key"—which she also underlined—

"immediately became covered with blood, some believe as a symbol of her perverse sexuality, or her perversity, her filth. And as she stands with the bloody key, who should return? The husband who had set her up, and is carrying the sword to kill her. In virtually all versions of the myth the bride is saved by her brothers, who arrive at the last possible second, and kill Bluebeard before he can add another woman to his collection of hooks."

She brushed the chalk dust off her hands, pushed up her glasses. "A strange story to tell in this class, maybe, except I think the modern readings of the myth are the right ones. What Bluebeard's bride, Fatima, represents is not disobedience or the poison of female curiosity. She is boldness and independence itself. She will not let a mystery remain unsolved. She will avenge the death of the other wives, which she somehow intuits. She will not accept luxury and wealth and ease at the cost of such vicious crimes. Fatima is the heroine of that story regardless of whether her brothers arrive—myths always have to have a male savior. But in this case, I think it's the woman with the key." She smiled at her wounded class. "So let's think of it that way—you are the heroines of your own stories. And you aren't waiting for Prince Charming to rescue you or kiss you or make your mermaid's tale go away; you are going to find that figure inside yourself. *You* will awaken yourself from your slumber. *You* will protect yourself from the hunter who is coming to cut out your heart. *You* will decide if you want to walk on dry land or stay in the ocean. *You* will decide whether or not to open the locked closet door. Literature will be the guidepost along the way, and these women around you—we will do it together."

There wasn't a dry eye in the room, except for Trace's. She was moved, a little, but mostly she was taken by the image of the hunter coming for her heart; the wooden casket in the story. She was remembering the details now—how the hunter saw Snow White and couldn't do it, he couldn't kill her after all, so he cut out the heart of a doe and took that back to her mother. The heart of a doe. A wooden casket. The original story had been twelve sons and a thirteenth child, a daughter. The father had declared if the child were female all twelve brothers would be slain, so their mother hid them in the woods. Eventually the sister found them and they loved one another, but she picked the lilies next to their house and the boys turned to ravens and flew away. Spirit birds. She had killed them.

The next two young women explained why they were taking the class and Dr. Cohen lectured in between each (in her fashion that wasn't so much like a lecture), and then their time was up, even though it was a ninety-minute class, meeting only on Tuesdays and Thursdays. The spotlight hadn't reached Trace and she wouldn't have spoken if it had; or else she would have lied, and then lied some more.

Dr. Cohen's groupies, self-declared, surrounded her at the front of the classroom as Trace put her books away and put on her coat.

"Is he back from Paris?" One of them asked.

"He is," Dr. Cohen said, raising an eyebrow. Playful.

"Are you seeing him tonight?"

The professor smiled. A lovely smile, Trace had to admit, the smile of money and an M.D., credentials, a Ph.D., a soon-to-be published dissertation; the smile of tenure and a rather homely woman approaching middle age who had somehow, miraculously, caught the big fish, and knew it. "I am indeed."

✝

Trace left campus and crossed the bridge over the Planck River, out of one town and into another. She went as far south as Fourth Street, to the Laundromat where no one knew her. The place was filled with women and their children, who, without exception, stole all the carts and used them as vehicles. It was irritating but still Trace loved the smell of the place—the soap and fabric softener and dryer sheets, the heat. She even loved the molded plastic chairs bolted into the floor. After getting her laundry started, she sat down and took out the stationery she had never used before. She longed for her favorite pen. Finally, after writing the date and the address of her campus mailbox, she began:

Dear Billy,

    It has been so long since I saw your face but I can see it in my mind as clear as a photograph or a mirror. You are my most beloved brother and the last of my kin. It might not be safe to write to you but you gave me your p.o. # and of course I'm using the other name and I would never cause you harm if I could help it.

    I know it isn't safe for you to come back here; I've known all along that I might never see you again. But Dusty Ann is in terrible trouble, and in fact it might be too late to save her already. The little girls (you've never met them—that's almost impossible for me to believe) are in trouble, too. I'm not even sure what I'm asking you for. Some part of me wants you to ride in and take us, take Dusty and the girls and Weeds and me and let us go back with you to Ontario, wherever and however you live. I have a dream of you saving us. I know it's unlikely, but if you would please just open up this conduit—write back to me and let me tell you what's happening and

    Billy you did what you had to do; we all did. I tell myself this every day. I pray to be forgiven even though I will never be— forgiveness isn't possible for me but it is for you. You acted as a hero would and I don't mean a fireman rushing in a burning building although sort of like that but more—a hero in a fairy tale. You are mythic. You are like the hunter sent to cut out the heart of a girl

and you didn't. a doe. A fawn. I sat under a tree with a fawn, Colt
had given me a kit and I was learning to make arrows, but I can't
remember the rest, if you would just come home.

Yours,
Tracey Sue

She dried her laundry and folded it; stopped at a pay phone to
call Candy, who said Skeet wasn't home, to come on over.

✛

Trace had planned to lay it all out—she'd even made *note cards.* She
would tell Candy about the timeline, the Hills, the template for the
accounts that followed. She would explain what happened during
the various conditions associated with parasomnia, how an episode
of sleep paralysis could convince anyone that something supernat-
ural had occurred.

But when she stepped out of her truck and saw the wind moving the tops of the trees, the way they swayed as if communicating
with one another; when she stepped over to the chicken wire fence
and saw just the tip of Blue's nose at the edge of the doghouse;
when she called and called him and he remained so still she wasn't
sure he was alive, she rethought what she might say.

The trailer was so clean Trace stopped in the doorway and wondered if she should take another step. The carpet appeared to have
been shampooed and every surface was shining. Trace looked over
at the table in the dining alcove and the plastic tablecloth was gone;
where it had been was wood, polished. "Candy?" she called, prepared to step backward, and leave.

"Hey, Tracey! Just a second," Candy was down the hallway,
probably trying to keep the clothes on one of the boys. When she

emerged, though, there were no babies hanging on her, and Trace noticed now the absence of the television noise.

Candy's Mall Hair was perfectly curled and sprayed, and she was wearing clean clothes—a white sweatshirt and jeans, with white tennis shoes. Both of her eyes were blackened, nearly swollen shut, and her top lip was so huge it had split open at one corner. "Well come in, silly, don't just stand there."

"Do you—do you want me to take off my boots? Your carpet looks brand new."

"No, are your serious? I've never asked anyone to take off their shoes in my house. Good heavens."

"Where are the boys?"

Candy headed into the kitchen, where Trace could smell coffee being made. "They're in bed."

"Isn't it—isn't it kind of early for them to be asleep?"

"We had a busy day today, wore them out, you want some coffee?"

Trace took off her coat and scarf, draped them over the couch. "Okay." She carried her bag to the table and sat down, then placed her hands on the wooden surface. It was smooth as glass, not a crumb on it.

Candy carried in two mugs, sat down. "How'd your first couple days go, at school? You gonna make it to the end?"

Trace shrugged. "You never know. What, uh, what's been happening here?" She looked around the trailer rather than directly at Candy's face.

"Ugh, I just got tired of it, you know, I wanted to see what it would feel like to live in a clean house for once. Since I got married, I mean. Turns out I like it."

"I bet. It looks great." Trace nodded, sipped at the fiercely bitter coffee. "What, uh. How's everything else?"

"Fine, pretty good, really, Skeet got more hours at the garage so he's working a lot later, but sometime soon, in the next paycheck or the one after that, maybe we'll see quite a difference. Pay off his truck, maybe."

"Mmm hmm. What about your—what happened to your face? What are those bruises on your neck?"

Candy reached up and touched her neck, a delicate gesture. "Oh, you know." She leaned across the table and whispered. "I'm not supposed to talk about it."

"With me?"

"With anyone. I'm a special case is the problem, I have a situation with—with the atmosphere. They told me that each time is like I just got born, you know how babies come out with their noses smashed and sometimes their eyes are bruised like this? It's like I don't fit through the . . . space, the space *between* is too narrow. I'm not supposed to talk about it."

"It's probably okay to talk to me, though, right? I can understand not talking to, I don't know, the media or a doctor, but you can talk to me?"

Candy shook her head. "No, especially not you, they said. They won't punish me, nothing like that, you know, but they say you aren't on my side and I shouldn't trust you."

"Did they tell you why? Why shouldn't you trust me? And what about Skeet, can he not see you?"

"No, he can't see me. I look just the same to him. They told me you're—building something, I can't remember the word. You're building something of lies, and you want to give it to me. You want to make me a part of it, but if I do go in this . . . thing they'll never come back."

Trace froze, her hand resting on top of the coffee mug, warming her fingers. "I'm sorry, are you saying you want them to come back? You want this to go on?"

Candy glanced around at the silent trailer. "Tracey Sue, I've come to understand something. I've come to understand that I've been chosen by them for a reason. I thought—at first I thought I was being tortured, but now I know that isn't the case. It's not easy, I'm not saying that, and I'm still scared most of the time, but I think they've come to *save* us. I don't know all of it but I think they're here for *love*."

Trace looked down into her lap, rubbed her forehead with her fingertips. "Why, what has made you change your mind?"

"Well, before I only saw the scary ones—the workers, you know. But now I've been introduced to another one, he's not like the little guys. He's tall, I think he's thin but I don't know because he wears a blue robe but it's almost like there's no *body* in there, it's like I can only see him at all, his face and eyes, because he wants me to. He's taken over all the work with me and anytime he comes into the room—no, before he comes into the room I can feel him, I can feel his love ahead of him."

"He loves you."

"Oh absolutely. I'm not—I can't say any more."

Trace said nothing, imagining her earlier hope. *Note cards.*

"I have to tell someone, Tracey, I'm pregnant, I'm pregnant with his baby. No one will ever have to know because their babies don't take so long to grow, just three months or so, and then they'll remove it and it will go into the nursery and I'll get to see it every night. He told me they might let me bring it home with me eventually, there are others, hybrids they're called, they're all over the place. Yesterday in the grocery store I was sure I saw one, I could tell by his eyes, but I didn't say anything and neither did he although he looked at me a long time." Candy pushed up the right sleeve of her sweatshirt, absentmindedly, and Trace could see purple and black bruises all over her wrists and forearm.

"Have you seen your mom and dad?" Trace asked, as if changing the subject.

"Not for a couple weeks." Candy drank her coffee. "I talked to Mom yesterday but I told her I was cleaning to beat the band and she said she'd stop by sometime later in the week."

"Will she"—Trace looked at Candy's eyes, her split lip—"be able to see you?"

"No, no. You're the only one who can see me."

Trace raised her eyebrows in surprise. "Me? Why am I the only one?"

"Because." Candy rubbed the rim of her mug with her thumb. "Because you're my enemy, they tell me."

Trace sat back hard in her chair, sending a jolt up her spine. "Your enemy."

"Aww." Candy waved the pronouncement away. "I don't think it's true, Tracey, they just want me to be careful. I have to be very careful with the baby, if anybody found out about it, you know, the government or, you know, they would take it and that would be the worst."

"What about Danny Rae and Duane? What about . . . the thing you told me?"

Candy didn't look up. She sat very still, her thumb stopped in its orbit. "They're fine now. I took care of them, I made sure. They're fine now."

✢

Sitting in bed with Weeds, the smaller heater blazing, the windows sealed, no light visible from the road, Trace wrote in her new dream journal.

I had a dream that I came to a beautiful lake and everyone I loved was there. We cooked meat on a grill and there was watermelon and after we all swam in the lake and it was a wonderful day.

CHAPTER SIX

Revenants

The *Enkekalymmenos* Fallacy: "Can you recognize your father?"
Yes. "Can you recognize this veiled one?" No. "This veiled one
is your father. Hence you can recognize your father and not
recognize him."

EUBULIDES THE MEGARIAN

Journal

I note that Candy never made mention of the craft in which she
was taken, as if she never saw it from the outside, meaning (obviously) that while she believes she is transported directly to an interior, the operative word is *interior*. It is in her, not outside. Abductees
differentiate themselves from ufologists in this way. For the devotee
of the flying saucer (and they go back, as Jung mentioned, to 1947),

the phenomenon is not only outside them, it's far away—in the sky. And it turns out that people have witnessed every imaginable shape and form (some phalluses, but mostly not). A by no means exhaustive list includes the *spherical* (subheadings: With Skirt; Featureless; Saturn Rings), the *elliptical* (Football; Egg; Egg with Tall Thing Sticking Up), *light forms* (Fireballs, etc.), the *discoid* (With Fins; With Little House on Top; With Handrail, Presumably for the Elderly; With Legs), and the *cylindrical* (uh-oh—the Cigar; the Cigar with "Dome"; the Cigar with Lights; the Bullet). The object in the sky is an inherited form; it's primordial, but I can't . . . I know what Jung says about . . . well, he says in *Mysterium Coniunctionis* that just because something can be read as psychical, as belonging to the psyche, doesn't mean it isn't physical, too. Then there's that whole Terence McKenna thing about mushroom spores, how the crafts are sending spores, like fungus, into our atmosphere. But also the sightings run in the tens, maybe hundreds, of thousands? by now, which means that our world, the very sky into which we gaze at night, is being interpenetrated by something funguslike, or else grossly incompetent.

Candy says she is pregnant, and it's Hillman (is it Hillman?) who says if you dream of being pregnant you are pregnant with *something.* Jung saw such dreams as ripe with *meaning;* one literally carried the material and meaning that was the key to the unconscious conflict. I was nine, I guess, when Loretta decided she needed to call in reinforcements—to be honest, I don't know if I was nine or ten, those years seem very similar now. I could never remember how we got where we were going, to the red table in the basement; it was almost as if my eyes were covered but I don't think that's the case. I remember taking her hand, even as I got taller and older, and letting her lead me out of the house and into her old station wagon, I can see everything—the drive down our road . . . and the nothing. What had that table been? I can't imagine. It wasn't a pool table, a

Ping-Pong table, it wasn't something from a doctor's office. Wait. Wait. It wasn't a table, it was a *chair,* it was a reclining chair from an old-fashioned barbershop, the kind in which a man was shaved. And who had it, what were their names, all these years I've expected to run into one of them, I've expected to turn a corner and see Brother —— or Sister ——, just the one, Margaret? But where are those people now? It's as if they arrived from the ether at Loretta's summons and vanished when she no longer needed them.

If there aren't UFOs, all the books ask, then why does the government work so hard at preventing us finding out about them? Well, indeed. The government does have to work long hard hours to keep information from us that doesn't exist. But there's also the possibility (slim, but I'm the Devil's Advocate—just ask my mother) that the discs and the rectangles and the ellipticals with handrails and the eggs with tall sticking-up things are real and the "government," whoever that is, takes the prevention of hysteria as its mandate. Hysteria is the Logos of depth psychology, as most everyone knows. Dear old Plato believed that the uterus (Gr. *hystera*) was an autonomous thing, an animal part of a woman that only wanted to become pregnant, the way certain moths have a single raison d'être, which is to implant eggs in a certain flower. I could be making that moth up but I don't think so. The uterus, the hysterical, has just the one job. Aretaeus the Cappadocian, second-century doctor writer, thought the uterus actually . . . floated around—all over the body—presumably looking for sperm. He even called it "erratic." Apparently the uterus loved pleasant smells and hated bad ones and fled from them, and on balance the uterus was an animal moving around freely inside another animal. The etymology of the word is actually rather scumbled about, with a Late Scientific Latin, and then the train from Latin to English may stem from the Indo-European root for *higher.* But whatever its history, hysteria found godfathers in Freud and Joseph Breuer, who did for the word (and its concomitant denotation) what Bach did for the Brandenburg Concertos. Now most people forget that Freud's earliest patients and case histories came to him with physical illnesses because he was a doctor, but this gave him the opportunity to question them— the talking, talking, talking Joseph Breuer had initiated—and during said conversation he discovered a single, irrefutable fact. Most illnesses were psychological in origin, disorders caused by their sexual lives. Take *acquired hysteria:* Katherina was unable to cope with sexual experiences. How about *hysterical amnesia:* an act of repression that allows one to forget infantile sexual experiences. *Hysterical illness:* overfondness for a father who died; somnambulism; a monotonous family life that provided nothing for her intellectual development (this would be the famous Anna O.); daydreaming. Oh, and sexual repression. Freud says, and I love this, I mean I think about it a lot, that hysteria is a form of neurotic defense, or pathological versions of normal psychical states: of *conflict* (hysteria), of *self-reproach* (obsessional something or other), of *mortification* (paranoia), and *mourning* (acute hallucinatory dementedness). He doesn't use the word dementedness I don't believe. He says in his Postscript to Dora—plain as day!—"The symptoms of the disease are nothing else than *the patient's sexual activity.*" Emphasis his! It is Jung who reminds us of the *globus hystericus,* the lump in the throat which is merely unswallowed tears. In Carl Gustav's opinion, nothing to do with the female reproductive system, god bless him.

So you see: a uterus floating around like an animal, trying to get impregnated, a uterus that furthermore can make one physically ill in peculiar ways because everyone is trying to repress traumatic early sexual experiences, and as if that weren't enough, the uterus bends our normal ways of conflict, self-reproach, mortification, and mourning. That's what the government is trying to prevent! That's why they won't acknowledge the presence of the flying saucers or the claims of the abductees. And frankly, if I were the government and Candy said to me, "I have been hypnotized, paralyzed, stolen from my bed, levitated out a window, experimented upon, found love with a disembodied alien, and am now pregnant," my response would be, "That is what your erratic uterus wanted all along, Mrs. Warner. Congratulations."

A barber's chair, a barber's pole. Now, without going to the library stacks I'm going to see if I remember that the reason the pole circulated red and white was because the barber was also a surgeon who performed bloodletting, and he wiped his razor on the pole, and that was how his patients knew he was in? I could have dreamed that, but I think that's where the pole comes from. And we invariably ended up in that red chair with the straps, the chair I thought was a table, and those poor people did everything they could to cast that demon/those demons out of my body and make me belong again to my mother who had once loved me but no longer could because I was a *changeling*. She was just trying to say, Loretta was, that her child was not her child, and the fact of that was driving her mad, it was heating her up to a dangerous temperature; it was affecting her relationship with Jesus; it was causing her to live beyond our means and not tell Colt, who worked as hard as he could. Where was her stolen baby girl? Where had she gone? If only I could be returned to her she would not—in the winter months when Colt's work was slow and he believed we were living on savings—take out loans, forging his signature, nor would those loans come due and there was no way to pay them and she couldn't tell her husband because as I may have mentioned he was whip-crack fast and he carried a switchblade and walked with a slight left-leaning swagger from a childhood accident. An A note in the upper range. She couldn't tell him because I was half in love with him already, I longed for him the way anyone in love longs for a particular object, and he loved me in return, nearly the same way but with more innocence, less understanding of the mythic dimensions that

I knew even then, at nine or ten. Errors were made on Loretta's part, and then they spiraled: the overspending, the demon child, the loans, the love between her husband and her bad seed, the rent coming due, the failure to renounce the spirits that inhabited my unnaturally colored eyes (the spirits didn't live there, that's a very awkward construction—they were merely a *mnemic trace,* as Freud would have it, an alteration of my very neurons), and she paid the way she could pay. As it happened, the Big Gun could not only lend her money and clear the debt, he happened to have a gift with wayward girls; he had a way of speaking to them very gently—a near hypnotic state, is what he promised—and he would extract the alien and put it in the body of the swine and drive it off the cliff, right back to Dis where it belonged. The room emptied of the brethren and sister(s); the floor—I remember now—was concrete, cement, whatever basement floors were if not dirt and mildew, and his bootfalls were loud upon it, sharp, a retort. I couldn't move from the chair. He carried a Bible, and something else. I don't know the something else. And very little else is clear to me, even though I had already been told two things: one by Dusty Ann, and the other by the man himself, clutching his heart. If I didn't sit on his lap, he would DIE! I had grown so used to that little black rabbit, his perfect, oversized hind legs, but that night there appeared instead a cat—not a normal domestic shorthair, but a solid black creature the size of an ocelot with eyes the color of a sky before a truly monstrous storm—that green. He was the most patient animal I ever met, and he led me home even as long as it took, no matter how often I had to stop and press my hand against the trunk of a tree in order to drive the bark into my flesh. The cat never left me, he never ran ahead. He waited. He returned. I can see him now, if I close my eyes. And Loretta was right to choose the man, because after that it was over and I never went back to the basement nor was the matter mentioned again. I began to spend my Sundays (once it became

cold outside) at the library; Colt took me in his truck, and I was allowed to check out twenty books at a time. Twenty. He marveled at
his daughter, he held my hand and I told him everything I had read
and everything that interested me, and I told him nothing else. I
kept Loretta's secret, I kept my own, although that secret was written in my language and it held me captive and I was never free of it.
As Wittgenstein well knew.

✝

"I'd like to get to know your names today," Dr. Scherring said,
straightening the sides of his hair with his flattened palms and trying to organize his valise, "and we really should talk about Adler before we talk about Jung, but also I want to discuss the idea of a
dream journal with you, so where to begin? Hmmmm." He looked
at his watch, he looked at the twelve silent students. "Let's skip
Adler."

Trace breathed a sigh of relief. In her notebook she wrote the
lyrics to the most recent Kate Bush song that had nearly frightened
her to death as she walked across campus. It was wonderful . . . the
river had frozen over? And she was alone, the girl, skating past trees
and cutting out lines in the ice, and Trace thought there was something about spitting, or splitting snow. Then there was the sound
Trace hated as much as any—sonar—and the skater realized there
was something moving under the ice, trying to *It's me* get out *It's me*
something someone help them *It's me.*

"Born in Switzerland in 1875. Think about that—he lived until
1961; he saw almost an entire century and two world wars. He considered a career in archaeology, or theology . . ." Dr. Scherring's
voice lulled her, as it had two days before, and she decided to tune
him out entirely, because she saw the connection in Jung's mind between archaeology and theology—he had been a tightrope walker,

only instead of walking he ran, he leapt, for all she knew there
wasn't even a rope. He took it as a given that there are things un-
dreamt of in our philosophy, things outside causality. He said there
were clocks that stopped at the moment of death, glasses that shattered of their own accord. She wrote 1900–1907, Jung's early years
as a physician. He took from Freud but he left Freud at almost the
same moment, because he believed beyond any doubt in the unconscious and the contents of the unconscious but he declared
them, as Dr. Matthias had said, *autonomous*. Trace underlined the
word; the idea was huge—it was bigger than Freud's work, as fear-
less as he had been. Jung had written, "One could almost say that if
all the world's traditions were cut off at a single blow, the whole
mythology and the whole history of religion would start all over
again with the next generation." He said that as if . . . it was a mas-
sively amplified version of the way people in small groups, left to
fend for themselves, tend not toward anarchy but toward attempts
to govern; they return precisely to what is so familiar it seems inborn. Except these patterns are not social or bureaucratic but the
patterns of reality itself: stories, fantasies, constellations of myths—
and not to explain an inexplicable world but because *they are true*.
And they exist without us, before and after.

We look up—Trace wrote—we have always looked at the sky.
The ancients saw the constellations and imposed upon them animals and heroes; and there were comets, meteor showers, it is just as
Carl Sagan said, we are either all alone in an infinite universe or we
are not, and either option is terrifying.

Dr. Scherring was about to get to the relationship with Freud,
and Trace had an inclination to stand up and say, "Please, let me,"
which she knew to be a problem because she had actually visited a
psychic once—she had been at her wit's end, to tell the truth, and
while she understood that suicidal ideations are the soul's call for
drastic change (so Jung said), she wasn't sure what method to use or

what *change* meant—and the psychic, whose name had been Mathilde, the same as Freud's firstborn, had said, "You have come back to this life to learn patience," and before Trace could stop herself she was snapping her fingers and saying, "Yeah yeah *what else?*" But it had been enough, that touch from Mathilde, because Trace had gone on, she was still.

It was easily summed up: the two men were nineteen years apart in age. Freud was an Austrian Jew, Jung was a Protestant from Switzerland, Freud declared the younger man an eldest son, adopting him as the crown prince and successor to the throne of psychotherapy. But what do you do when you give yourself a son? You write your own obituary is what you do, and the next thing Freud knew he was sailing from Bremen to America with Jung, and Jung was very interested in corpses extracted from some peat bogs in North America, Iron Age corpses perfectly preserved; now if you ask me, Trace thought, I too would be quite enthusiastic to see such things—indeed, I would venture to any museum to view Ice Age Peat Bog Men and I am no fan of museums, but Freud became increasingly anxious about Jung's interest in the corpses and at dinner suddenly fainted, having decided that Jung had death wishes against him, which *ibid.*—father/son.

Trace drew a vector from one generation to the next, wrote: Jung attempted to analyze Freud's dreams and Freud stopped him because, as rumor has it, he was sleeping with his wife's younger sister, and because Freud believed in dream *content,* the manifest would be clear, and he couldn't see that because Jung believed in *archetypes* he would not have seen the affair the same way, but Freud suddenly ended the session, saying he could not reveal more or he would be risking his authority.

A PROBLEM right there, authority. Colt couldn't stand it, he couldn't bear to be told what to do; he couldn't have a boss, he couldn't do another man's work for pay. He couldn't follow another man's design or footprints and it's impossible to enumerate all the problems this created and how deeply it connected me to him. I was just the same with a single, notable exception: Colt had complete authority over me, so I understand Freud—I understand that while he despised religion, he *formed* a religion around himself and called it science. After a certain point I would bend to no one and I wouldn't bow or tip my bloody hat, and yet I had a god and he knew it well enough to hide my soul in the cleft of the rock. Too late, but he tried.

"In 1910, Freud fought for Jung to be appointed the Permanent President for Life, the Grand Dragon Forever After of the Association of Psycho-Analysis." Dr. Scherring waited for a laugh, and one young man in the front gave it to him, but grudgingly, as if to speed things along. The professor opened his notes and read, " 'My dear Jung,' he urged on this occasion, 'promise me never to abandon the sexual theory. That is the most essential thing of all. You see, we must make a dogma of it, an unshakable bulwark.' "

Trace was already writing in her notebook, *A bulwark against what?*

"In some astonishment, Jung asked him, 'A bulwark—against what?' To which Freud replied—"

Against the black tide of mud

" 'Against the black tide of mud'—and here he hesitated a moment, then added—'of occultism.' "

Trace wrote: Make a dogma of it. Dog. Ma. Of it. Jung thought the sexual theory was occult as it got, and that while it might serve a community of analysands for the moment, he couldn't declare it an article of faith for all time, duh, I forget the third thing that happened between Freud and Jung but it had to do with Aknahton, Ikhnahton, something like that, and he replaced his own face as the god's face over his father's because that's what he was supposed to do and Freud fell off his chair in a faint. He fainted a lot, but nobody ever mentions that, maybe it had less to do with the Father/Son dynamic and the death impulses than his relationship to cocaine and also he had cancer in his jaw.

"My favorite line from Jung about his break with Freud," Dr. Scherring said, "is, 'I could not accept Freud's placing authority over truth.' " He waited for . . . Trace thought perhaps for applause, but these were Hoosier farm girls and boys and it took a great deal to get them animated. Basketball was the only thing she could think of that could move them as much as the truth moved Jung.

Today her professor's suit was brown, an unfortunate brown, and she couldn't escape the feeling again that she had even *seen* him at the moment he chose his vocation, standing on the staircase of a sprawling academic house, enamored of some mentor, enthralled by the man's marriage and by his fecund and still beautiful wife, their children all well-behaved and sleeping soundly, and the freezing gin in the beautiful saucer-shaped glass, pearl onions impaled and ghostly. Scherring was less a man than a character in a short story, and it was a story Trace rather liked; she liked how the years had disappointed him, and ruined that perfect family, and revealed gin to be poison to the liver. She thought it poignant that this Cheever manqué would find himself in Jonah, Indiana—the winters that offered no reward, the sullen children, the dead dead deadness of it—and yet he would try to hold on to that principle of Jung's, his love of truth. There were no houses like the house of his mentor, no wives, no babies tucked snugly in their flannels. All gone. The professor was writing on the board: REALIZATIONS ON ARCHETYPES.

Oh, Trace wrote, if we could only get to Hillman, if we could only get to his phrase—that the room in which analysis takes place could be a "cell of revolution."

"Now, many of you have probably taken the test that determines whether you are an Introvert or an Extrovert . . ." Dr. Scherring proceeded to explicate the two descriptors, as well as Thought and Feeling, but he didn't—and here Trace was seconds from holding up her hand—give a moment to *enantiodromia*. Why didn't anyone *anyone* believe it was the most important part of Jung's work? Enantiodromia: *running the other way,* borrowed from Heraclitus and working on all pairs in opposition or conflict. Thought/feeling, masculine/feminine, up/down, good/evil. If the conscious mind was dominated by one element, say, *animus* or the masculine, an abundance of *anima* energy would build up in the unconscious and eventually push forward and out. In this way even evil inclinations could become good.

"The aim of one's life is to know thyself," Dr. Scherring said, and Trace wondered how much that applied to him and if she could find out in . . . three questions? Two?

"We're out of time," he said, glancing at his watch and rubbing chalk dust on his brown trousers. "Please read the pages in *The Portable Jung,* pages listed in your syllabus, before Friday. Thank you, it's been a pleasure."

The world had been beautiful for him at Colgate, 1962. Trace closed her eyes as her classmates departed; she scrolled through an inventory until she came to 1962. The Port Huron Statement? *Silent Spring*? Kennedy had spoken at Yale that year, yes? But what was Scherring the Younger listening to, standing there with his freezing drink and his awe? It was a huge year for Elvis but Trace would put her money on Sinatra, and the sound track to *Days of Wine and Roses.* "Moon River," André Previn, Stan Kenton.

"Miss?"

Trace opened her eyes and there he stood, the Professor of Manifest Despair. "I'm sorry," she said, "I was daydreaming."

He smiled. "You know what Freud says about daydreamers."

Trace grabbed her bag and her coat, returned the smile. "I do, yes. Wish fulfillment? No, that's not it. At puberty I failed to relinquish my obsession with the *family romance*?"

Scherring nodded in admiration, a sinister twitch in one eyelid.

✝

She couldn't sit in his class; she was going to faint like Freud. She was nauseated, filled with dread, absolutely existential, and there was Myka sitting in the next row and a seat ahead of her, looking even more Ophelia-esque than ever, or perhaps today she was Half Sick of Shadows. Trace closed her eyes and breathed deeply; this was going to kill her and she didn't even know what it was. A man who had lost his suitcase. A speeding ticket. Dust on wax-covered wine bottles; dear god, to have just one person to ask, what is this what is this what is this.

He was late again and then was suddenly flying through the door all apologies, and today he was wearing a different white shirt under an oddly colored vintage sport coat; it was moss green but with a faint gold thread running through it, and the cuffs were ragged (again, again with her heart). Blue jeans, hiking boots. His hair was standing on end but there was yet to be a hat in sight, and his dark eyes behind his glasses. Trace swallowed, put her hand on her chest.

"Whew. Another day." And he just stood there, Dr. J. Matthias, smiling at them, taking their measure. "Oh, before I forget." He reached into his satchel and took something out, Trace couldn't see exactly what it was, and he was walking toward her. She didn't take her eyes off him, didn't blink, didn't breathe. It was her favorite pen, and he had tied a small red ribbon around it, and he placed it on her desk with a grave gentleness, did so in front of all the other students. He smiled at her, he turned and walked back to his desk, and he too lectured on Jung, and Trace didn't write down a word, she only listened to him because he was so *right* the air in the room had turned to crystal. He drew on the board the illustration for how living signs become symbols: The cross. The river on which that sign flowed from a historical crucifixion to a symbol pointing to the unknown, Jung's "inconceivable God," to whom Jesus had gone when he left his body behind on the beams; or more beautifully, what was already present in the beams; or even *more* sublime, what is present in all bodies at the crossing point of the four directions. To think, to see, to transcend; this man understood the Good, and Trace watched him as she had watched her father, and she did not confuse the cross ties of the beams with the crossroads at which Hekate was waiting for her sacrifice. Trace was gripped and yet felt new liberty, even though Jung had said and she well knew, "Freedom is one of the more difficult things."

☩

She took the key from Wanda and ran back to the women's shower room. It was absurd to shower every day in the winter in Indiana, but she was doing it, and she was considering buying an actual blow-dryer with a cord, she was considering all sorts of things, and she was clean and dressed—her hair dripping wet and causing her to shake—in what seemed minutes. Trace all but ran to her truck, and as she unlocked the driver's-side door she heard them, the murmur of the women and the truck drivers, the shadows moving between the monstrous vehicles—flitting, disappearing. Fine, she thought, take this, Hekate, Astarte, Poor Persephone. Take this as an offering. It is left for you every night, it is Hell on earth, enantiodromia—take it, please, and *pass me by.*

. . .

The back door wasn't locked. Trace sat down on the floral glider and on a whim lit what remained of the candles. She took out the Northrop Frye essay and read it, making notes as she proceeded, using the pen with the ribbon still tied to it, she did this in the mostly dark. An hour passed, and the door was opening and he was stepping in, smiling at her.

"Hello," he said with a sigh, sitting down beside her. He dropped his bag, which was overflowing with books and papers and campus mail envelopes, on the floor beside the table.

"Did your suitcase ever arrive?"

"It did! It came to my office today. And I opened it and it puzzled me, I looked at the things in it and couldn't imagine why I thought I needed them, it was as if they didn't even belong to me. Why did I need that suitcase so?"

Trace shrugged. "Because it *is* yours?"

"Like something handed to you in a dream, you mean."

"Yes. And you can say, 'I don't want this, I don't recognize it,' but it's yours after all, and you must accept it."

Dr. J. Matthias turned his body around until he was facing her. Neither spoke, but she could hear his breathing, a slight shudder in his lungs, and her own was the same except her heart hurt, her chest hurt, she was probably going to have some sort of stroke or seizure and that would be that.

"*You're very odd,* aren't you?" he asked, finally, and for some reason the question, the way he phrased it, hauled up in Trace a grief that left her speechless. (The third daughter is not gold, not silver, but lead. And she is dumb. A dumb show, a puppet. But she is chosen, and she becomes both Beauty and Death. Trace was leaden.)

"I mean, look at the color of your eyes. Are those some sort of . . . contact lenses? Is it a trick? Because violets are one of my earli-

est memories, gathering them for my mother; their stems are almost liquid, they're so delicate. But your eyes are that color, they are
the color of my own memory, and that strikes me as . . . well, very
odd."

"I'm"—Trace swallowed, the *globus hystericus*—"I'm a changeling."

He nodded. "That would explain it. Now come inside with me.
I understand that youth enjoys testing itself, but I am old and I want
to go into my kitchen."

Undoubtedly against the wishes—or without the knowledge—of
the Westside Historical District Board of Directors, Dr. Matthias's
kitchen was a mixture of the modern (an impressive gas stove, a
large chrome refrigerator hidden behind old barn doors) and that
of a French peasant. He even had a freestanding cabinet painted a
lost shade of pale green, which contained its own flour pantry, with
a sifter in the glass door. The harvest table in the center of the room
was long, scarred; none of the chairs around it matched. In the center was a porcelain pot containing a flower Trace had never seen before. "What is this?"

"*Tibouchina urvilleana*—the Princess Flower. Enjoy it while you
may, because as soon as I take it outside in the spring it will die for
reasons that cannot be explained to me."

"Do you garden?"

Dr. Matthias was busily pouring milk into a saucepan on the
stove, taking out two cups, a box of Dutch chocolate. "I plant, and
then I kill. That is my dark gift. Sit, give me your coat and scarf, and
sit."

Trace did as she was told. She spread her hands out on the tabletop, as she had at Candy's, and the wood was not of the same
species. Trace could see words written in the surface, all sorts of different handwriting, as if dozens of children had done their home-

work here, or an entire monastery had transcribed sacred texts with the sharp nibs of fountain pens.

"Are you reading my table?"

"Where did it come from?"

Dr. Matthias stirred the milk, turned the fire down so low it flickered. "My father made it. Look to your right, where the middle chair is. You'll see: Jacob Was Hear. Someday I Shall Be Imporent."

Trace laughed, ran her finger over the carving. It wasn't deep, but it was still legible. He had been a little boy, and he knew something about himself. "All day I've been thinking of Freud's essay 'The Theme of the Three Caskets.' "

"I love that piece. I rarely teach it; I just can't get my students to engage with it. He jumps too fast, in too small a space. What part of it are you thinking of?"

There were three daughters, and it was always the youngest who was chosen. She couldn't speak, she was lead. "I was thinking of how Fate, in Homer, Moira, was joined by two sister goddesses."

"Related to the Graces."

"Yes, and to the goddesses of the seasons, the Horae, and the Horae were originally—well, you know all this."

"No, go on. I haven't taught it in years."

"They were water goddesses—clouds in the sky, rain—well, water in the sky is the point, but in the Mediterranean, where the sun is prime, they became vegetation goddesses, and even through such change as . . . building a new calendar, they retained their names, which all signified time."

Dr. Matthias stopped stirring. "Their names all signified time." He reached for a sugar bowl, stirred some into the milk and the chocolate.

"Yes, they translate as What Was, What Is, What Shall Be."

He poured their hot chocolate without speaking, served Trace hers first. He brought her a linen napkin and a teaspoon. He opened the barn doors and took a plate of strawberries and a soft French cheese from the refrigerator and set them in front of her. He sat down across from her, his hands cupped around the mug, leaning on his elbows, leaning toward her.

Trace couldn't pick up the mug or even the spoon. She saw the strawberries but could not have named them. Her life was hanging in the balance and everything seemed too precarious to support whatever came next; even the table, so firmly constructed, feathered beneath her arms.

"I'm forty-seven years old," he said, and Trace realized he was a lecturer, he *professed,* and professing required a certain kind of voice, the timbre of which soothed beasts and quieted the imbalanced. "I have age spots on my hands." He spread them out before her and Trace first ran her finger over the backs, the fingers, then she lifted his right hand and held it to her face. "I will never have children. I'll never leave this university; I missed the chance. My wife of twenty years left me, and my cholesterol is high. I love to sing but I have no ear, and I listen to NPR at the top of the hour, every hour, regardless of whether the headlines change."

Trace held his hand, which was warm and wide. His fingers were lovely, and there were, indeed, spots on the back from age and from sun. Tears streamed down her face and rolled onto his fingers, but she didn't feel as if she would die; she had just sprung a leak, she was old, too, after all. Her mechanisms had been faulty to begin with and were, by now, ruined.

"You are twenty-one and are first in your graduating class. But no one knows a thing about you, and frankly I'm afraid of this. I've never, ever so much as looked sideways at a student, particularly one so—well, you *are* very odd, aren't you, and maybe antisocial. Perhaps there is something very wrong with you, perhaps you have some horror-movie history and I am stepping off the edge of a plank into shark-filled waters."

"Perhaps you are playing loose with metaphors."

He raised his left hand, the free one, in a gesture of submission. "That's my point exactly. You aren't supposed to say such a thing at this juncture—I am asking you for comfort and a degree of confidence. You are supposed to *reassure* me, not hand me the gun and then debate what Chekhov would say about it."

Trace let go of his hand and they both drank their hot chocolate, and in silence they each ate some strawberries and tiny spoonfuls of the melting French cheese, which was undoubtedly terrible for his cholesterol. Every bite was an ache. He dated Dr. Cohen, who was age-appropriate and wore those shoes and that hair. Her T-shirt declared her flawlessly correct political optimism, and she had money and a birthright and a history. The strawberries were ripe; they were bright red and sweet. How he came to have them, to have them there for her, waiting, was a miracle, and she would remember it always.

He stood and took her hand. They walked through the large formal dining room and into a parlor, where Dr. Matthias turned on a gas log in what had once been a coal-burning fireplace. He said, Lie down with me, and she saw that there was an animal skin on the floor, and she nearly turned at that point, because the violation of that particular taboo was cause for wailing and terrible moaning, according to Freud. A bearskin, a grizzly from the size, and old, moth-eaten. Its face didn't seem remotely real—the glass eyes, the snarling teeth, the lips painted a ghastly red. But it was real, it was fur, it was a bear, and Trace lowered herself down in prayer and a plea for forgiveness, a bear, a *fucking bear,* there was that Galway Kinnell poem that he had spoken at a reading at their visiting writers' series, Galway with the largest hands she'd ever seen on a man, and his head, too—he was a tempest, a genius, and he spoke the poem without ever looking at his book—and every woman wanted to sleep with him but only Trace was able to track him, she found him, Dr. Matthias was lowering her down onto the hide, she was facing the fire and he was lying behind her, his arms wrapped around her with such warmth as she had not known in many years. Galway tracks the bear by his blood and his scat, one of them is dying and the other is freezing. "Please," Dr. Matthias said, his body pressed against her back, "please do three things for me. No, four. Maybe five or six. Turn and face me."

Trace turned and faced him; his glasses were off and his eyes were very nice although they weren't the damning, feminine eyes of Colt Pennington.

"Take off some of these sweaters."

She sat up and began removing them, the cardigan, the boat-neck, the black cashmere, the silk first layer. Her skin was translucent in the firelight; she feared he could see through her.

"Lie back down." His hands on her skin were a shock; his fingertips were slightly rough, and she knew she must feel more like silk than silk itself, an otherwordly tactile blessing to a man of forty-seven. That's what Galway had said to her, he had told her as she was leaving, "I know who you are; you will be the biggest surprise of some man's life."

She was surprising him all right, surprising this man she couldn't call Jacob, although someday he would be Imporent. He was already Imporent, he had lowered her onto the carcass of an animal, which revealed her brute ingratitude, and yet she lay there, warm in the body of the bear.

"Tell me two things. Who are your parents and where do you come from?"

Her eyes were violet, her eyelashes black as Colt's had been; she gazed at him, from his forehead to his lips and back again, because hers were eyes that could make him forget such a question, they could silence him. But she answered anyway. "I am an orphan in all the wide world; I have no kin, and I came from nowhere." She spoke the words quietly, as one would stopped at the top of the Ferris wheel.

Jacob kissed her forehead, her eyelids, the tip of her nose, the tear-dampened cheek. "You are a liar."

"Liars and orphans are cousins, Dr. Matthias, and their names still signify time."

He lowered one hand to the dip of her waist, and made his final request. "How did you come to be called by your name? If you are an orphan in all the wide world, who christened you Ianthe Covington?"

She smiled at him, just as his lips grazed hers. She smiled in admiration, because that was the question that really mattered, and he had proven himself to her. This was a man who was a physician of the secrets buried in texts; he peeled away old layers and fabrications; he tore down the moldy velvet theater curtain and exposed the bare stage and then told those dull and witless children in his classes that the stage was true, it made life worth living, it was the floor of civilization. But Ianthe was not a text, nor would he ever read her as such, if she had her way. Ianthe Covington was a child born in March of 1965 who died a month later, and Trace and her father had often stood silent over her tombstone, which was flat on the ground and upon which a stone lamb lay sleeping. And they pondered how that might have been Tracey Sue herself, her father's child bride although he didn't know it, because he was an innocent man. It had taken work; it had taken the exchange of money and talismans in the basements of clubs blackened with cigarette smoke; she had procured drugs for the children of petty bureaucrats; and once she had even slept all night in the County Records Office, in order to steal their forms and their seals, but in the end she had gotten it all, following Loretta's lead. A birth certificate, a driver's license, a high school transcript, a shocking SAT score, and admittance to the only school she could imagine attending because of

Candy and her parents, and Dusty and the girls. Two worlds, two paths, and Trace had chosen the one entirely untraveled.

"It was the name I was left with. It has no history," she said, which was nearly true.

"You are a liar," Jacob said, and he hacked a ravine in her thigh, he ate and drank, he tore down the length of her, and they both slept briefly. When she rose and began gathering her clothes he told her he wanted her, he wanted *only* her, but there were two conditions: no children, ever, and no dogs. He would never have a dog in his house, was he being as clear as possible, and she nodded. Did she truly understand him, no children ever? And no dogs, ever. She nodded again, and went home.

CHAPTER SEVEN

Nekyia

Journal

Colt coughed. It seemed he always coughed—not anything alarming, just a steady bit of thunder every morning. Most of the time I didn't notice. He had me, his truck, his black dog, Weeds, his bike, his Marlboro red pack. We had a scare one afternoon, home alone on a Sunday. I was walking past the bathroom door and I saw him leaning against the wall, struggling to breathe, and there was blood on his hand and on his blue work shirt and I did the unforgivable. I would do it again, which I assume is at the root of why I should never be forgiven. I lay my hand on his back and I experienced a deep inward swell of gratitude that he was too sick to stop me, because I could feel the muscles in his shoulders, I could feel *him,* his frantic living spirit. He was trapped there, coughing, and that gave me time to study the curve of his neck, his knotty biceps straining inside his shirt. I didn't say a word; I didn't ask him what I should do. I didn't panic, because we were alone and I had him, I had him to myself. I'm not sure how long we would have stayed that way— would I have let him die?—but he broke the spell; he said he needed to go to the doctor, the words rang in my ear, and as he spoke, tiny, pale blue moths flew from his mouth and every time he coughed there were more, and they never landed on anything because they were too light. Too pale. *Do you hear me?* he asked, which was an odd thing; was I ever listening to anything else?

I ran for his truck keys; I was fourteen but I'd been driving for years. When I got back to the bathroom I wiped his mouth with a cold washcloth and I whispered in his ear. I can't recall exactly what I said. I might have told him he couldn't be ill because he was my genesis; he inspirited me, I would return to nothingness without him. I might have reminded him of the week before, when we had stood at the edge of a neighbor's cornfield and watched a flock of starlings rise up in a cloud—how they all flew first to the east and then turned in a great spiral, a black pirouette. Perhaps I even pleaded with him, told the truth (or part of it): without him something terrible would happen to me, it would happen at the hands of my mother. I didn't know it already had. For fourteen years (I *might* have said) Colt had been my sentry and even that hadn't stopped her. At night I lay awake, listening to her pacing outside my gate, Colt's gate, like a starving mountain lion, I never lost sight of her.

He was admitted to the hospital and it wasn't the worst. The doctors first suspected idiopathic pulmonary fibrosis, or emphysema, or even tuberculosis, which still reared up periodically in our county. It was none of those; he had chronic bronchitis and acid reflux disease, and the blood was from his esophagus. He lay in the white bed and his skin against the sheets, in the sterile room, was so novel I could only stare at him; I sat next to the bed stroking his forearm—I couldn't take my eyes off the place the IV shunt entered the back of his hand. They had pierced him. Right there, right where I was looking, was an entrance into his veins. A nurse came in and gave him morphine to stop the coughing and let his lungs and throat rest, and I saw it hit him, I saw it reach his eyes. He gestured for me to come to him, and I climbed into his bed, I held him like a lover, I wanted to unbutton my own skin. Lying there he said, Billy. He said, Your brother. In my mind I was writing the story of a man who has had a great fright, and in his delirium decides to make arrangements. Not financial; not insurance or trusts; but something as simple as *I have employed Billy to stand in my place against your mother, and against the uncles in Kentucky you don't know you have, and against any animal that might turn on you. I have asked him to spare you the winters, and the invisible.* There were things I would have said to him, too: I would have said the Underworld isn't really under anything. It is the needle in the hand of an adored man, and it's in the morgue where other men and women are lying chilled. It is in the purple curtain of the crematorium, behind which caskets slide, and in the cheap urns people keep on mantelpieces. Colt blinked, his eyes were unsteady. He said, *If anything happens to me, take care of my dog. Don't let her have my truck.* That's the story he was writing, but I held him anyway, and swore the oath he asked of me, and I didn't let anyone know where we were, not for an entire day and night, and it was the happiest I had been in years and years. I fancied myself a poet at the time and when we were back home I wrote him a sonnet entitled "Evensong"—that's what I called it originally. I eventually changed the title to "Vesperal"; I've forgotten most of it now, except for the final couplet.

> *I accept this shadowy grace and nod.*
> *I am your bride; I have forsaken God.*

Idiopathic idiopathic that's how I feel, not a diagnosis but how I *feel,* that I am of unknown cause, sitting in this bed and the wind is battering the farmhouse but none comes through the shrink-wrapped windows of my bedroom, the bedroom I share with the dog who is the dog of my most sacred vow. I live with him in trust. I live with him because he is the link to the other side, I'm not stupid I know he is my totem, it might have been any of them, it might have been the pig or the snake or the horse (or the black birds or) but it isn't, it is Weeds, his gentle face and feathered tail, his bright bright gaze, he was a dowry, a bridal gift from the father of the bride to the groom, who was also the father of the bride. Freud said, *We are ignorant of the horror of incest and cannot even tell in what direction to look for it. None of the solutions of the enigma that have been proposed seem satisfactory.* Those were his words. He looked at what he called primitives and he saw that the incest taboo among members of the same totem clan was far stronger than among civilized people, and why would that be when the primitive people had no notion of biology or the dangers of inbreeding? Jung had a different take but let's leave him out of it for now, just this once, and let Freud stand as the authority and say the incest taboo is arbitrary, as love is arbitrary and the movements of atoms and the pandemonium of the universe, and speaking of the universe or glacial time or any naked singularity, how much can it matter anyway, how can it matter at all? I have read too many fairy tales—the real ones—where the little man comes to my cell and spins straw into gold for me, not once or twice but the holy thrice and in return I owe him my firstborn child. I've read Bluebeard, seen the six prior wives hung limp on wooden pegs. Dear god, the mistakes that are made in the classics—Ariadne, Medea, Iphigenia, Agamemnon—and in Grimms', and the *reckonings,* they are worse than anything we read about in the news. I'm not talking about the self-dug trenches or the Storm Troopers or the German shepherds who were sometimes kept in basket muzzles and sometimes not—one never knew what to expect—I'm talking about the *way down* story of consequences, personal decisions, the Fleece stolen from your own country, your abandonment at Naxos. Jacob says he has chosen me and the only price is this, it must seem like nothing to him, and to me it is the pearl of great price. No children, he said, and I could see the fear on his face, because he expects me to fight that—not now, maybe not for a few years—but someday and like a viper. Never, never, I wanted to say, I cannot, I would not. But the addendum. That line of fine print *And no dogs, ever, do you understand what I'm saying?* If I had told him the truth, if I had said, "If you make me leave my dog, my soul will wither and die, you will destroy me as you will kill the Princess Flower come spring," that would have been the end and I would not be the youngest child, the third of the women who became three daughters. He didn't choose Myka, who was gold. He didn't choose Dr. Cohen, who was silver. He chose lead; he chose my silence, my opacity. Weeds doesn't know it and I'll never tell him, it would be too much for his sweet shoulders to bear: he is my tribe and my temple, he eats my sins, he runs across the graves of all I loved, and he leads the way down, he will lead me down on that day. And Jacob didn't even say why. He didn't say he's allergic, or that he can't bear the smell or the dirt or the exuberance or the pests. He didn't admit to being afraid of dogs, he didn't say he was bitten as a child and has never recovered. The matter must be so trivial he didn't feel the need to justify it. *I'm not a dog person,* people say, I hear it all the time. Oh? Oh, you're not a dog person? Are you a zombie, an automaton, a marionette? Is it about your *carpet*? Your *beige* carpet? Or is it the nuisance, the caretaking, the ritual? Is it about how you'd prefer not to be bothered, or how you find a certain level of sterility necessary in order to support your loveless marriage and your absurd career and your rapid decline and death? The death you will go to without the irritant of dog hair on that black suit, split up the back by the undertaker? Is it because you don't understand that dogs are Other, they are messengers and wild animals—they could survive just fine without us—and they are *carnivores*, they are *dangerous*, they could kill us (and do), and yet virtually all of them choose to live in harmony with us for reasons we will never understand? There is no species of mammal on earth with greater diversity: a papillon is a dog, and a Neapolitan mastiff is a dog, and a greyhound is a dog, and a mutt scavenging at the edge of a garbage heap in Calcutta is a dog, and so is a Pharaoh hound, an Irish wolfhound, Weeds. A medium-sized black dog who looks like a retriever and is all that binds me to this earth. Is a dog.

I will leave him here, in this house. I will find a way to install a dog door so he can come and go, and while Jacob and I are keeping the relationship a secret I will be with Weeds as much as I can, and when I move in with Jacob I will come out here every day and he will never know the difference, and I will do the best I can. Tomorrow I must drop his class. I won't graduate. He says I should stay in the other two because if I am missing a single credit I can walk with my classmates through commencement and take the last class in the summer, he has told me what to do.

The silence in Dr. Cohen's class was rich, and the other students, particularly the groupies, glanced at one another repeatedly but didn't speak. Dr. Cohen came in on time, organized, well-kept. She wore a long brown skirt with her brown lace-up shoes, a different T-shirt (Emma Goldman: *Understand One Another*) under a quilted jacket made of dozens of brightly colored squares. She hung her bag on a chair, took out her class list and her notes without a sound; under her glasses her eyes were red and swollen, and her cheeks were flushed, veiny. He had told her *already,* he had told her at lunch, just as he said he would. The what, not the who.

"Good afternoon, everyone." Dr. Cohen paused, gave a tentative smile. "As you can see, I'm not having the best day. I've suffered a loss—a romantic one, which is nothing compared to . . . but it hurts nonetheless, and I would be dishonest if I didn't admit it. Odd, isn't it"—she looked down at her shirt—"that I would wear this today. It was Emma Goldman who said, 'The higher mental development of woman, the less possible it is for her to meet a congenial male who will see in her, not only sex, but also the human being, the friend, the comrade and strong individuality, who cannot and ought not lose a single trait of her character.' Too much to print on a T-shirt." She laughed, but a tear ran down her face. "I memorized those lines from a poster I had in my office when I was a doctor, because it seemed truer then than it does now. Or did, until today. Now"—she sat on the desk, put her fists into the pockets of her jacket—"I would like to *not* talk about myself anymore. I'd like to talk about you, and the reading we did for today. It will be a relief to me to focus on something other than . . . him." Dr. Cohen looked around the room, at the chairs arranged in a circle, nodded at the women with whom she was most familiar, and said, "Let's start with you, shall we? I don't believe we've met."

Ianthe swallowed—so soon, all of it?—as if her sympathy for her professor had left her a bit stupefied, and said, "No, we haven't met. I'm Ianthe Covington, and . . . this is the last course I need to complete a minor in Women's Studies. My focus has been mainly on women in antiquity, and the history of women in psychology, so this is new, umm, a new format for me."

Her professor nodded, but Ianthe could see that she was fighting off the powerful distraction of heartsickness and surprise, humiliation even. A hard thing to watch, particularly if one were the cause. "And would you say—Ianthe? an unusual name—that you are a Wounded Woman?"

A wounded woman. "I . . ." Oh to be sucked into a magical vortex, a transporter, anything. "Maybe I'm not clear on the definition. I don't know the answer."

"Let's talk about this book, then." Dr. Cohen held up the previous night's reading, which Ianthe had found in the Self-Help section of the bookshop. "The author presupposes—and I agree with her entirely, by the way—that the father/daughter relationship leaves a scar. It's not the same for all of us"—she stood and walked to the blackboard—"is it? Some of us are sacrificed. Some become dolls, the 'little squirrel' in Ibsen's *A Doll's House,* what Jung calls the *puella aeterna,* the Eternal Girl. And there is the Amazon, which is as far as we were to read today. The Amazon is . . . let me hear from you."

Kaitlyn said, "An overachiever, a star."

Dr. Cohen wrote *star* on the board. "What else?"

Jessica said, "Overly dutiful, a martyr."

Dr. Cohen wrote those words on the board. "And of course she can be a warrior, someone so strong she's willing to cut off her right breast in order to be a more accurate archer." She turned back to the class. "Ianthe, did you see yourself in any of those descriptions? No, wait. First, if I may, how did you come to have that name?"

"My parents read it on a tombstone in an old cemetery." She did *not* say, Later I went there alone and three dogs ran toward me from behind an enormous tree, and terrified me. "It's not so interesting a story, I'm afraid."

"Still," Dr. Cohen said, brushing the chalk off her hands, "a lovely name. Now, what about the reading we did?"

"Honestly?" Ianthe glanced down at her notes, feigning humility. "I feel too young to know yet. The case histories the author gives are all of women who have reached crises, and are trying to resolve them. I don't think I'll know how . . . damaged I am until my life begins to . . . crack?"

"A thoughtful answer." Dr. Cohen nodded. "What about your father? What if we, this gathering, were a group of fortune-tellers, and our task was to determine the crisis you might reach, or the category that applies to you, by your relationship with him?"

Torturous, this was torturous to Ianthe, the entire miasma of political correctness, therapeutic language, attempts to right the wrongs of *history.* The university was overwhelmed by the zeitgeist, which had only recently reached the Midwest. People like Dr. Cohen actually wanted to mend the *culture,* the dead of a hundred, a thousand years before? What cause would they take up next? *Bruising? Humidity?*

Ianthe licked her lips, leveled her violet eyes at Dr. Cohen. *Press me,* she thought, you are an amateur, and besides I have already won. "I'm the youngest of three sisters," she began, "the quiet one." She remembered Lear saying, in act I, scene I, *Thy paleness moves me more than eloquence.* But she didn't say it aloud.

✝

She left the building quickly, raced down the stairs and through the glass doors of the old Humanities building. The cold wind was fine, it was glorious, if she could get to the English building in the next five minutes she could see him, she could see him pass even, and then she would know he was real.

All the students changing classes moved out of her way, they clung to an invisible wall at the edges of the sidewalk, most without realizing it or even seeing her. She was *that* girl, Ianthe Diana Covington, who had ridden the black mare to the end. Or she was the girl who had dropped her line through the ice and for the first time felt a pull upon it almost too strong to counter, and she was on her

way to see her lover, the Senior Professor, the man in line for the
chairmanship of the department, one whose name had been mentioned in connection with a search for a new dean of Arts and Humanities. She could already give him four or five epithets, as the
Greeks had done with the Olympians: *High-Thundering Zeus.*
Bright-Eyed Athena. Crooked-Footed Hephaestus. Silver-Footed, Decep-
tive Aphrodite. Ianthe could call him Jacob of the Lost Suitcase.
Wild-Haired Professor. Jacob the Francophile. He of the Yellow
Speeding Ticket. Bearer of Ripe Strawberries.

She flew through the open doors of the English building as
someone else departed, passing the classrooms on the first floor
where she had taken the American and British surveys; where she
had first read *Beowulf* and *Gilgamesh* and Emerson and Dickinson
and Gerard Manley Hopkins and *Faust.* She opened the door to the
staircase and ran up to the landing, turned to run the next ten stairs
to the second floor, and Jacob was just running down, his face when
he saw her was so luminous, he smiled at her so hugely and with
such joy she laughed out loud and so did he; he grabbed her, lifted
her off the floor, said, "I've never been so happy to see another person in my life," and she buried her face in his neck, breathed him in,
a feeling so intense and complete it was nearly pain, she said, "I'm
gladder. I'm even gladder, if you can imagine it."

✢

"And what is this?"

"It's angel hair pasta in a mushroom, anchovy, and virgin olive
oil sauce. That is bok choy on the side, and this bread I got at that little bakery on the south side of town no one seems to know about."

"I know that bakery! Thelma's Baked Goods!" Ianthe raised her
arms in the air as if witnessing a miracle.

"That's the one—a very fine place."

"And what is this wine?"

"Well, when I was a young Ph.D. and training myself to be sufficiently serious, I drank what I was told to drink, which was a fine claret. The claret was general; Europeans preferred it as a table wine as well. And then the claret seemed to disappear, which was a source of consternation to me until I realized it had simply been renamed. Except it isn't the same, the name has altered it and stolen my connection to it, even the word 'claret' sounds *old* and *fusty* and *established*. That is how the wine should taste, as well." Jacob took a bite of his pasta, wiped his lips with his napkin. "Okay, tell me. Let me swallow and then tell me."

Ianthe sipped her wine, sat back in her chair. She cleared her throat and affected the posture of a young actress with a burgeoning reputation, entering stage left. "He said, 'I earned my master's and Ph.D. from a little place called Yale, maybe you've heard of it?' "

Jacob of the Great Laugh paused a moment, as if allowing the scene to enter him fully, and then his head fell back against the wooden kitchen chair and he roared. He shook with laughter, he had to wipe his eyes, and Ianthe too came completely undone; she had to rest her head on the table to ease the ache in her side.

"He also said, 'I played football at Colgate—not an Ivy, but the Patriot League—I have pictures to prove it.' "

"Stop! Oh dear god, I can't." Jacob took off his glasses and dropped them on the table. "I can't take any more."

Ianthe wiped her own eyes, took a deep, shuddering breath.

"Ah." Jacob blinked, shook his head. "Tell the part about Yale again."

· · ·

The upstairs, which she had not seen before, was expansive but cold. Only the woodwork, the doors, glowed warmly. There were four bedrooms, each painted a peculiar, jarring color.

"Are these colors"—Ianthe hesitated—"historical?"

Jacob sighed. "Allegedly. Rita chose them, but how can they be right? This—what is this color?" He pointed toward one of the bedrooms, which was empty except for a stationary bicycle, an old metal typing table, and a clothes basket filled with what appeared to be gloves.

"I'm no expert, but I think that's called neon pink."

"Yes? That's what I call it, too, I call it flamingo pink, and I simply can't believe that it's appropriate to the Queen Anne era."

"I agree."

"Sadly, that will be your office. So you'll need to adjust."

Jacob's study was a light-sucking, unnatural green. It was also disastrously disorganized: all the bookshelves were filled and then filled again with books lying on their sides, and there were towers of books about to topple. There was a stack of what appeared to be twenty dissertation manuscripts, file folders everywhere, and scraps—little pieces of paper bearing a single word or a phrase— that seemed to be floating. Jacob picked one up and read it. "Mask," he said. "Hmmm. These are ideas for my next book. I wonder what I meant by that."

"What's the book about?"

"Masks," he said, leading her down the hallway. "This was Rita's room." He opened a door onto a decor fit for Myka Holloway and her delicate, wasting sickness. This room alone was painted a normal color, a flat blue, and there was Rita's antique brass bed, a handmade quilt in pastel shades. There were her pillows and white lace curtains at the two tall windows, a Victorian dressing table on which a tray of toiletries and brushes remained. A pink robe hung on a hook by the door, and under it Ianthe could see the edge of a matching gown. She turned and looked at Jacob, who shrugged, a flicker of pain on his face. "I guess she didn't want any of it. Nothing." They backed out of the room and he closed the door with a soft click.

"Now this," he said, opening the final bedroom door, "is what I was given."

"Jacob," Ianthe said, turning around in a circle, "this room is orange."

"It is orange."

"And your bed has no frame. And where did you get that table next to the bed—out of the trash? Where is your dresser?"

"It's built into the closet, thank heavens." He stood with his hands on his hips, surveying the scarcity. "It's also always freezing in here."

Ianthe turned and looked at him. She took a step toward him and he took a step toward her. "You've slept in a cold bed. You had separate bedrooms. You don't understand the colors of your own home. What are you saying? What happened here?"

Jacob pulled her to him, wrapped his arms around her as she slipped her own under his sweater, his dress shirt, his white T-shirt. "I don't know. I don't know what happened."

Ianthe rubbed her lips over his ear, whispered, "Until I can set this all in order, go get the quilt off her bed. Finders keepers."

Hours later Jacob said, "I'm warm." He was wrapped around Ianthe from behind, so that every part of her back was touching every part of his front.

"I'm warm. You have bony ankles."

"How did you do this? Was it just the quilt?"

Ianthe rubbed his arm, the one resting in the dip of her waist. "I also turned up the thermostat."

Jacob buried his face in her hair. "You," he said, "are the biggest surprise of my life."

"I've got to go home. I've . . . I have responsibilities . . ."

"One more hour," Jacob said, almost asleep.

She drifted; fell into the horizon dream, which was sometimes a comfort and sometimes disconcerting. That's all the dream was: an endless horizon, everywhere she turned, no ground beneath her feet, no sky above. A line where two concepts either met or parted ways. No sun rose, no moon. The Horae were the seasons and their names signified time (*heure*): Lachesis, experience, or the accident in destiny. Clotho, the inborn disposition. And Atropos, the ineluctable, Death Herself. Ianthe dreamed warm, the horizon did not alter, she thought of Weeds, and of the dark freezing house down the lane no one could see. Colt never entered her mind.

CHAPTER EIGHT

Kerberos

How pale the paint of the birdhouse. How ghastly pale
The sound of the cry coming closer . . . If I forsake
The dogs? . . . If I forsake the mummers? . . . If I step
BRIGIT PEGEEN KELLY, from "Sheet Music"

Journal

Every morning Jacob makes me coffee in a French press pot he
brought back from a conference in Seattle; the coffee is so strong
and dark it makes my toes curl and yet I have come to love it and it's
the first thing I think about when I wake up in the morning. I turn,
and if he is beside me he is the first thing, but if he's gone I know
he's making the coffee, and he'll bring it to the bedroom with orange juice and fresh bread and cheeses, he does this every day. Like

the original Ianthe Covington I was born in March and my birthday is tomorrow and when Jacob asked this morning to describe the best birthday I ever had I tell him that my Grandmother Covington once made me a cake that was half lion, half lamb. Not one of Hicks's *Peaceable Kingdom* paintings; more like the weather. The weather of my ephemera: sun, moon, ascendant. I tell him the icing on the lion's half was close to the color our bedroom had been in January, and the lamb had been frosted with white buttercream in little swirls and arcs. Was I close to my grandmother? he asks. And I tell him I was, I adored her; I say she was from very old Philadelphia money, much of it made on Civil War bonds, and that she had memories of speakeasies. To her dying day she believed that the way one cast a vote in a presidential election was a secret as sacred as any told to a priest. *Democracy,* I tell him. I imitate her accent, just a few words, and I describe the scent of her house, her favorite style of shoes. He asks if I ever dream of her and I tell him most assuredly: I dreamed of her only a few nights ago. I was lost in Center City, far from her neighborhood, and I tried to call her on a pay phone but there were no numbers, no buttons. I set out walking and all the row houses looked alike. I saw a man named Tony and I knew him to be a tailor in the garment district, and as I passed him a man was hit by a car right beside me. The man flew into the air and vanished. Eventually I found my grandmother in a park, sitting on a bench someone had crocheted out of cobwebs, and she told me to go home, she said, "This isn't even your zip code."

"What was her first name?" Jacob asks, spreading butter on his bread.

"Cecile."

"You're lying. Every word. You are an orphan and alone in all the world."

"That is correct."

"You have no grandmother Cecile Covington, and you had no such cake."

"Also correct."

He moves the tray aside and slides closer to me. He presses his face against mine, and he loves me so dearly I can hear his heart pounding just because we're sitting so close, on this ordinary day.

A week ago he gave me a brand-new black Volvo sedan as an early birthday gift; he said we'd sell the truck. I told him I wanted to donate it to the homeless shelter, and I drove it out to the farmhouse to leave it there. But something happened, it's a peculiar thing: I couldn't find the lane. I drove past it, saw it in my rearview mirror, turned around, drove past it, saw it in my rearview mirror. I began to panic, because in the two months I've been gone—even though I come out every day—I sometimes can't find him, I can't find Weeds. He is nowhere in the house. I walk through it and it's terrible to me now, I can't believe the stripped shell of the piano, the bloodred spray paint, *La Dolce Vita!* The layers are nauseating, I can't imagine how I endured them. When I arrived at Jacob's I had two boxes of notebooks, my two hundred file folders, most of my music, a trunk filled with clothing, and three cartons of books. I left everything else behind. He had even bought me a new toothbrush, expensive shampoo, I walked away from the house like everyone before me. But twice, three times? I have gone up to the bedroom and there is the mattress and the blankets Weeds and I slept under, and there's no sign of him, his food hasn't been touched, there is an absence of him that takes my breath away. I go outside, I stand beside the discarded grills, the bathroom cabinet missing its bathroom, and I call him. I walk around the outbuildings, I call him. I go into the woods, the path he and I have always followed, I walk down the lane, down the dirt road, and finally he appears, he runs to me with a frightening joy, and

I spend as much time with him as I can. His fur is matted in places; there are burrs in his feathery tale. I've noticed he's grown some white on his chin, and a patch of white on his chest. I park the truck behind the house—I'll hitchhike back to town—and then I don't know how to keep him from following me, I have to keep turning, shouting, Go home! He stares at me as if in mourning; I've become incomprehensible. I cry as I shout at him, and between the crying and the yelling and the stomping of my feet he eventually turns and heads down the lane toward the house and I watch him go, I see he is limping. He limps just slightly.

"That is *perfect* on you," Jacob says, standing back to admire the dress he has just given me. It's a simple, flattering design of soft black cotton with a boatneck and a narrow skirt that stops just above the knees. He has also given me a pair of black patent leather boots that zip up the back and reach nearly to the hem of the dress, and a pair of lavender topaz earrings. The closet in our bedroom, painted now the gray of a dove's chest, can barely hold all the clothes he's given me; they fit me like a second skin, and they resemble a palette in the middle range: black, white, gray. And shoes. All black, some of buttery leather, some that are punishing and make me taller than any other woman in the room, taller than women. Tonight we're having a party, a coming-out as it were, and this is what I will wear. I dropped both other classes; I had no choice. I couldn't sit in Dr. Cohen's class and look at her, I couldn't revel in what she continued to exhibit as a loss, day after day. When I told her I was withdrawing she asked me to come to her office and I did; I intended to be gracious and show fortitude.

I found myself sitting uncomfortably close to her, our knees nearly touching, and even more unnervingly near a gigantic poster of Virginia Woolf. While I agree that Woolf is one of the geniuses of Western literature (there can be no doubt), the size of the poster seemed to me gratuitous, and heaven knows what I was thinking but I pointed to Woolf's familiar profile and said, *"Saxa loquuntur,"* to which Dr. Cohen offered a puzzled expression. I said, "Stones talk," the definition of a ruin. It was a misstep; she looked at me as if I had not only been profane, but morbid, and she, Dr. Cohen, had left epidemiology to heal people in another, more meaningful way, a way that precluded morbidity.

"Ianthe, tell me what the problem is. I don't want to lose a student like you, and if I'm doing something wrong I hope you'll tell me. My style might not be right for everyone."

I shook my head. "It isn't you, honestly. You're a wonderful professor and I have such admiration for your . . ." Words failed me. Her earnestness? Her variety of T-shirts? Her lack of vanity? ". . . compassion. And your commitment, to your students, and to the process, and to the literature. I admire all of that."

She leaned forward, earnestly. I preferred that she not, but I had nowhere to go. "I wonder," she said, her face a picture of concern, "why it is that you share so little in class. I know we aren't conducting actual therapy, but the class does offer the possibility of catharsis, as you've witnessed."

I wanted to remind her that Aristotle assigned catharsis to *tragedy*, not to the narcissism of the Midwestern *puella aeterna,* the girl whose father sometimes couldn't attend her volleyball games. "I'm . . ." I pursed my lips, searched for the right word. "I'm very private, I suppose. Being a private person has never interfered with my academic performance."

"No! No, of course not. The work you've done, your papers have been . . . I'm afraid my praise will be superfluous. Your essay on Plath's use of the Dostoyevskian double in 'Daddy,' the husband/father figure that creates a double wound; your knowledge of weapons . . . the way you tied it all together with the Jungian tarot figures." Dr. Cohen held her hands out, near exasperation. "It's publishable, as I said when I returned it to you. I think you should submit it as is, I'll even give you the contact information at various journals."

"I appreciate that," I said, and I did. But I would never submit that paper to a scholarly journal; I hadn't broken new ground. Anyone who knew the first thing about Plath knew she wrote her thesis on Dostoyevsky's use of the double, and that she employed it herself *all the time.* Applying the theory and a close reading to "Daddy" was akin to using . . . leaves as an example of leaves. A tautology. I also couldn't say that while I had studied Jungian tarot images before, I actually found a deck of them in a shop in Gloucestershire, when Jacob and I had toured England in late January. He had attended a legitimate conference; I had feigned illness to get out of class.

"What I wonder"—Dr. Cohen looked at her lap—"is if you aren't closed—emotionally—for some reason that could be served by staying the course, and joining your peers. I wonder if there isn't something you aren't—"

"Dr. Cohen," I said, so suddenly I myself was taken aback, "there is something I haven't told you or the class, and it's simple. I'm the woman Jacob Matthias left you for; I'm his lover, and we live together. The situation—I'm sorry, this has become untenable."

She froze, and went so long without moving I had to look away. I didn't know whether to stay or to go; I was trapped by her silence. After what seemed hours, she said, "You have done me a terrible wrong. You have wronged another woman, a sister. And you have deceived me for weeks now by withholding this information."

I knew she wasn't just angry; her righteousness filled the room like smoke. There was no denying her charge. I stood to leave, a penitent. Except I'm not really *made* that way—it's a crying shame and I would *love* to be a better person. "I accept your claim, Dr. Cohen, and I apologize. But I would like to point out that while you came late to literature, you surely know the definition of irony.

You quote Emma Goldman and Andrea Dworkin and use phrases like 'the meta-ethics of gyno-feminism,' and yet you are fighting like a cheerleader over *a man*." I left her office, and promptly went to Jacob's office and wrote her a sincere apology. I had been cruel and wrong. I used Jacob's letterhead.

Withdrawing from the other class was infinitely more simple. I took the Late/Drop slip to Dr. Scherring during his office hours, where I found him disheveled and reading a comic book. I knocked and he invited me in without looking up; when he realized a woman was in his office he took his feet off his desk, hid the comic book, and smoothed the sides of his hair, which I have come to recognize as his form of genuflecting.

"Miss Covington," he said, revealing a nicotine-stained smile. "What brings you by?"

"I'm withdrawing from your class, and I need you to sign the Drop slip."

He held his hand out and I gave him the form. "So," he said, "are you withdrawing because you're tired of lying about what you dream, or because you're shtupping Matthias?"

I thought about it. "Both, really."

He handed the form back to me. "Best of luck to you. I really like the way he's dressed you up—this new look you've got. He definitely saw the raw material. I'll give the man credit even though fifteen years ago he dicked me over and my salary will never catch up to his, still. Credit where credit is due."

I laughed, shook his hand. I just loved the man, but I could hardly tell him why. I couldn't describe for him the fully rounded character he had become in a tawdry short story about a dead era, a story that existed entirely in my head. Especially not when his bitterness only deepened his pathos, made him all the more believable. Sad.

• • •

Living with Jacob is infinitely more satisfying than taking a class with Jacob, because I can ask him a question, any question, and we can talk about it as long as we want to, we can go around and around; he quotes from sources he could never ask a class to read, but I read all of it, anything, our conversation never ends. We spent an entire Sunday on *The Dream and the Underworld,* and at a particular moment we both felt it—the scope of Hillman's idea that the figures of the Underworld are autochthonic—they aren't condensations or compensations; they aren't symbols or the fulfillment of wishes. They do not guard our sleep. They are not Jung's objective "the people themselves," or his subjective "the characterological essence," of whomever we see. My former neighbor, in the Underworld of my dream, is neither a piece of me nor a reflection of himself. *The images are the dead themselves, they are literally autonomous.* "What one knows about life may not be relevant for what is below life," Hillman writes, he says there is a *downward love,* he says, "The less underworld, the less depth, and the more horizontally spread out becomes one's life." I am shaking by this point, the horror of the horizontal life, my dream of an infinite horizon, and Jacob comes around the table, takes me by the shoulders, and leads me to the living room. We sit on the couch and he gathers me up. He will ask me a question about my imaginary family—my lies bring him enormous pleasure, as if he were a child and every day I give him a new tale—and it will be calming to me, as well, I can forget the ramifications of Hillman, and not just in that book but in the others as well, and Jacob asks me, "So who was your best friend growing up?"

I see it very clearly, the story I should tell about the strange girl who invented her own language because she was raised by wolves; how she had been found and institutionalized, and eventually sent to the Catholic orphanage where I lived; I see the shape of her birthmark, the deformity of her feet from running in a pack, I will give her curiously colored hair and a name like—"Candy Buck was my best friend," I say. "Candace." I tell him everything: the coyote, the picnic, the chicken, the mulberry pail, the rock in my neck. I run up to the top of the hill and over the rise and there she is on her grandfather's porch and we know one another right away, and when her grandfather offers to drive me home he asks where I live and I tell him the truth: I don't have the slightest idea.

Jacob rubs his lips over my shoulder, my collarbone. "You're a liar."

"That is correct."

"You had no friends, no kin, you are alone in all the world."

"Also correct." I take his hand, I hold it against my heart, my cheek, my lips. "Not anymore, though. I'm not alone anymore."

"No, no, you are now two, I am your *permanence*. It is fixed."

✝

The caterers arrived on time and began setting up in the dining room. Jacob had ordered shiitake-mushroom-and-goat-cheese-filled miniature puff pastries; chicken satay; smoked salmon topped with mild green horseradish sauce, in butter lettuce cups; a fruit salad; small hummus sandwiches; caviar, sour cream, water crackers. There were two cases of claret, two of chardonnay, and Italian lemon soda for the nondrinkers, whoever they might be.

Ianthe zipped the back of the black boots; they fit her perfectly and added an inch to her height. She slipped in the earrings, brushed her hair. Jacob stepped out of the closet, knotting his tie.

"Sweetheart?"

"Yes?" Ianthe turned to him, hoping he didn't need help with the tie, as she had no idea how they worked.

"I got you a little something—I wonder if you'll try it?"

"Of course."

He took a white box out of the closet and brought it over the ornate vanity table they'd found at an antiques store. "I took three photographs of you to a woman at the Lancôme counter, and she put together this collection of cosmetics specifically for your skin tone. I got one of everything, just to be safe, and in case you like it. You start with this—just a dot under the eyes, yes? It brightens, I think. And then you move on to this liquid foundation but only a tiny bit because your skin is perfect. Hmmm." He watched as she smoothed the foundation over her cheeks, following his directions. "That's lovely. And then this powder—I bought the softest brush they had, it's like—it feels almost like feathers. Now. Use this eye-liner—I don't want to get near your eyes." Ianthe applied it quickly. "Wow, you're really good at that—you did that so fast. Now look at these colors, aren't they . . . ? The silver-gray goes on your lower eyelid, the lighter up near your brow. Right—and this is the pièce de résistance: at the fold of your eyelid, make a single streak of this wine color and watch what it does to the color of your eyes." He stepped backward, clutching his chest. "My heart. Now the mascara—you don't need much, your eyelashes are already so dark. Whoa, though, that really—they seem twice as wide, they're magnificent. And finally, try this shade of lipstick, it's a silvery plum . . . flawless. She recommended this clear gloss over it, to keep it from drying out. Let's . . . okay, look away from me, and then turn your head quickly and look me in the eye." She did so, and Jacob knelt before her. He studied her face, her throat, the fit of the dress. "That sound you hear, beloved, it isn't bells. It isn't music. That's Aphrodite laughing, she is rising from the sea, laughing with joy, because of you. You."

The house was filled with people; she had had no idea there would be so many. She recognized some faculty members from the English department, a man from Classics, two women from Philosophy, but there were far more strangers. Architects and historians and physicists and a group of people from the Drama department. She recognized a scandalous sculptor, a man who had made all the furniture in his house out of six-packs of beer, which he then proceeded to drink, until the house was empty and he could start over.

Jacob put a glass of red wine in her hand and he initiated the evening with his arm around her waist, and then he mingled while she stood still and the guests came to her. It was as if he were a satellite, she a planet. He reappeared regularly; he kissed her brow; he refilled her glass. The same things were said to her a hundred times, Jacob was a wonderful man, an exemplary professor, and a wise administrator. Such a combination was rare. He was a man of integrity, a champion of intellectual freedom, a rigorous scholar and thinker. Ianthe's feet began to ache, her head hurt from the red wine, faces had begun to blend into a single, academic jowl. She caught sight—the merest glimpse—of Elizabeth Cohen coming through the door and walking toward the kitchen with a familiarity that made Ianthe sick with anger and jealousy, but when Jacob appeared beside her moments later she asked if she had been correct, if Elizabeth had been invited. Jacob said he had sent her an invitation as a gesture but had received an R.S.V.P., regrets. He looked around, went into the kitchen, came out. He shrugged, no sign of her. And Ianthe didn't see her again, either.

A few at a time they left; then in larger groups, until finally the only people remaining were ten or twelve faculty members Jacob had warned Ianthe would be hard to shake. Carcass pickers, he'd called them, and indeed that's what they were doing. By the time they were finished, only the skewers from the chicken satay would remain. Ianthe remained planted in her spot in the library, near the fireplace, afraid if she moved her feet would either swell to such an extent she would never get the boots off, or that the boots would fill with blood, which might be thought gauche. She wasn't drunk; she had never been drunk, but she felt unwell; she was finished.

Surely, she thought, she could tell Jacob she needed to retire and he could entertain the last of the guests, but before she had even completed the thought, two of the carcass pickers were standing in front of her, a woman and a man. The man was tall and bearlike, with a white fringe of hair and an enormous white beard. He had a plate filled with food and as he systematically laid waste to it, he breathed loudly through his mouth, as if he'd just climbed six flights of stairs. Ianthe felt a wave of nausea, and hardly dared glance at him; part of everything he'd eaten was resting in his beard.

The woman was short, portly. Her gray hair was coiled into a tight permanent wave and her glasses sat crookedly on her nose. She had obviously made the green sweater she was wearing. She had a plate of food resting on her palm; a terrible handbag hung from her opposite forearm, and that too had been created with knitting needles.

Ianthe didn't catch their names, if in fact they were offered.

"Jacob is wonderful," the woman said.

"Hmmk," the man agreed.

"And you are just stunning, pretty as a picture, the two of you make a dashing couple. I'm sure you'll travel. Jacob loves to travel and he always went alone, what a delight you will be for him. I don't know how he stood it, living with Rita so long. I don't know how he managed."

Ianthe became attentive; her malaise vanished. No one ever talked about Rita, including Jacob. She was about to ask what the woman meant when the man said, "Oh come on, I don't know how Rita ever put up with *him*. Twenty years with that crap, that ego, writing a book about masks, *I ask you*. What could be more obvious? He might as well write a book about asses."

The woman ignored her companion and continued to speak directly to Ianthe. "She was no intellectual, Rita. I mean, she taught at the university but she was a nutritionist. I'm, I'm not even sure what that means, I don't know why she was employed with us rather than in a . . . hospital, or a nursing home or what have you. I'm sure he could never talk to her about ideas. She hated these functions, she hated *abstractions,* that's the word Jacob used."

"*(A)* Rita was an athlete, she ran marathons. *(B)* She taught in the nursing school. *(C)* Jacob belittled her and thought she was too stupid to know it but he was wrong. Yes, she was a regular person, she was a *real* person. She was kind and thoughtful and remembered birthdays and always had something good to say, he should have fallen at her feet for *not* being obsessed with literary theory and the contents of her own psyche, for the love of god." The man panted; food fell from his beard to his shirt, landing on his hugely swollen abdomen.

The woman chewed. Her eyes were unfocused, looking toward the fireplace rather than at Ianthe. "Well. At least there weren't any children."

The man chewed, took gulping breaths. Ianthe looked at him and saw that his lips were pulp, his eyes a milky blue. He squinted, cocked his head, said, "Wasn't there a child?"

They were gone. Jacob walked toward her as if he too could barely stand another moment. "Whatever the caterers don't clean up we'll deal with in the morning. I've got to lie down."

"Yes, please."

They hobbled up the stairs and took turns getting ready for bed. Ianthe wasn't accustomed to wearing so much makeup, and had to wash her face twice to get it all off. Her skin stung and her eyes ached. She brushed her teeth, walked down the hall, but could barely feel the floor beneath her feet. Their bedroom was so pretty, opalescent; it was warm and smelled like candles and almonds.

Ianthe climbed into bed and let her body go loose as Jacob wrapped himself around her.

"You were so . . . I was enormously proud of you, tonight. You do me a great honor, sharing my life."

Ianthe's eyes filled with tears. She loved him, she was so tired. "Jacob?"

"Hmm?"

"Did you and Rita have a child?"

He had been motionless before the question and he remained motionless, and yet every atom in the room shifted, scattered so as not to be seen. The mystical properties of physics applied in every moment, Jacob was fond of saying. He was currently reading *The Dancing Wu Li Masters;* he wanted access to the quantum universe.

"Who told you that?" he asked quietly, with a dash of rage.

"I don't know who they were, they didn't say their names. A man and woman—I—I didn't know them."

They lay in silence. Jacob's body was tense, tight. He gradually moved away from her.

"Sweetheart? Will you just tell me?"

"Yes!" He sat up so swiftly Ianthe grew afraid; she wasn't sure whether she could look at him. "We had a child who was born with magical powers. He could fly, and he could put on a special hat and become invisible, and he could talk to the animals, and he could even eat the dishes! Then one day he put on his helmet and flew away."

Ianthe raised a hand to her mouth and bit down on her index finger. She kept biting until the feeling passed, a primitive panic—Freud would say primitive and Jung would say Pan. Ic. The God Pan. She lowered her hand, pulled the blankets back over her shoulder. "You're a liar," she said, looking away from him.

"That is correct." Jacob lay down but with his back to her, and all night she waited but he did not relent.

CHAPTER NINE

Eros

Journal

As if the gods had said I could love him but not see him (there is always a sliver withheld); which meant I *had* to see him and with my gaze made him disappear. Until that moment I had as much of Colt as I wanted, nearly, my arms around his waist as we drove through town. Sitting up against him watching movies after Loretta had gone to sleep. *The Night of the Hunter* was coming on—the late show—and I said yes let's watch this and Colt said no. I turned and looked at him, cocked an eyebrow. "Why not?"

"I've seen it before and I don't care to see it again. And I don't want you to see it."

"But I *want* to," I said, pushing my forehead against his shoulder.

"Well, you're not *going* to." He flipped through the *TV Guide,* bit at a hangnail with his teeth.

"What would it cost me?"

"Not for sale." He shook his head. His profile was lamplit and his hair was braided, the braid hanging over his right shoulder. With his eyes cast down at the television listings he appeared to be sleeping, and his eyelashes cast a shadow on his high cheekbones. Those are the only answers I can give.

"Colt." I whispered in his ear. I didn't move away; my bottom lip grazed his earlobe.

That was the moment, the signal event. In literature it's always so much more dramatic and memorable: a woman places her hand against a rearing stallion and calms him, or she opens her front door and there a man stands, unprotected from a terrible storm. At any rate, she knows: he knows. And that knowledge—bidden or unbidden—is like a snake striking the ankle. Colt would tell me whether the bite was delicious or unwelcome, he would tell me with

He turned very slowly. He looked at me. The moment hung poised; it hangs to this day.

In the kitchen I would reach past him for something I didn't need, just to press myself against him. He would slip away. A certain song would come on, "Maybe You'll Be There," and for a moment he'd forget and we would dance, and then he'd drop my hand as if coming to his senses. One day my Winchester disappeared from the gun cabinet. He unlocked my hands around his waist and gently pushed them down to my own thighs, even while taking sharp curves, but he denied me in no other way. Steady, strung-tight, unconditional. We glanced at one another, he knew I was biding my time. If we passed each other on the stairs he moved hard to the right but I kept walking straight up the center, I didn't give an inch. More than once I was awakened by the strike of his lighter, the quick glint of flame, as he stood in my room in the dead of night. I pretended to sleep, there was nothing I wouldn't have done, and he left, he wouldn't stay, but no matter. A part of him remained.

Loretta. She feigned ignorance, singing along with the radio in the kitchen, her voice clear and sure, Colt loved to hear her sing. I imagined wolves—or just a single wolf, my own—who by *nature,* not by my *command,* would leap upon her in the backyard

rain was coming and she'd left clothes on the line and it was already getting dark, *Doggone it,* she'd say, grabbing her wicker clothes basket as she headed out the back door, *What was I thinking leaving them sheets out all day*

mincing down the three back steps and into the yard, small steps because she was so top-heavy, her feet so small, and she had to really reach up to squeeze the clothespins, a shadow rounding the chokecherry tree, his head dipped low just prior to the leap, he would rip her throat out and she'd never know what hit her. Loretta pretended not to notice about Colt and me but she turned up some heat between them—she thought a little less of others and a little more of him. *How do you like this dress, Colt darlin',* something she'd made herself, white with red polka dots I can almost touch that dress it's so clear to me, and Colt would say, *That's real sweet Loretta,* although what did he know from dresses? Not the first thing. A sartorial disaster, the red dots in furious competition with her red hair, no winner there but I just sat and watched her. Sometimes she'd stroke my back and say, *I wish you'd let me make a dress like this for you, we could match like me and Dusty used to do.* Wouldn't that be nice, I'd say. Colt standing behind her, even if he was closer to the door he was the one trapped. I could look right over the top of her head, directly into his eyes, Loretta pretended not to notice. She slept in the same bed with him every night; this was incomprehensible, intolerable. Many a 3 A.M. I snuck down the hallway and stood outside their bedroom door, my ear pressed to the wood. I never heard a thing.

✛

For two weeks they'd been preparing for this visit; cleaning and re-fining every corner of the house, stocking the pantry, driving to In-dianapolis for the better wines and coffee beans. Jacob saw the house as if for the first time, and suddenly a cushion that had served them well had to go, and why was the upstairs bathroom cluttered with so many *shampoo* bottles? Because you keep buying them, Ianthe answered calmly. Yes, but why are there so *many*? Poor Jacob, she had not known it was possible for him to be intimidated—she had imagined him at the top of the food chain. He wasn't intimi-dated, he insisted, he just wanted everything to be perfect for this man, this old friend.

Gianni Loria had taught in the English department with Jacob for just two years, fifteen years prior, but in those two years the two had formed a deeply held bond. Loria was older than Jacob, an aca-demic nomad whose idea of torture was tenure. He saw himself as an outlaw, a gun for hire—those were the very words Jacob had used to describe him—causing Ianthe to laugh helplessly. Academ-ics! They really used such metaphors for themselves! His relation-ship to the Law (and guns) aside, Ianthe knew only a few things about the man coming to stay with them for a week. His parents were Sicilian, from a village called Poggioreale. Gianni and his sister Anna were the first in their families to go to college, and Gianni had been treasured for his great successes. There was money—Ianthe didn't know who had earned it or how. Gianni had traversed not just the universities of America but of the world, teaching a year or two at an institution and then moving on. He was retired now, living in a small town off the Pacific Coast Highway, near Big Sur.

"Now I don't want *you* to be intimidated by Gianni, Ianthe—he can be a bit overwhelming at first but he has a heart of gold, hand me the pencil? I need to mark this spot." Jacob was on the ladder in the guest room, which was also Ianthe's study, hanging new curtains.

"Why would I be intimidated by him?" She did not want *anyone* staying in her study. She didn't want a strange man in the sleigh bed she and Jacob had bought at an auction; she didn't want him looking at the things on her desk. She didn't want him *near* the desk: black mahogany, drawers that locked without keys, as heavy as an elephant. This was her room, good lord the hours she and Jacob had spent on the paint alone. It was his idea to take the dove gray of their bedroom and mix it with lavender to draw out Ianthe's eyes, a concept she had at first found—whatever is beyond a folly—but which had turned out to be a small stroke of genius on Jacob's part. Not because she saw herself reflected in the walls, nothing like that, but because the color was otherworldly, and it made her *happy,* and it made the room *hers.*

"Oh ho—that man!" Jacob all but clapped like a child. "He's been everywhere, done everything. He met everyone, knows the most interesting people. Just ask him a question and you can sit back and enjoy yourself for hours. Ask him about Hunter S. Thompson, for instance—that's a helluva story."

Ianthe smiled at Jacob. "I can't wait."

"Oh, and darling"—he finished marking the place he would drill—"don't bring up Jung or archetypalism, any of that. Loria has no patience with the topic."

"He has no patience with your . . . work?"

"Well, that's not so unusual for English departments. Disciples of one approach having no patience with disciples of another."

They both laughed hard and with an edge; what an absurd understatement. Jacob had wondered aloud at dinner just a few nights before if 1987 might be the year, finally, that his colleagues began poisoning one another.

"Maybe you should make a list of the schools of thought with which Dr. Loria has no patience?"

Jacob adopted a professorial pose on the ladder. "Let's see: Feminism, Post-Colonialism, Structuralism, Post-Structuralism—I can't stress enough how much he hates the French critics and anything that bears the tag 'Postmodern'—Semiotics, Reader-Response, Social, Psychoanalytic, Narratological, Historicism."

Ianthe nodded. "I think the only thing left is New Criticism. Which isn't so new anymore."

"He's a man of his time, as we all are."

"I'll try to keep all of it in mind. Do you want the level?" She didn't say what must have been clear to Jacob for years. *If he appoints you his son and successor, you'll have no option but to kill him and put your own face on the flag.* On the mask. Or maybe one could actually dismiss psychoanalytic theory so thoroughly it ceased to apply to one's own life? It became nothing but an idea ghost? A thought castrato?

"Darling?"

She blinked. "Sorry—daydreaming."

"I do need the level. You know what Freud says about daydreaming, don't you?"

"Yes, Jacob. I know."

The faculty directory contained the data for each department, and included a one-inch-by-one-inch black-and-white photograph of every professor. Ianthe had gone through Jacob's directories covering the past five years and could find neither the tall repulsive man with the food-filled beard nor his wiry-haired companion. She looked forward and back through each one compulsively, because they *had* to be in there somewhere, she was turning the pages too quickly, she didn't recognize them, perhaps the woman, whom

Ianthe now thought of as Toad's Wild Ride, would take off her eye-glasses for a photograph? What if Gasping Santa dyed his hair, or had been thinner in years past? Nothing. She had tried asking Jacob to tell her who all had been at the party; she'd asked pointedly who the carcass pickers were, and he described everyone he could remember but not those two. And she couldn't very well say so baldly, "There were two who told me . . ."

She had lunch with Jacob every day at the faculty club; she never saw them there. She walked down the hallways of the English department with him, arm in arm—they weren't English profes-sors. Jacob was obliged to attend a university function almost every week, and Ianthe accompanied him. Never.

They knew Rita, they had known Rita, they were the only two people besides Jacob ever to mention her name. The man had surely been close to her; he said pointedly that Rita remembered birth-days, and how would he know that unless she had remembered his? In the public spaces in the house, the drawers to which she had ac-cess, Ianthe looked for her. There wasn't much: Some photographs of an athletic blond woman who had spent too much time in the sun. Jacob and Rita together at the beach; Rita painting the master bedroom orange; the two of them dancing at a wedding. And strangely, even though Ianthe found herself prone to fits of murder-ous jealousy with the slightest provocation, the photographs didn't bother her at all. It was as if Jacob were sitting with a mannequin, or the cardboard figure of a woman. No matter how Ianthe looked at her, from every angle Rita was already gone.

There were the photographs, and in a downstairs coat closet, a terrible oil portrait of her in an oversized white wooden frame. Her wedding dress. Ianthe took it out of the closet, held it up to the light. What kind of woman left her wedding dress hanging in a coat closet? It wasn't even in a dry cleaner's bag—the wire hanger was rusting right through the fabric. The dress itself was unattractive, mercilessly dated. Ianthe carried it into the downstairs bathroom, held it up to herself in the full-length mirror. Rita had been tall, very thin. Much thinner than Ianthe. As if on a note card, she made a list of what she knew: a runner, a nutritionist, taught in the nursing school, was uncomfortable with abstractions. Was probably not vain, was unsentimental but kind, married twenty years, left almost no mark. She had no family, and so far Ianthe hadn't met anyone who had been friends with Rita and Jacob as a couple, which was odd, given Jacob's . . . ebullience, his affability, his way with . . . everything. Very odd.

Ianthe hung the dress where she'd found it. She searched for the woman as gently as possible, so Jacob wouldn't know.

✢

She told Jacob to go to the airport without her—she would stay home and put the last touches on the house. She'd make sure all of the appetizers Jacob prepared were out at the right moment; she'd let the wine breathe.

"When we get home, you won't be listening to . . . any sort of . . ." He shook his head, unable to find the language for his distaste.

"To what? Listening to what, Jacob?"

He sighed. "You don't have to make me say it, Ianthe."

"Oh but I do." They stood in the doorway, facing one another and holding hands. Jacob was dressed so beautifully he could have been in an anti-advertisement: the Middle-Aged Man Every Middle-Aged Woman Knows Does Not Exist. Ianthe was wearing what Jacob had chosen: an Egyptian cotton man's shirt—deliciously too big for her, according to him—with French cuffs. Jacob had given her the cuff links on some anniversary or another (two weeks, two months): the *Birth of Venus*. She was also wearing a white lace camisole, and the shirt was unbuttoned to reveal it. Black cigarette pants. Black-and-white spectator pumps. Her hair was loose, brushed to a high gloss. The earrings, and two new additions: an heirloom platinum engagement ring, and a platinum bracelet—a delicate chain with square-cut aquamarines—on her right wrist.

"Darling, you know I adore you, but please don't—I don't want Gianni to walk in and the first thing he hears is some banal—or worse, some—"

"Enough. Tell me what you want to be playing when Gianni comes through the door."

Jacob kissed her on the nose. "It's already set up. Just push Play at seven-thirty. Don't forget?"

Ianthe laughed out loud. "Just push Play. I won't forget."

At her desk she took out the calfskin-covered journal Jacob had given her. She'd nearly filled it already, but that was fine—the cover slipped off and he'd given her three additional inserts. Ianthe rarely reread what she wrote; never the dreams. But she'd begun working on poems again, now that she wasn't in school and had a lot of time to consider her options.

She turned on her beautiful little black IBM word processor, took out her printed pages, turned to the notes she'd written in the journal. *Technological angels,* Jung had said, and she had thought and thought about it—how really the two words had to be pulled apart and placed in separate rooms, like disruptive, symbiotic children. She had begun making notes for Candy, so she would have a systematic way of addressing her, and then the notes had evolved. Of course she understood the New Criticism, and that it was déclassé ever to assume that the voice of any work of literature was the voice of the author, rather than that of an autonomous creation. Nonetheless, Ianthe had been surprised to find another voice taking over her poem, a speaker who both was and was not herself.

And to whom was she speaking? The title had been reduced to "Angel." It was in four parts; Ianthe studied them one at a time.

> 1.
> *A woman is pacing, your name in her mouth*
> *are sheep grazing on a steep hillside.*
> *She is your shepherdess, she watches*
> *the lioness who is watching her*
> *from a place not distant and nearing.*
> *Your name on her tongue gives her*
> *courage—she will lead these lambs*
> *to a fortress. And if you demand it*
> *she will waste them, ear to silken*
> *ear, open in their throats a second*
> *smile. They were born*
> *to bloom like roses. Oh their whiteness,*
> *their lashes, their black, heart-shaped noses!*

She was dissatisfied with "from a place"—that place should be named, it should be specific, except Ianthe herself didn't know for certain where the lion was, she never knew where the lion was, that was

> 2.
> *The woman is pacing, her heart blisters.*
> *She is the most beautiful of three*
> *beautiful sisters, and you have said no*
> *to her after the angels said yes.*
> *What is that small planet, the secret*
> *concealed in her dress?*
> *It is something she swallowed that once*
> *grew but ceased growing. She will carry it*

through the orchard, to the seaport, and all
the way home; it is her stone
child. It is your child turned to stone,
white as winter birch, and on this rock
the angels are building their church.

Six-thirty. In a few minutes she would go down and take out the
cheeses, so they could begin to soften, and she'd open the wine.

3.
Consider the angels fucking
or at play. Multiply the dalliance
of eagles with mating lions at midday.
When the angels descend and penetrate
Time, whole herds of panicked
deer lie down and die. Young girls
are bound, bereft, made mute
as ruined brides. In dreams you
are pricked by the Architect's quill,
watch the flexing of His muscle. Giant
bats in flight. It is your name the Angel
spoke: you He wished good night.

This whole section surprised her, frankly. She wouldn't place
bets on it. Giant bats in flight? To whom is she speaking, this
woman?

4.
Loved, loved, loved this way once
and never again, you who creep back
into habit when the Angel attends.
Vanished: the sheep in their snow

white hoods. Even the earth that absorbed
it has forgotten their blood. The lions
are hobbled and losing their teeth;
what once we called sacrifice is now
simply meat. Your woman, her profane grief,
has dissolved into history. She is buried
with your baby and his infinite memory.
Consider that child, how stern his closed
eyes, his fingernails like crescent moons,
his marbled skin blue. The final sky.

She thought she would throw it away; she gathered up the pages and straightened them, in order to throw them away. It wasn't what she'd meant to write: where was Jung, where were his saucers, everything she'd meant to say? The Sphinx, when Oedipus meets her, has the body of a lion and the head of a woman. *After a while he returned to marry her, and he turned aside to see the carcass of the lion, and there was a swarm of bees in the body of the lion, and honey. He scraped it out with his hands, and went on, eating as he went.* Judges 14:8. Or Gilgamesh: "The joyful will stoop with sorrow, and when you have gone to earth I will let my hair grow long for your sake, I will wander through the wilderness in the skin of a lion." Who had come in and taken over her poem? She straightened the pages, slipped them back in the top desk drawer. *Oh*—she nearly laughed out loud. My Grandmother Covington made me a cake—not the *Peaceable Kingdom* but the weather of my birth. Tomorrow she would throw the mess away.

✢

At eight, when the two men burst through the kitchen door in a flurry of talk, Ianthe had gotten everything right. Scarlatti was, she assumed, at exactly the measure Jacob had intended for Gianni's entrance. Everything was on the table just as she'd been told—the antipasto and the array of small dishes Jacob had spent all day preparing; the cheese plate; the fruits. The wine had been breathing, the glasses were waiting. Jacob came in first—he smiled at her and raised a hand in recognition, then the hand became one finger that meant, "Don't say anything yet—he's right in the middle of something," and behind Jacob was Gianni Loria, a short man in his early sixties who was talking loudly and gesticulating. He wore a black overcoat and white silk scarf (although the weather was balmy). His story concluded with, "And I told *him,*" then turning and whispering something in Italian to Jacob, who laughed loudly.

They were carrying shopping bags, or Jacob was. He set them down, dashed to the end of the table to give Ianthe a quick kiss, and in the flurry Gianni was still talking. "So move all this aside, what is all this taking up space? I'm going to *cook.* I'm *Sicilian,* and I am preparing the meal, give me *space.*"

So far he hadn't acknowledged her, so Ianthe stepped forward and said, "Gianni, it's a pleasure to meet you—I'm Ianthe," holding out her hand.

Gianni looked up at her, looked up and down at her, said, "I know who you are, now help me clear this table. Jacob!" He shouted toward the front of the house, where Jacob was hanging Gianni's coat. "Very nice, this girl, good choice!"

Ianthe picked up the cheese plate. "I'm sorry, I thought Jacob said you were from Hoboken."

Gianni straightened to his full height, such as it was, and gave her a narrow-eyed smile. He shook his head no, and said, "Nu-uh-uh, don't play the high-hat with me, little girl."

Jacob sailed into the room. ". . . I know, I know, isn't she divine? The two of you are going to *love* one another."

• • •

Of course he hadn't been able to find the right ingredients, he couldn't believe Jacob still lived in this provincial swamp—no, Jonah *aspired* to provincialism—it couldn't claim even that denigration. He had had to make do with pathetic substitutes, as one would during a war, bartering for rations. The caprese salad would have been fine were it not that Jacob and Ianthe's balsamic vinegar (*aceto balsamico!*) wasn't even real, it was neither *Aceto Balsamico Tradizionale di Modena* nor *Aceto Balsamico Tradizionale di Reggio Emilia,* it was—he made an eloquent spitting gesture—suitable only for the sponge and the windowpane. The mozzarella was "fresh," but fourth-rate. The tomatoes, the basil! Ianthe wanted to say, They aren't in season! Surely even Hoboken has seasons! But she was quiet.

The gnocchi in red sauce with anchovies would have been a tremendous dish, Gianni claimed, but where did they go to get handmade pasta, or did Ianthe make it herself? The greens for the salad—he had wanted a particular spicy leaf—toasted pine nuts and red raspberries. Where did they get the proper raspberries? On and on, the wine was off, it bit his tongue, and all the while Jacob apologized, smiled like a schoolboy with a crush, praised his old friend to the heavens for what he had done with such limited resources.

Hours passed and they remained at the table, Jacob and Ianthe's inadequacies hardening on the dishes, as Gianni told story after story: the grapevines on Ezra Pound's estate in Rapallo, from which Gianni had stolen a cutting to replant on his estate (it was thriving). Hunter S. Thompson: indeed it was a tale, similar to the one many people told of Thompson. Cocaine, guns, the night sky in Colorado. A weekend with Bukowski in San Francisco that had ended dreadfully. Ginsberg, Corso, Peter Orlovsky. Chögyam Trungpa Rinpoche. Gianni railed against the poets who were wrongly considered the successors to Pound, men who should have taken the outlaw mantle from Burroughs; he called the lot the Impotence School, or the Castration School. Bly Bly Bly, sensitive nature boy Galway, the master of chicanery, James Wright. He described a run-in with Bly in which Gianni had insulted the poet with earnestness and vigor, and Bly's response. Any sane person, Ianthe believed, would see that Bly had been the victor with his kindness, his refusal to engage. If she and Jacob were talking alone they would have agreed, first and foremost, that Bly was a *fine* poet, a man whose mind was enviably deep and broad and inquisitive; they would agree that he deserved all the recognition he received, for his honest love of both poetry and humanity (humanity!). He was so tireless an ambassador he made himself vulnerable to people like Gianni Loria and the thousands of critics like him, he was vulnerable deliberately, and that was his strength.

She looked at Jacob, at this man who placed the ring on her finger. He was nodding in agreement with his old friend, not saying he agreed but not arguing, and Jacob, Ianthe's betrothed, would have raised the question of where were the women, why was there never a mention of the women, past or present? Even on Planet Ginsberg there was Anne Waldman, and how could you talk about James Wright without mentioning Anne Sexton? If Gianni had seen Bly he had probably seen Sharon Olds—but oh, she got it, it wasn't that women writers were contemptible, they did not exist. *Capisce?*

"Gianni, shall we have coffee and brandy in the living room, make ourselves comfortable? Ianthe, yes?"

"And Snyder—I used to have some respect for Snyder, he was a real—" Gianni was standing, folding his linen napkin and placing it carefully next to his plate.

"You two go on," Ianthe said. Jacob had to turn his head back and forth from her face to Gianni's, who was still talking. "I'll bring you coffee and start cleaning up in here." He smiled at her gratefully, pressed his lips to her temple, followed the Sicilian.

They escorted him upstairs at two-thirty in the morning, all of them exhausted. Jacob said, "We've put you in Ianthe's study—I think you're going to love the bed. We found the frame at—"

"What have you done?" Gianni stopped cold in the hallway, looking through the open doors into the bedrooms. "What have you done with Rita's beautiful colors?" He was aggrieved, his voice shaking. Ianthe turned and looked at Jacob, who was sickly pale.

"Gianni," he began.

"This is all wrong! What—these aren't the right curtains for a Queen Anne!" He strode into Ianthe's study, looked around. "Jacob, you *had* to do this? You had to erase her *completely*, huh, get her out of the way so you could move a new bird into the nest."

Ianthe reached out and took Jacob's hand; he was trembling. His face changed from white to a yellowish green, his eyes and beard in sharp contrast. Ianthe, too, was shaking, not only from the ugliness but for fear of what Gianni was saying. What was he saying, *get her out of the way COMPLETELY*. She was looking at Gianni (who was not looking at her) and Jacob let go of her hand and took one long step toward his friend; Jacob wrapped him in his arms with such swiftness Ianthe could hear Gianni's forehead hit Jacob's chest. Both men were crying, Gianni in a big Hoboken/Sicilian/The Most Famous Person You've Never Heard Of way, Jacob with tenderness.

"Why did you have to do this, Jacob? Why her *colors*?"

They lay entwined in their warm bed, Jacob still so distraught he couldn't speak. Ianthe traced the contours of his face, his neck, she kissed him lightly on the shoulder. What would become of a person who had found the love of her life, not once but twice, and lost him both times? Gianni had said it himself: *This was* HER *house. This is* HER *house.*

✛

Her only relief from him was when Jacob took him to campus, where Gianni spent the day consorting with old colleagues, the few who remained. From Jacob she gathered that he was given the hero's welcome with those men, too, who endured his insults, his stories, his pity. Late at night, when they hoped he was sleeping, she and Jacob fought in fierce whispers. She told him she didn't expect him to defend or protect her as the time for that had come and gone the moment Gianni walked through the door, but she sorely wished Jacob would protect himself, that he would show some pride in the face of Gianni's condescension, a word that failed to describe the scope of the man's insufferability but was the best she could do in a whisper.

Maybe it was the hour, or the too-high level of feeling, days of it, but Jacob sat up and pulled her up with him, he forced her into a sitting position and held her shoulders as he spit words at her. They popped, they exploded in the cadence of a furious snake about to strike. "Do you know what it has been like for me to live in this godforsaken pit of hillbillies and—the stupid filthy retarded 'patriots,' the unshaven cavemen in their trucks and their—to be stuck here and know I would never get away, I would never get the job I deserved, in part because *Rita* didn't want to go, she loved her job and this town, that you come home from buying paper towels at Kmart and say, 'Listen to what I heard this woman say to her husband,' and it takes all of my *will,* it takes a *Schopenhauerian amount of will* to stop myself from saying, 'I don't want to hear a *word* about the people at Kmart, have they not already ruined the world and destroyed the possibility for anything decent or meaningful?' That with the exception of the two years *that man* was here I have never, not one single time, been able to communicate with someone on my own level, there hasn't been one person?"

Ianthe bit her lip; the *jaw-dropping* level of hubris and arrogance was so hilarious she wished there were someone she could tell, someone to whom she could say, "And then he said . . . ," just to watch his or her face at the moment of the punch line. The punch.

"Stuck here in part because of *her,* and don't even start, don't even ask me if I could talk to *her,* because about what, oh, I don't know, nursing school gossip, whole proteins, shin splints, no matter how much I loved her and did for her she had to run run run, she wouldn't have anything to do with my career, she wouldn't travel with me. And irony of ironies, *that man* in there, who was like a life-line to me, *loved* her. He loved the respect she showed him, how quiet she was, her old-fashioned diligence and up-at-five-in-the-morning-to-run, her work ethic. He thought she was what a woman ought to be, he came to visit us twice a year and I know in part he was coming to see her but that was fine with me because I still got him. Since the day she walked out that door downstairs he has never stopped looking for her—if she could be found he would find her. So I have to endure his grief, his attacks, which by the way break my heart, and then I get it from you at night, and sweetheart, the best part? *She hated him.* She thought he was the biggest ass in the *universe,* a black hole."

She couldn't help herself; Ianthe covered her mouth, but still anyone in the house could have heard her laughing. She turned and buried her face in the pillow. Jacob began laughing as well, he lay down beside her and she pulled him close, the two of them so over-come the bed began to bounce. *She hated him.* Ianthe wiped her eyes, said, "That Rita."

Jacob sighed, laughed. "Oh my. Yes, that Rita."

+

He was finally leaving, I couldn't believe it—I had grown accustomed to him the way one does to poison ivy, or an ache in the side—I thought he was going to be on my skin forever, and then the day came he was finally going home and I walked out of our bedroom and down the hall toward my study, he was vacating my study, to ask what time we needed to leave for the airport, and I saw Gianni and Jacob bent over my desk, intent on something. I slowed down, tried to be as quiet as possible, but neither looked in my direction even after I'd walked into the room.

"Now you see here—this line," Gianni was saying, "it's overwrought, the whole thing is melodramatic and forced, but I think it shows real promise. Her use of the word *meat,* for instance, I think is muscular, direct—if she could strip away all other tendencies and find where that came from . . . I'm"—he shrugged—"I'm thinking she has potential. There were instances in everything I read that surprised me, that made me—"

Jacob was holding the two pages of the poem, scanning them. He read the end, went back to the beginning, he looked up and saw me. He came toward me so fast I backed out of the room, I would have fallen down the staircase if I'd veered slightly to the left, he was saying

I tried to explain it was just—I didn't know where it had come from, it wasn't about him, it wasn't directed at him—I thought he was going to hit me. Gianni was saying, *Hey hey, Jacob, enough, friend,* Jacob was in my face, we were nose to nose, he was saying, *What do you think you know, what do you think you KNOW?*

I don't know anything.

. . .

Jacob tore the poem into pieces and ran toward the bathroom. He slammed the door behind him but we could hear him vomiting. I said to Gianni, "I'll take you to the airport."

"Now Ianthe, I'm an old man, entertain me here, I don't have many fears but I'm afraid of cars, I'm afraid of dying in a car wreck, so we'll need to take it slow. I'm sure you understand." I pulled away from the house as he fastened his seat belt. I locked the doors, drove slowly to the corner.

"Thank you, I appreciate your caution. You know, I've been in countless situations where my life was in danger and I rarely even felt it, it was some distance from me, you understand, but cars seem immediate . . ." He went on and on, his sisters shared this fear, he thought he'd never have a driver's license himself but it was necessary although he found cars on the whole to be representations of the trivial, I continued to slowly drive out of town. I reached the exit for the highway, four lanes that would eventually lead me to the bigger highway and then to I-465, the loop around Indianapolis, I said, "Gianni, shut the fuck up." I pushed in the cassette I'd been listening to and turned it up until my rearview mirror was vibrating, I let Gianni bathe in the banal as I sang along, "Bela Lugosi's Dead." The Volvo is a very safe car, *Il Volvo è una macchina molto sicura!* I shouted, as we reached ninety, then a hundred miles an hour; very safe and very fast.

Jacob slept that night with his back to me, I wept and begged him, I pressed my body against his, he slipped away. I had the first nightmare I'd had in his house: the little black rabbit, my demon, had grown huge and was dead, hanging on a hook in our bedroom, hanging by his mouth. He was in profile to me, swaying, the size of a horse, and all I could do was lie still and watch him, massive, black. His eye was open, a circle of gold. Sometimes I thought he was looking at me; at other times I feared he was not. No matter how hard I cried Jacob wouldn't bend, and I could feel it happening just like I knew it would he took my dog from me and now in the spring my soul is dying, I have to get Weeds back I have to go back to him, I fear Jacob did something to his wife, I try not to give shape to the thought but

Please Jacob, I say, *tell me what I did* but he doesn't move he doesn't bend, and I will dream of the black rabbit on the hook, and worse still I will dream of Rita hanging in the same spot, only she never looks away. She's had her eye on me from the moment I broke into this house. Her house.

CHAPTER TEN

Familiaris

She was no longer protected by the dog from the dog. The dog was now ruling her land of sleep, her sleeping earth, digging up all sorts of bones and dirt. A *nekyia* had begun.

JAMES HILLMAN, *The Dream and the Underworld*

Journal

Tomorrow we leave for San Francisco, this is another. It's another thing Jacob *must* attend, an event known by an acronym—at some of these he interviews people for positions in the department, at others he delivers scholarly papers and sits on panel discussions, and there are others I don't understand at all—it is April, imagine being Eliot and having the strength to convince so many that a month is cruel, "The Waste Land" was published in 1922, the year Freud at-

tended his final conference of the Psych i—I forget what it was
called. But he never went again. Here is the thing: I waited until
Jacob had gone to campus and then I tried to go into her room but
the door was locked. Why would the door be locked. He doesn't
know I know that all the doors in this house open with a skeleton
key, it hangs flush against the trim around the bathroom door, up
high, on a small nail, it is virtually invisible. But it's very important
in all locations to see a lock and locate a key, this is most vital when
the key doesn't come in a recognizable shape or the lock is
metaphorical. I saw it the first time he ever took me upstairs, as we
stood in the bleak expanse of the hallway and considered Rita's colors, we were standing between the bathroom and his study and my
eyes traced the frame of the door and I saw not the key but the nail
and I knew. So I unlocked the door and went in her room, he has
returned the quilt and we have a new one, a light down duvet with
interlocking something. I didn't touch anything at first I just
walked around I asked myself would I leave this, would I leave that,
and it was okay I would leave most everything I could see and then
I tried the closet and it was locked. Jacob is disturbed (as am I) by
something that has begun happening at night. I have the same
dream at the same hour—3 A.M. or thereabouts—it was Bradbury,
I believe, who called 3 A.M. "the soul's midnight," as if what ani-
mates us breaks free and travels abroad and might not return. The
soul's midnight. Just because a thing is *psychical* doesn't mean it isn't
also *physical*. Every night I dream the same thing but for the first
time in my life I can't recall a single detail. The moment comes
round and I sit up and scream *Oh my god what is it?!?* or sometimes
Oh my god what is that?!? I am terrified, and Jacob is scared out of his
sleep and can't comfort me. I've begun to sleepwalk, too—a few
nights ago I got up and walked into the closet and just kept going, I
walked at full speed right into the wall, facefirst, and when Jacob
came and gathered me up he asked where I had thought I was

going and I said I had absolutely no idea. I bruised my forehead, somehow in the process I hit my lip and it's swollen, I bent my left wrist backward. Earlier in the night or later in the morning I have dreams I do remember, and they are very similar to one another in that they all involve predators. A few nights ago I dreamed I was standing on a vast plain; the only other thing in sight was a dead . . . bull? An elk? I felt nothing for the animal, and then I heard hissing, a deep guttural sound such as Hitler would have made if he had been robbed of words but still had a Reich to install. I looked up and there were vultures circling, but one vulture got to land first, she was the Chancellor. The others landed behind her, keeping a distance. She looked at me, and *then* I felt something for the animal on the ground, a mute indwelling old pity. An arcane pity. The vulture craned her neck and it stretched out straight and long, like the tubing plumbers call a snake, and she narrowed her face to the point of her beak and inserted her head in the dead bull's rectum, her face and all the way up that long tube of a neck, and then she withdrew it, grasping his intestines. She pulled them out a foot at a time, walking backward and tugging and of course they seemed to stretch for miles, but as soon as she had withdrawn the entire length the other vultures descended. I didn't tell Jacob this dream, I didn't need to, I know it was a ceremonial meal, and—while there are no nutrients in Hell—such images are the soul's food, should one be brave enough to take, and eat. I know it is Aeropagus, I read about her in Hillman, who arrives with an agitation of black wings, the "great one" who gives birth to Justice, I know Jung, quoting the *Hieroglyphica,* says vultures are always female and symbolize the mother. They conceive on the wind (*pneuma*), pneumonia, chronic bronchitis, idiopathic pulmonary disorder. I unlocked Rita's closet and turned on the light, and I don't know whether I saw a question or an answer: all of her clothes, hanging like shed skins, not even a gap where a favorite dress had once hung. All of her shoes, her winter clothes in marked boxes, her summer clothes, her running shorts. A pink box before which I hesitated; it held the most-loved 45 records of her youth—cataloged in the order of her affection and cross-referenced by labels and B sides. Her yearbooks, her diaries, a very old stuffed rabbit missing an eye, a wax-coated box marked Mother's China.

"What the *hell* do you think you're doing?" Jacob had snuck in, I never heard him coming at all. His face was scarlet, his voice shaking. I held the rabbit out to him and he recoiled. I said, "Tell me where she is, give me her address." He shook his head, "I don't *know* where she is, how many times—I don't *know* where she is." I said tell me the names of her parents, her siblings, *someone* knows where she is. He said she had no parents, no siblings, he was her only family. I walked past him, I kept the rabbit, he shouted at me that locked doors mean something, I shouted back they mean more than he would admit. I didn't complete my degree but I am an A student, and Jacob made a mistake, the clichéd slip of the tongue. In his anger and cruel haste, in bed that night after the party, he said his baby was born with magical powers, he could fly, he had a *special hat,* as if I didn't know that it is Hermes' cap, the one that renders the wearer invisible; the little hat Hermes lent to Hades, the better to abduct a bride through a hole in the fabric of conscience. And pigs trampled the crime scene and fell into Hell with her. A downward-dragging love.

They were sent to me: that nasty Santa with his beard full of ceremonial food, the short woman with hair the color of steel, they were messengers or guides, trolls, elfin, beasts, shadows.

I drive up and down the dirt road and cannot find the lane. I walk the road and cannot find the lane. I blaze my way through overgrowth and nettles, I call him and call him. The last time I was here I caught a glimpse of him at twilight, he was starved, feral. His paws were bleeding and I followed the prints until they vanished. The dirt road is finite but has no name, and it is crossed at each half mile by roads without names. If I don't find the house. If I don't find the house.

At Jacob's I pull off the clothes I was wearing—they are covered with burrs and leaves—and I pretend I am Jacob dressing me for his pleasure. I drive to the police station in Jonah, I say to a bald man behind a desk that I want to report a missing person, I want to know the status of a vanished person. He pretends he can't hear me, because he's studiously writing the last word on a report; he's gripping the pen so hard I fear it will snap, and the tip of his tongue is exposed. It is all very hard work, I sympathize. At last he presses the tip of the pen down and produces a dramatic period, and he reads over the words he has written in big blocky letters, I would like to offer him crayons, the rabbit I have clutched under my arm, and minutes pass. The woman who gave birth to you + the bride you chose + the woman who destroys you = three daughters, three metals, the Graces, the seasons whose names signify time.

"Can I help you?" he asks, as if just noticing my presence.

"Yes, I'm wondering if you ever received a report of a missing woman, this would have been . . . three years ago, I think, Rita Matthias, if anyone called or looked for her, or—"

"Whoa." He holds up his hand like a crossing guard. His name tag reads Ballard. "You need to start at the beginning."

I realize the mistake I made. I stand up very straight, I am taller than women. I am wearing a three-hundred-dollar cashmere sweater, a black linen skirt from a boutique on Fifth Avenue, black boots. My hair is jackal black, I wear opals tinted lavender in my ears, even though opals bring terrible luck. I level my gaze at him and don't blink. Through the force of my will he'll see the funeral horse between my legs, our ride through the merciless dark, and Sergeant Ballard stands with a groan, favoring his right hip, and walks over to a wall of dun-colored filing cabinets. He doesn't ask me to repeat her name because he heard every word, just as the dead are busily working but pretend to be at rest. He limps back to the desk, tosses a file folder in front of me; I can see there is almost nothing in it. I will not open it. He can do his own work.

He takes a deep breath, pulls the file toward him, licks his thumb to open it. "Let's see, one Rita Maria Matthias, reported missing January ninth, nineteen-eighty-four. Never located, case dropped."

He reported her missing. I breathe. He made this effort. "Who filed the report?"

"Officer Jackson took the notes. Husband did. Talked like college. Wore a big black overcoat. Jackson shoulda been a writer, huh. Husband alibied; wife had left on other occasions, had suffered a trauma from which, Officer Jackson says, she did not. Recover."

I stare at him.

"Adults have a right to leave, you know. She mighta always wanted to hitch a ride on the Orient Express, yeah? Me? I daydream. I stay. Miss Rita here said sayonara."

"There's never been any sign of her, ever, anywhere else in the world? That's what you're saying?"

Officer Daydream shrugs. "You'd have to ask the rest of the world. My jurisdiction is as they say *limited*."

I let my eyes close slowly, I open them slowly, I say, "Thank you."

He smiles, he shows me, as dogs will, that he would walk backward down a basement staircase for me, into standing water, rats swimming to safety around his knees.

"I'll bet you were *something*," I say, turning to leave.

"Before that train left the station, maybe."

I look back at him; he is gripping his pen like a stake, a make-do dagger to wound the daughter waiting for him at home, in front of the television. Give that little anima projection the ink pen she *deserves.*

✛

On the harvest table in the very nice kitchen, on the table where young Jacob had first declared his ambition, Ianthe found a note apologizing for his behavior. He hoped she would understand that some injuries linger; that grief, too, is a rapid descent and he was not, alas, fully well. He loved her, loved Ianthe desperately, he had packed for her so she could relax. He'd run over to the travel agent's to pick up their tickets; he'd bring home dinner, she would love San Francisco, she would love the very air of the place. And the event they were attending boasted a pantheon of stars: he listed poets, critical luminaries, beloved old scholars, two gluttonous bad boys of contemporary fiction, notorious for turning every event into a food-drink-cocaine orgiastic bacchanalia. He added, in the shy tone (he even wrote smaller) he adopted for malice, that there were a few heads he'd like to see on pikes.

She sat down at the table and held the note, studied his elegant handwriting, his rigid grammar. He had been educated in a time when boys could do nothing less than write beautifully, and construct elaborate trees on which to hang the parts of speech. Archetypes are local; lexicons are tied to time. He spoke a different language, written in a different hand. Those things were not the measure of his character, they were accidents buried in destiny. She loved him, she thought, she had certainly mythologized him: she had amplified the red ribbon around the pen to an image no less potent than a mandala; the red had alchemized into blood and melon. The strawberries he fed her; the skin of the bear on which he proved Hillman's maxim that *Soul is made in the rout of the world.*

She pressed her forehead into the palms of her tingling hands. Myth. Animus. Animus. Who was she to tell him that he had no right to declare the hour of bed, every night, without fail? *Ahhhh,* yawning, the stretch of his arms: *It's bedtime, let's call it a night.* If she said, But I'm not tired, or I'm reading, I want to finish what I'm doing, he would say, *But I'm ready for bed. We go to bed together.* There flared in him a solar authority, a bright force, Hillman's *Cœur de Lion:* kingly, sulfurous, red.

He *suggested* her reading list. He purchased the tickets to a film festival in which they endured every single film by Kurosawa, and told her a day or two before it was to begin. He had standards, his lion's heart was aesthetic by design. Jacob was a man of means and integrity; he was bilingual; he mourned the passage of a good claret. He had lifted her up like a sleeping child and not once had he justified his conditions: no children, no dogs. And she had not asked. Ianthe laughed aloud, a single exhalation; she had reversed the fallacy of Eubulides: Jacob stood before her and she was asked is this your father? No. A veil was lowered over his face: Is this your father? *Yes.*

The closet has been breached, so he hasn't bothered to relock it. I walk in, turn on the light. I feel it again, a lure. Not the pink box of records, and not Mother's China. Rita had no mother, no father. The China of Revenants, it should read. Something else. I scan the shelves but there is so much, there is an entire life, a body plucked away clean. Not even her husk left behind.

Boxes, seasons, photographs, mementos. But where was her work? Banker's boxes, in the far corner. I tear off the lids, find scores of course materials, student evaluations, copies of her vita for the salary committee, year after year, a dependable, tedious employee but she would keep them . . . here. Her own medical records. I don't read them all, I have no desire to violate her, what is left of her, I just want to get to a single year, a cluster of months. And then they are in my hands: a series of faded sonogram pictures, beginning with an undifferentiated tug at the edge of the uterus; a month later a little gilled thing with a cleft nose, enormous black eye sockets; and then a baby, hands with wide fingertips and rudimentary fingernails, perfect feet and toes, his chin tucked, arms pulled up near his ears. In the upper left corner: MATTHIAS, RITA. In the lower left: BABY MATTHIAS. I hold that image as long as I can, well aware there is another behind it. I just want to look at him, small spark of the sunlit world, the daylit, green world. But I move on; there is no profit in hiding from the thing hiding from you, or attempting to outtrick the god of shocks and robbery, with his quicksilver feet and his magic cap.

One more, a fourth image, beautiful in its way: black as the night sky, dotted even with what appear to be points of light, *ephemera hysterica,* perhaps. The limitless, unknowable universe and empty. No baby.

She sat on the floor of the closet and waited for Jacob to come home. A Leonard Cohen song was stuck in her head; strains, phrases repeated, faded. The house was quiet but for the slight hiss of the radiators. She could go down and pour herself a glass of wine; she could spend an hour artfully arranging fruits and cheeses and herbs on a yellow plate. The worst dream had been a week ago. She was being chased through a dark junkyard by a man she never saw. All the cars had faces, some were friendly, some were glowering. The dream was deathly silent; she ran and hid and could hear nothing but her own footfalls, and if she stopped, his. And when it seemed she would get away—just when she thought she had seen an opening in a barbed fence, one of the cars reached out and grabbed her pant leg and she couldn't tear it free. The man chasing her realized she was caught, and this was where the dream had become unmanageable: he stopped running. He slowed down, he strolled in her direction. His boot falls were languid, a deep tone like the blast of a late and distant train. She pulled frantically at her pant leg, and certainly Pan had cantered in somewhere, goat-footed and reeking, a miasma of musk, because she was the nymph in a blind panic. A very bad dream, but not as bad as what was happening in the upper world, unbeknownst to her, the world where she had mistaken the lace scarf on her vanity table for her pant leg, and was pulling on it with all her strength. She pulled until an old brass lamp, a thing heavy enough to kill a man, had toppled over and hit her directly on the bridge of the nose, breaking the bone like a toothpick. Jacob had been heroically calm, driving her to the emergency room in his pajamas, Ianthe barely conscious, her face covered in blood. The doctor who treated her made Jacob leave her bedside; he pulled the curtain for effect. "You don't have to live like this," he'd said angrily, as if Ianthe had failed him through parasomnia. "There are places you can go, people who will help you."

She stared at the cruel hospital lights in the ceiling. "It wasn't him," she said. "Trust me." But she didn't care what he thought, and the doctor heard it in her voice.

"Suit yourself," he said, flinging the curtain open and nearly running over Jacob, who had been standing on the other side all along.

When they got home from the hospital Ianthe picked up the

newspaper, which Jacob had folded open to a particular article. At first she wasn't sure what she was seeing; she had to read the headline three times:

PROMINENT BUSINESSMAN AND HIS WIFE LOSE CUSTODY BID FOR GRANDDAUGHTERS

In a surprise decision yesterday, Family Court Judge Lois Peacock refused to award physical custody of two minor children, Erin and Jessie Wilson of Mason, to their maternal grandparents, Loretta and Martin Morrison. The children have been in foster care since January, when their parents, Phillip and Dusty Ann Wilson, were arrested in a major narcotics sting operation. More than 200 people were arrested and charged with possession with the intent to distribute methamphetamine. The local sheriff's office seized approximately $725,000 worth of the drug, much of which had been distributed through the Wilson home. Announcing her decision to place the children up for adoption, Judge Peacock cited Mr. Morrison's three arrests for lewd and lascivious conduct with minor children. Morrison's attorneys argued that all three cases had been dismissed, and that Mr. Morrison and his wife were devoted churchgoers and upstanding members of the community. Judge Peacock declined to comment, stating only that the parental rights of Phillip and Dusty Ann Wilson were permanently severed, and that the Morrisons would not be granted visitation rights. No other family members could be reached when the matter of physical custody arose in January. The girls will "most likely" be adopted by their foster parents, according to a social worker familiar with the case. The name of the family was not released, and the adoption records will be sealed.

"Have you been following that story?" Jacob had asked from behind her, carrying in her bags from the pharmacy.

"No—I didn't know anything about it until today."

"It's very sad. Very shocking. We've traveled so much—wine?—I missed the beginning. It must have been dramatic, arresting two hundred people at once. And there were a lot of children involved, all of them placed in foster care. That article is going to be repeated in one form or another every day for a while."

"It makes me . . ."

"I know," Jacob had said, squeezing her shoulder. "Me, too."

Ianthe leaned back into the corner, clutching the black sheets of film without bending them, trying to. The bells were ringing, church bells, she assumed, and they must have been ringing for Dusty and Erin and Jessie, and for Baby Matthias as well. Her head hurt, her fingers were nearly completely numb. I'll wait in the kitchen, she thought, opening her eyes, just as the closet door opened. Only it didn't open as if pushed; it simply moved. It was compelled. And standing in front of her wasn't her husband, or even the thing she feared the worst—Rita herself, hanging limp, or dressed for her morning run. The first thing she saw was a curved black claw on which hung a silver pail, emptied of summer's mulberries. He was standing on his hind legs and was dressed like a scarecrow: jeans shredded below the knee, a flannel shirt, a floppy cap. But it was him, the smell of him was unmistakable.

"Hello," she said.

"Hello." His voice was deeper than she remembered. But she had been very small then. "I came to tell you what you're seeing there."

Ianthe spread the films out like a deck of cards.

"As you can see," the coyote began, "this was Jacob's son, eighteen weeks' gestation. This one, with his hand up next to his face, was made one week later, and this"—with a sharp claw he pointed to the last—"was the next morning."

Ianthe swallowed, wished they were back at the clear stream. "Where is the baby?"

He squatted down closer to her, set the bucket between them. It was rusted at the edges, as if it had never held another summer's gathering. "They had a dog named Marcus, a golden retriever, typical of his breed. Neither Jacob nor Marcus awakened during what followed, which Rita described under hypnosis."

Tears streamed down Ianthe's face, but the coyote seemed not to notice. He probably had a scrap of handkerchief somewhere in the mess he was wearing, but she didn't ask. "Here's what she told them: She said that she had seen the bedroom window open and three— she called them 'trolls'—came in but they didn't make any sound. They pressed a silver thing to Marcus's head, the silver thing Rita compared to a tire pressure gauge, and then they did the same to Jacob, and neither of them struggled at all. She was flown out the window and across the backyard. There were blank spaces in her memory, and then she remembered being on a table and the 'trolls' were talking to her but they didn't have mouths. She understood them. They said they would be taking the baby and putting it in an incubator, and she could see it every night and even maybe bring it home someday but in truth it belonged to them, because Jacob had not been the 'donor.' The one in the black robe had made the donation."

She knew she was making a terrible scene, crying so hard she had begun to hiccup, her face pressed against one of Rita's old dresses.

"Rita told them, 'They unzipped me, and took him out. I knew he was too small to live and I tried to say so but I couldn't speak or move. Then they zipped me back up and took the baby away and I never saw him again.' In the meantime"—the coyote cocked his head as if to deliver some unfortunate news—"Jacob was being held for questioning; the fetus was being searched for everywhere, and a gang of volunteer sheriff's deputies came out and shot the dog, Marcus, in order to have him necropsied. Of course he had not harmed the baby." A look of disgust passed over his muzzle. "Barbarians."

Ianthe gasped, wiped her face. "I'm sorry, you've never told me your name."

He smiled a canine grin that sent a chill down her spine. "Cleonus."

"Cleonus, you have to help me get back to Candy; you remember, you gave Candy to me in the first place, and this rock here"—she pressed against the back of her neck—"it belongs to you, it binds us. I have to tell her certain things. She believes they love her, those are the words she used, they are here for love, but that isn't true and you and I both know it—they love no one, they are incapable—"

Cleonus shook his head in disgust, rumbled a low growl. Ianthe believed he was expressing his hatred of the blues, the Nordics, the policemen.

". . . I know exactly what they'll do to her if they haven't already, she is the *perfect* candidate for them because she can be made to believe they share something, they share values . . ."

The coyote growled more deeply, his head swiveling toward the closet door, and there stood her husband, his hair askew, his raincoat glistening with a scattering of drops. She tried to say Jacob, she tried to put her body between his and Cleonus, she tried to shout or otherwise intervene, but the coyote was merely bending over to pick up his pail, the emptiness of it a shock to Ianthe's heart again. He picked it up with his teeth and slunk like a dog out of the closet, right past Jacob's legs. Her husband had a phone in his hand, he was calling for an ambulance, as she held the ultrasound screens out to him and said, *I understand, I understand. This happened to me; you've got to take me to Candy's; I know how to make it stop. Jacob, put the phone down, help me. Help me.*

✝

Around and around, just as Jung's mandala suggested; here she was strapped back to the barber's chair in the basement. Except she was more comfortable, and there was a needle in her arm, a steady cold drip, she was strapped down, yes, but she had a pillow and she was tired.

Jacob said something, and a deep-voiced man answered. "There is definite activity in the temporal lobe—this spiking—but I want to test her too for lesions of the hippocampus and amygdala." He was silent a moment, flipping pages. "I'm looking at her chart and there are things I don't understand. It appears her medical history began when she entered the university."

"I don't—"

"No one ever *noticed* that she had a seizure disorder? Transient global amnesia, that she was completely disassociative, she probably hallucinated, lost autobiographical details. You?" Trace thought he was turning toward Jacob. "Have you noticed anything unusual about your wife?"

Jacob sighed. "She sleeps with her eyes open. She has terrible nightmares and can't remember the content. She sleepwalks, she talks, she wakes up in the night convinced I'm going to kill her. Runs from me, hides. Some part of her is convinced I killed my first wife, Rita, who divorced me, just because I don't know where she is."

The doctor scribbled something audibly. "Rita's in Santa Fe. She's a lesbian now. Goes by Ree."

Jacob said, "Oh."

"I can't find any family doctor listed in these records, only her vaccination history at the health center. No parents, no siblings. I don't understand how she survived alone, in frequent fugue states if not entirely disassociated. How did she live? I assume you've come to terms with the fact that you're probably dealing with an alias, and one of many?"

"What?" Jacob sounded angry. "No, she doesn't have an alias; we were married in the courthouse, I saw her birth certificate, her driver's license. She has a passport, for heaven's sake, we travel to Europe every summer."

"But she came from nowhere." The doctor spoke more quietly now. Trace's eyes fluttered behind her eyelids. She was tired and leaden, she felt as if she couldn't move a muscle.

"She has no one; she's alone in the world except for me. It can't be the first time you've met such a person."

"Does she lie to you, Dr. Matthias?"

"Lie to me?" Jacob seemed to be considering his answer carefully. "Not if she knows the truth, no."

"What would you say her level of intelligence is?"

"It's off the charts. But, I. I took her out of school her final semester. She was about to graduate summa cum laude from the Honors College, top of her class, and I made her drop her courses. Because she didn't seem okay to me, I was worried about her."

"Do you frequently watch her?"

"Are you accusing me of something?" Jacob asked. Trace could hear him stand fast, pushing back his chair. "How could I know she had this form of epilepsy; *you* barely know what it is."

"True enough. And no, I'm just wondering how much care she needs."

Jacob was quiet. If she had to guess, he was taking off his glasses and rubbing his eyes. "A lot. A fair amount. But I don't mind, and I don't want you digging around in her past. I know who I married and I know who she is and that's enough for me, so let it go."

The doctor made a last notation, hung the chart at the end of the bed. "We'll see how she does with the anticonvulsants. My guess is that she'll turn quickly. If not, we'll test her for lesions, other problems."

"What causes this, what triggers—"

"Couldn't tell you. Most often it's stress, lack of sleep, hormone fluctuations. Some people have seizures because they're afraid, and some people are constantly afraid because they have seizures. But it would take a while to learn your wife's particular triggers."

Jacob took an audible breath. "How will I know?"

"She'll have halos, auras. She'll smell something unusual, hear a bell ringing, her extremities will go numb. Ask her. Pay attention. How long have you been married, Mr. Matthias?"

From her bed Trace tried to say, *Four months,* because she remembered it exactly.

Jacob said, "Four years and four months to the day."

Then they were alone and he was kissing her forehead, her eyelids, and she went under.

CHAPTER ELEVEN

Hekate

We must go over the bridge and let it fall behind us, and if it will
not fall, then let it burn.

JAMES HILLMAN, *The Dream and the Underworld*

Jacob of the Deep Sleep does not know—imagine my surprise—
the difference between a rifle and a shotgun. When he is called
upon to mention one he uses them interchangeably, as if he is em-
ploying a category called "long gun" and everything falls in it. Sadly,
he would be wrong about the definition of long gun, too. He hasn't
watched enough television, he has lived too vertically. The gun Colt
gave me was the wondrous Winchester Model 52B, it is a fine instrument, walnut stock, a velvet trigger system. The cocking mechanism is on the rear of the bolt, so it's easy to see the cocking status;
the safety is thumb-operated, just forward of the bolt handle. If

Jacob were with me I would say think of it as something fluid; a complement to the human arm. The butt plate is tucked against your shoulder, the fore end rests on your forearm and is sensitive to pressure, the safety is engaged/disengaged at the same location as the cocking bolt and the ejection port. Very near the trigger is the magazine release button; each magazine holds five shots. Five bullets, Jacob—a rifle fires bullets through a barrel with a pattern of grooves, compelling the bullet to spin around an axis, and the conservation of movement at the point of departure increases accuracy, just as a tightly spinning football is more likely to be caught than one wobbling through the air, although Jacob is not a football fan either.

But when Colt gave the gun to me it was temperamental—it was disagreeable—because some moron had tried to install a peep sight without the aid of a gunsmith, and the process had thrown everything out of whack. I took out the manual, the cleaning kit with its soft yellow cloth and metal dowels and special oil, and I disassembled the entire gun, and I should say I was ten years old and the Winchester 52B is not a junior rifle; it doesn't rely on compressed air for shooting at varmints at your bird feeder. I got the gun, the cleaning kit, a box of ammunition, just standard Winchesters for target practice. I reassembled it and that attention gave it new life and I snuck out a hundred early-morning hours and practiced with beer bottles, with cans, with crab apples, and then I started making paper targets and I learned to count off fifty yards, because the Winchester ought to be accurate at fifty yards, if the forearm adjustment screw is right. I shot it until I developed a black bruise under my collarbone that looked like some panic-inducing fungus. I breathed with that gun; I loaded the magazine, I threw the bolt on the cock, I aimed, I fired; I cocked, I aimed, I fired, one two three four five times as fast as possible, and I hit the magazine feed and reloaded, stole money from Dusty Ann or just asked for it from

Billy and bought more ammunition, and then one weekend morning I asked Colt to go with me into the clearing where I'd hung targets on trees and on hay bales. I'd hung them so I had to turn while aiming—I shot the first, I pivoted, aimed, shot the second. I had choreographed the display like a dying swan, and when I was finished Colt stood silent, looking from one target to the next, each blown through the center with some stippling because I didn't have high-end ammunition, and the air was heavy with cordite. He stood very still and even then, even at that age, when I looked at him he was a boy in the top car of the Ferris wheel and I was beside him, looking at his eyes, his profile, and seeing my future. I saw us fleeing from a lightning storm, I saw us skin to skin, maybe just our arms, our knees. His feet entwined with mine as we napped in a hammock, a cradle between two trees we didn't own, behind a house we hadn't yet built or bought, I could smell him there in the clearing, I could smell him young on the ride at the carnival, the way that scent would deepen just as the line of hair on his belly grew darker and his skin more tawny, every inch of a mile marker pointing forward and down, I loved him with an ache like a hillbilly song, I loved him with my field of violets and their tender stems, when I dreamed of him, which wasn't often enough, I dreamed of honey, or drunkenness. I stood barefoot in the clearing, the Winchester's barrel and muzzle branding the part of my shin they were touching, and I waited. I waited. He looked at me, the fierce shadow of his eyes, his brow, I hoped he was about to issue the order, the cut that would break me open into who I was meant to be for him, and he slowly raised his hand, I would give everything to see it again, his hand lifting into the air, coming down like parachute silk on the crown of my head. We stood there in the morning light, twin jackals, the children of Anubis, and he said so quietly I had to stand very close to him, *Oh god, oh my god what have I done.* He looked at the targets with their hearts blown out, his eyes filled with tears, he looked at each one as if it were a yearling, a lamb, a falcon, a son. I sobbed and sobbed, he held my face against his belly and I cried until my throat burned, he stroked my hair and whispered, *What I have done to my girl, my god.* The air grew hot but the sacred river is icy and its children are the children of Hate; I never let go of that gun, not in my moment of failure, not later, not yesterday, not now.

Jacob. Jacob unfolds: the red ribbon he tied around my pen is also the red of poppies in Lethe's fields, the divine land where we are allowed to forget, oh I have forgotten that, I will say to him, and he'll say what have you forgotten and I'll shake my head and say I don't remember. I will ask him if he has forgotten and he'll say, Forgotten what? And there will be nothing but the red of those hellish flowers and the red of his gift, the red of the story we will tell and then forget. Three times he let slip what he should have concealed: Hermes' cap. The Children of Phillip and Dusty Ann Wilson are forever severed from that root and their adoption will be sealed. And with his thumb counting down the vertebrae, as if he were playing my spine, tonight he said, *The moon is full.* A red statement, the mortal wound of his golden retriever, his wife unzipped by thieves, and all his treasure squandered—even if he claims those are all metaphors, and he watches me take my three pills daily. There are men. Jacob is a man.

Don't sort this out, I tell myself, just hold fast to it and sit inside your lack of understanding, as Keats advised, then died. Hekate: Her cult was in *Thrace,* she is depicted as *triplicity*—three heads—a dog, a serpent, a horse. She slices the throats of sheep and then uses that knife to cut umbilical cords and the link between life and death. God she is such a *bitch,* I'm so fucking *sick* of her, her attendant and her familiar is a *bitch,* all right already, we get it, here are some of her fucking names:

- ☠ Chthonian Hekate (Underworld Goddess)
- ☠ Crataeis Hekate (Mighty One)
- ☠ Enodia Hekate (Goddess of the Paths)
- ☠ Antania Hekate (Enemy of Mankind)
- ☠ Propylaia Hekate (At the Gate)
- ☠ Prytania Hekate (Invincible Queen of the Dead)
- ☠ Trioditis (Greek), Trivia (Latin), Hekate (Goddess of the Three Roads)
- ☠ Klêidouchos (Keeper of the Keys)
- ☠ Tricephalus or Triceps (Three-Headed)

She is also the usurper of the rightful Moon Goddess, Artemis, but you know what? That doesn't matter a bit in the end because Hekate is just Hades in a black robe, standing in the dirt demanding meat. And yes, fine, she is extremely powerful, she is distinct, she is *it,* and she's too powerful to marry or even haul around a eunuch as her consort, but there are rumors of many children, all of them monsters. And Hekate gets everything; she gets dogs, ravens, owls, scorpions, lions, bats—I could make up some animals—they're hers. And all the plants and herbs, every poisonous berry and every deadly plant: hers. So why not all wild areas, and borders, city walls, crossroads, thresholds, doorways, graveyards, I don't know it's like one day you wake up and you've given that old woman all you can. You've worn her costumes and listened to her music and slept in her pestilent swamps. You've gone to her parties and watched *Blue Velvet,* forward and backward. That was Hekate's razor in the silly girl's hand; Hekate's leather on the disaffected boys; her cigarettes, her spilled sticky liquor, her mold in the bathroom, her vomit on

the carpet. Hekate's theatrics, and I know one of her most endur-
ing aspects is Wisdom but maybe by Wisdom she means, get the
hell out of Hekateville. I'd like to tell her, though, if I happen to run
into her, that when I began seeing Jacob I became the scourge of
the Goth nest at the University of the Midwest. The last time I
saw Anastasia and Myka they were walking down the main avenue
and as they passed me, little Anastasia, who I could keep in a Habi-
trail, hissed, *"Jew whore,"* and Myka floated on unseeing, blinded by
loss, Jacob was meant to be hers and I took him, which is like
money, which is like bankers, like Shylock, ergo I may well be a bit
of a Jew, like Plath. With my Gypsy luck and my taroc pack. And my
taroc pack.

The moon is rising as I pull into the Warners' driveway. The senior
Warners' house is dark and looks deserted, and as I traverse the vicious ruts leading to Candy's trailer I notice that weeds and grasses,
those species of the horticultural world that stumble like the homeless and the mad, bungle their way up through hubcaps and the
rusted bones of lawn mowers, are thriving even in April. They are
making their retarded, suicidal stand, and I offer them a salute. The
trailer itself is a crypt, it has come all undone, but I get out anyway
and I stop at the chicken wire fence but of course there is *worse* than
nothing there. A chasm into which some girl fell, and behind her a
blue tick and a redbone coon hound, their long, graceful legs beat-
ing at the black air. I climb the stairs. The screen door is missing; the
storm door, that peculiar white vinyl used for mobile homes, is
standing open. *Then enter in,* Dickinson said, and there was damn
sure some Underworld, some Goddess of the Paths in that one. I'd
write *that* paper for Elizabeth Cohen, if I didn't hate her so much. I
pull the Maglite out of my coat pocket and shine it around the
room, and what I see causes me to sway, I almost fall. The furniture
is gone, except for the television in front of which Danny Rae used

to sleep; someone has put a bowling ball through it. That's it—that's all that remains of a human occupation. The walls, carpeting, the kitchen linoleum have all been clawed apart, clawed to shreds. There are red stains on the floor, in patterns like rain on what is left of the walls, but it looks like paint. Rust. Candy said she had taken care of the boys, she had solved that problem, and I'm about to take a step back toward the shallow pits of their bedrooms when I

I pound on the front door of Skeet's parents' house but it is empty too, and the vertigo, my periodically too close relationship to gravity, returns because *this house has been empty for years,* and so has that trailer. I am doubled over, gasping, but I don't fall this time, I reach out and steady myself against the abandoned house, which is covered with roofing shingles, and the texture, the graininess, the paint just barely concealing the sticky black, pulls me back into my body and I run to my car, which is my car, it's a masterwork of engineering and its's in my name, and I fly, hell-bent for leather as Candy used to say, out of that driveway.

I drive into Mason and farther north, to Paul and Esther's. I will just tell the truth: I'll say I meant to come see you every Friday but something. I meant to come see you every Friday for the last five years but ssom. I meant to. Where their house stood is a Village Pantry. I get out of the car and walk across the parking lot, I leave my car running and the door open because this is the one, *this is the phone I used to call Billy,* I reach out and pick up the receiver, it is as cold as I remember it being. I turn to my left, I turn so fast I almost keep going, and to the right, but there are no landmarks, nothing stands out—which direction had I come from, did I enter from there? On that corner? From that street? I run back to the car, dump out my purse, I don't need to keep quarters for laundry anymore but his number is here, and now I have a phone credit card.

The overhead light isn't bright enough—I use the flashlight, and Jesus. I don't have the number, I kept that church bulletin with me at all times, I thought, and it's gone but something else remains: the letter I wrote him at the Laundromat, the letter I remember mailing but here it is, unstamped, no return address. All that's written on the front is: *Billy*

I have moved the Winchester from the trunk to the front seat, as I drive around the gas station in quadrants, I will not miss a block. Jacob, I will say, a rifle is one thing: a shotgun is another, they are different as material and dream. That's hyperbole, for heaven's sake, they aren't even remotely that distant. Rifles shoot bullets; mine only a few at a time and each one has to be cocked into the chamber. My Winchester is like a dolphin at SeaWorld; there are rifles that are great white sharks: semiautomatics, automatics, assault rifles, carbines, recoilless, snipers. There are those that fall under General Brutal Death at Sea or on Land: the Mauser, the machine gun, the Walther MKb42, and the modern sniper, the *anti matériel*. The McMillan TAC-50, which killed a man in Afghanistan at a distance of *one and a half miles.*

But a shotgun, particularly the 12-gauge, is altogether different. For one thing it's the exclusive choice for skeet shooting, which seems a rather wholesome exercise. And the shotgun is really the only choice for hunting—everything from game birds to deer. They are the weapon of choice for homeowners, too, because just the shape of a shotgun arouses an animal instinct, the one that says *Run,* or if the criminal is world-weary, *Later.* Say you've got a 12-gauge in your closet, Mr. Detroit, Mr. Gary, Indiana. The amount of buckshot in each shell is referred to as the *load,* and a self-defense load is, I don't know, ten to twenty-five large lead pellets, because *if* you are going to take that step and remove the shotgun from your closet, and if it happens to be a pump-action model (it's okay—Freud is dead), one of two things is going to happen. Well, *one* thing is going to happen, which is you, Mr. Detroit, will fire the weapon in the direction of the person of the intruder, and if you are some distance from him and an unskilled shot, the odds of you hitting him with some percentage of the multiple large lead pellets, creating multiple large holes, is pretty good. It's okay. However. Should you fire that particular load at close range, say ten to fifteen feet, the load will not expand beyond a few inches. And if you get closer than that? All twenty-five scalding lead pellets, moving at the speed of . . . I have no idea, at the speed of death, will enter your intruder as a single mass, leaving a hole, well. Leaving a hole from which one doesn't recover.

I drive block after block and never see anything I recognize; not a building, not a parking lot, not a city wall, a threshold, a door. I'm in the right neighborhood, but the entrance to the building where the wolverine was waiting beside the dresser, and the stairwell, the hallway, the doorway, the room within the building: concealed. *Physis kryptesthai philei,* Heraclitus said. *Nature loves to hide.*

I take a familiar two-lane highway leading out of town, and I know exactly where to turn: at a corner, the V of a fence row, and just inside it a withered old dogwood tree. The road turns to gravel, narrows. I look for the red mailbox on the left, but I don't see it before the road dead-ends. I turn around, drive more slowly, and there is an old wooden stake, the kind that once held a mailbox. There's no visible drive, so I park at the edge of the grass and, using the flashlight, walk toward the house, Candy's granddad, who died when we were seventeen. I never asked what became of the house and land, but now I have an answer: there is no house. The moon is nearly at its zenith, and I can clearly see the place I topped the hill—it's like a ridge, or a sandbar. I could go backward, I suppose, I could stand at the crest and go running down to the picnic spot, the creek. The silver pail dangling from a black, hooked claw. Not tonight. I go back to the car, stop, look up at the clear sky. There. Imagine people getting so worked up about flying saucers or cigars, when we can stand on terra firma and on our own two human feet and admire the light of stars *that are no longer there.* Isn't that . . . weird enough?

Colt and Billy hunted together through every season. They were both excellent marksmen, they were patient and quiet, they abided by whatever code it is that allows men to find the killing of unsuspecting animals a transcendent experience. They competed a little, probably, not out in the open, but we always knew who shot what and under what conditions. One year Billy got a six-point buck with a clean heart shot, and Colt had it shoulder-mounted for him, a gesture of respect. But the next year Colt shot a big, meaty young buck and his aim was so clean there was no wound. He and Billy puzzled and puzzled over it, they turned the animal every possible direction but there was no bullet hole. It wasn't until they got him home and hoisted to bleed out that Billy saw the shot: straight up the rectum. Not a mark on the hide, but ten thousand jokes about what a pain in the ass Colt could be.

Fathers and sons. Outside the psychic realm, in, say, just the living room realm, the dynamic is so much more subtle and complicated than between mothers and daughters. With mothers and daughters there is no living room: there is only the primordial drama of a woman yielding her sexual dominance and her fertility to her daughter. Or not doing so, as is much more often the case. At some point a father is expected to say to his son, *Here is the key to the kingdom,* and hand it over. But mothers? They say, *Here is the key to your catastrophe,* and they keep it on their key ring as a sign, nestled among the spare change, the linty gum, and the used Kleenex at the bottom of their decaying bags.

• • •

I know every dip in these roads, every curve, the slightest irregularity in the pavement. What is the value of that knowledge? I guess the way Colt and Billy spoke, or worked it out, was that Colt had the slightly better gun—in my opinion anyway. His was a Winchester 1300 Ranger, sleek as a cat. It was a pump-action, and even the pump was narrow and graceful. There were things about it I didn't understand completely; a mechanism in the recoil timing that minimized the space between shots, allowing the shooter to pump sooner than on lesser guns. Billy had a Mossberg 500, also a great gun. It held six shells, including one in the chamber, also a pump-action. Maybe I had it backward, I don't know, but the Mossberg looked more like a workhorse, a gun that could accomplish a clean heart shot, whereas Colt's Winchester? I try not to think about it.

✝

The night is as bright as it's going to get, and I have come back to the farmhouse to find Weeds, and to kill him. If he's already dead, I will pick his bones clean. I'm taking him home one way or the other.

I walk the dirt road with the flashlight off. If I hear the slightest sound I whistle or call his name. I want to see him in this silver light; I don't want to scare him with the Maglite's blue glare. He wandered up to us that day in late summer, out of nowhere, and Colt said, "Look at this new kind of weed we've got growin'," and that was his name. Colt picked him up, he named him, but he was always my dog. He is *my dog,* and who would have thought I could do worse things than have already been done? I did this? He is my dog and I belong to him equally, that's the contract we make between species if we dare to call it *love* and not a zoo, or an abattoir. I leave the road, press back to where I think the house is, that's the

Leonard song I've got running on the tracks in my head. *You let me love you till I was a failure; your beauty on my bruise like iodine.* I don't get to listen to him, the genius ladies' man, so much these days, as Jacob has his own ideas about music and they're mostly the Modern Jazz Quartet, those ideas. Loretta said at first Weeds could never come in the house, which just made me sigh, the woman was like a little red-haired Tyrannosaurus rex, flapping her flippers around and making do with a brain the size of a peanut. I wanted to say, "How is Weeds worse than the pig, or the bobcat?" I would never tell her about the sheep; he'd been in *her* room, eating her favorite wool scarf when I found him. That one puzzled me in two ways: was he my sheep, or Loretta's, and what did it mean, him eating wool? In the end I led him out into the yard and told him to keep the scarf, my gift to him and his, and he trotted away.

I brought the dog in anyway. I'll say this for Loretta: once she thought she'd completely broken me, once the deal was hammered out and I was her coin, she was pretty much finished with me. I stayed out of her way—I didn't want to test her, but her victory had been so thorough, the battle waged so long, that by the time it was over I think she barely saw me. I was Dresden, she was the carpet bomb, and who cared, ultimately, if a handful of people climbed out of the basement of a vitamin factory? The city was *gone,* her daughter was *in ribbons.* She could put on a puppet show when she needed to, if she was getting her churchy on with her Church Hens and I happened to wander in, and I mean by the worst kind of accident, she would act as if she knew me, she would put her arm around me or stroke my hair, say to the Hens, "Isn't she beautiful? And such a mystery, those eyes, whenever otherwise she's the spittin' image of Colt, don't you think?" Where she had touched me I would sizzle, blister. Sometimes if we were alone in the house she'd call me in her room and put on a fashion show. She'd make me sit on the bed and she'd parade around in her costumes and laugh her

high, hollow laugh, and I would applaud. I still remember the smell
of her things, the drawer in which she kept her rubber girdles and
bras the size of shopping bags, that aging rubber in the straps, the
odor trapped in the girdle as it rotted away. I would say to her,
"Now tell me the truth, Mama, where did you come from?" And
she'd bat her eyes at me and say, "I came from the Lord's love, angel,
just like you did." She knew so many recipes—fried chicken, drop
dumplin's, collards, corn bread, every kind of cobbler. Once when I
had a fever she stayed up all night, moving me from the iced tub to
the bed and giving me alcohol baths, her hands were so small and
her touch was light *Compassion with the sting of iodine* and truth be
told about Loretta, I mean if I were honest I loved

    and she

I've made my way back to the road and walked east, and I hear
something, the moon is on the decline and I can't see as well anymore, it's a draggy—I whisper, "Weeds? My boy?" There is something moving slowly down the road with no name, the north/south
road with no name, and suddenly I'm afraid, I don't have that deep
and abiding feeling of rightness anymore, who. Why—why in the
world would I believe I owe Weeds his death, whoever could declare such a thing a truth? Oh my god, there is so much movement
in the tall grass, I am standing in the middle of the night in the middle of a road that appears on no map with a rifle in order to kill the
dog I loved and to whom I committed myself and failed? I could
have a panic attack, I could hyperventilate, I hold the gun above my
head as if in surrender and I'm turning in circles in the road. I say
the word *instinct,* I actually pray the word *instinct,* and he appears, I
see him; or what I see is bones and fur and the long teeth of the
dying animal, he is moving so slowly and without a second's
thought I've slammed the gun against my shoulder, tripped the
safety, cocked it. I pull the trigger

I'm deafened by the gun blast, I'd forgotten, and the place I once trained to take the kick is tender now, I'm not that girl anymore, I walk toward the cross where the four directions meet and there is barely any light remaining, I drop the gun, I reach in my pocket for the flashlight although I don't want to see him, I don't want this, I tilt my head back and breathe, I look at the nonexistent stars, the dog is my dog but the dog in the Underworld is not my dog, not me, not mine, I can't remember any of it anymore, so I turn the blue light on him, I look directly at him, at my Weeds, my black dog, and there is nothing there, there is nothing, not even a bit of his hair I could carry with me, there is nothing, I am a dead-on straight shot: that bullet is still flying.

I decide to lie down at the crossroads, lie down directly in the dirt. I point my arms and legs in the Four Cardinal Directions, the Four Noble Truths, the Three Stooges, and I am laughing and wailing at the same time, like a schizophrenic. Jung wrote a book about the disease when it was called *Dementia Praecox,* and that just makes me laugh harder; imagine saying to someone who believes George Washington is telling him to wear aluminum foil underwear that he's suffering from *Dementia Praecox,* I cannot breathe, I—oh my god, poor Candy, every time I wipe my face I become more caked with mud, as if I'm applying my own death mask, but I can't stop crying for her, I had a plan. I was going to show up there and we would sit at the table I would ask her as I have always asked her if she'd like to hear a bit of poetry, a passage of a play, something I had memorized that day. Yes, she . . . yes, without exception. I was going to say this to her, from *Faust, Part II,* act V . . .

I knew what I was going to say to her but I've lost it. It, right— I was going to tell her that she is wrong to think they love her—*they do not love anyone or anything*—I had an analogy. Something something.

I was going to tell her they aren't as sophisticated as people think. Yes, they have certain gifts we lack and once you are in their laser beam there's nothing to do but endure it. But they are easily confused by humankind. I was going to tell her that what would save her is to become invisible to them through enantiodromia, through an abundance of presence in the world, *this* world. This was going to be hard with Candy, I already knew it because she feels without thinking; she is often irrational; she lacks judgment. Jung said, "Only one thing is effective against the unconscious, and that is *hard outer necessity*" (emphasis mine). It was going to be a task just convincing her that she wasn't standing on the event horizon of some evolutionary miracle, but to actually convince her to follow my plan? And I was too late? *Oh my god,* it's so horrifying I just have to laugh; I finally saw what I needed to see—the empty sonogram film—and I knew what to do after not knowing for months, and by the time I arrive there is no Candy?

Colt coughed, he had always coughed, but the next time in the hospital wasn't the same. When the doctor described the treatments, the prognosis, the percentages, I saw it on his face, he wasn't going to do it. There wasn't a chance in this world he was going to suffer those indignities just to die harder and slower. We left the oncologist's office and talked all the way home; the wind was blowing so violently I had to sit right up against him to hear what he was saying. He was worried about college for me; he wanted to arrange things in such a way that his life insurance policies were honored because I was the beneficiary of the largest one. He didn't want Loretta to lose the house and so some years ago he'd refinanced and added mortgage life and if we could just work out

I stopped him. I told him to pull over for a minute. And sitting there in the howling wind I told him everything, I told him about the red chair and the barber's pole, and how Loretta had been forg-

ing his name on liens for so long he didn't own the house anymore
and he had no life insurance policies except the one in my name, because Loretta didn't know about it and I had the file; I told him I was
the collateral on every debt to Marty, it had already been decided.
Telling him about what happened in the church basement was
worse than the experience itself—the look in his eyes, I said you are
my genesis, you inspirited me, without you something terrible is
going to happen to me, we were holding one another, I was nearly
hysterical but Colt had turned to stone. And then, I don't know, I
just found my voice, I calmed down and was able to speak reasonably.

What is the worst thing that can happen to a man? I asked him.

This, he said.

You are dying, you know I will suffer unspeakable things in
your absence, and there's nothing you can do about it, because there
isn't time. That's the worst?

He looked at me, Colt had gravity, he was in every way a work
of art. He understood I was offering him something, offering him a
chance out of the jaws of an iron trap.

"I want—"

He turned his eyes back to the parking lot, started the truck. The
rain began just as we turned onto our road. "Is it a deal?"

And I swear, I swear that when he said *Deal* he raised one eyebrow just slightly as if I were the biggest surprise of his life.

The rain was so hard, I don't think I had time to put on shoes, he
grabbed our guns, made sure they were both loaded, we just set off
because we couldn't take the time to think about it, if you say this is
a good day to die you have to mean it, Weeds followed us he ran in
circles of happiness, I wasn't wearing any shoes and our guns were
getting wet. We came to the clearing and Colt reached back and
broke the band holding his ponytail, and he swung his hair around
in a black sheet and water flew like diamonds. Then he pulled me to

him and broke the band in my hair and I spun around and around and Weeds ran and barked. I intended to run my father to the ground. I wanted to hiss at him as I tore his shirt in half; to watch the water gather in pools on his brown belly; to drink it. We would be skin to skin at the top of the Ferris wheel, our feet entwined, my body open like a petal and all the years he kept his distance, my attempts to sit on his lap or wrap my arms around him as we took sharp corners on his bike, I had been absurdly right: you take something that marks you and you push and push and push and eventually like grace it rolls right out of your hand and generates its own opposing force. After years and years I was to be the object of Colt's force.

But it turns again, that would be the problem in a nutshell, it rolls back sometimes much faster than one is prepared, I had taken off my clothes and he hadn't, the rain was still battering us, I couldn't shake the nearly drunken rapture, the honeyed intoxicated

He took my .22 and handed me the 12-gauge, he couldn't, he said, he couldn't love me that way and he could not cut me in half. But you already have, I said, still not

The point was the rest of our lives, that was the point for both of us except his names signifying time weren't the same as mine, even though he'd gotten everything else right, the woman who gives birth to you, the woman you marry, the woman who destroys you, he raised my own gun barrel at me. The truth is I wasn't afraid of being killed; I would have died without blinking. But *I* couldn't shoot *him,* and . . . Here's the key to your catastrophe, daughter.

It was just moments, a few shaken down to the bone but they are the

. . .

I said I won't, I will *not,* we have to rethink this, if you can break your part of the promise so can I, I saw then he never intended to go through with it. He simply didn't. There had been a moment. A sick and dying man, it's harder to shoot yourself with a 12-gauge than it is to be shot with one, I said I will *not* and he answered with one sentence: If you do not agree to shoot me on the count of three, I will turn the gun on your dog. Weeds, who was just sitting there watching us, puzzled and dear and clever. I screamed at him I begged him, he gave me sixty seconds to decide and for the whole sixty seconds I begged and tried to get near him but he kept the rifle barrel pointed at me, and damn if, at the moment he said sixty, he didn't turn and shoot that dog right in the chest; he blew a hole in him bigger than a grapefruit

There was a second, maybe two, of wet silence, and then I watched Colt's chest explode, a red poppy, the Red Falls of our honeymoon, and there was Billy on a rock not ten feet from me, it turned out the Mossburg was a fucking cannon, that sweet Billy my angel brother who slept on the floor for a year between me and the window; but inner necessity is the very definition of instinct, and I shot him in the heart, a full load in the shell like a battering ram made of molten lead, I cut my brother in half. It was Dusty who called the sheriff, and he came himself, he smelled disaster, and he found me naked, trying to bury Weeds in mud I was clawing out of the ground with my bloody hands as Colt and Billy lay on their backs, faceup in the rain. It was like a photograph, taken at Appomattox after the Union army had turned flank, and without mercy mown down their own countrymen.

There is only one thing left for me to do: take the box of journals, the hundreds of file folders out of my trunk and burn them, I don't know what's in them, I don't want to know.

✛

Jacob raised his head, squinted at Ianthe sleepily. "Hey, whatcha doin'? Where did you go? I woke up . . . I don't know when, and you were gone. Your hair is wet."

"I took a shower, then recorded some things in my dream journal," she said, closing it. "You want to know what I did this evening?"

Jacob put his head back on his pillow, smiled. "I'd love to know."

"Well," she began, "because it was a full moon I decided to go shoot the ghost of my black dog at a crossroad, in order to appease the terrible goddess Hekate."

"Is Hekate displeased with you for something?"

She shook her head. "No, I don't think so." She kissed Jacob's cheek. "Not anymore."

Acknowledgments

I would like to thank Hall Farm Center for the Arts, Wylie O'Sullivan, Christopher Schelling, John Svara, Amy Scheibe, Delonda Hartmann, Fred Neumann, Miriam Parker, Joel Moore, Sarah Messer, Martha Levin, Dominick Anfuso, Carisa Hays, Jill Browning, and everyone at Free Press. Thank you dearly to Leslie Staub and Tim Sommer. My love to Bryan Block and Jeff Keller. And as always, my heart: Kat, Obadiah, Baby Augusten, Big Augusten, Dennis, Christopher, Robert, Jeffrey. Thank you, Dianne Freund, who knows all the reasons why.

This novel was inspired, in part, by the work of Dr. James Hillman, a writer and psychoanalyst of such depth and sublimity I barely dare include his name here. The books that would have been most important to this narrator are *The Dream and the Underworld, Suicide and the Soul, Pan and the Nightmare,* and *The Thought of the Heart and the Soul of the World.*

About the Author

HAVEN KIMMEL is the author of *The Used World, She Got Up Off the Couch, Something Rising (Light and Swift), The Solace of Leaving Early,* and *A Girl Named Zippy.* She studied English and creative writing at Ball State University and attended seminary at the Earlham School of Religion. She lives in Durham, North Carolina.